Faith Crossfire

Standing for God in Zyngola

Stephen L. Thompson

Faith Crossfire

Books by Stephen L. Thompson

The Crossfire Series

Colorado Crossfire
International Crossfire
Israeli Crossfire
Believer's Crossfire
Spirit Crossfire
Faith Crossfire
Chinese Crossfire
Texas Crossfire
Dark Crossfire
Island Crossfire
Jagged Crossfire
Violent Crossfire
Russian Crossfire
Nuclear Crossfire
End Times Crossfire
Revelation Crossfire
Gates of Hell Crossfire
Assassin's Crossfire
Albatross Crossfire
Global Crossfire
Far East Crossfire

The SFO Series

Station Force One - Onset

Faith Crossfire

When the Crossfire Team attempts to help Victor Chamberlain take back his food processing plant in Zyngola, Africa they become embroiled in Zyngolian politics.

The majority of the people in Zyngola call Zultar their god and the religious leaders are attempting to evict all other religions, especially Jews and Christians. The team is tasked by Yahveh God to prevent the murder of thousands of Jews and Christians in a clash between the Zyngolian moon god Zarthon and Yahveh God of the universe.

Putting their lives on the line to defend the condemned believers, each member of the Crossfire Team realizes that this may be their last act as they stand unarmed against thousands of people who want to see them die.

- Stephen L. Thompson

Faith Crossfire

Published by
Stephen L. Thompson
Facebook.com/CrossfireNovelSeries

Unless otherwise noted, Scripture quotations are taken from
the HOLY BIBLE, NEW INTERNATIONAL VERSION®.
Copyright© 1973, 1978, 1984 by International Bible Society.
Used by permission of Zondervan Publishing House. All
rights reserved.

ISBN- 978-1-943879-99-1

Published in the United States of America

Foreword

To my Christian readers –
The Crossfire continuing series of action-adventure novels include depictions of violence which are unusual in Christian literature. It would be nice if there were no conflict or violence in our world. But we live in a time when evil is increasing instead of diminishing, when some men seem to be controlled by selfishness, madness, or evil forces. When the enemies of decent mankind are bent on subjugation of other men and women, righteous men and women must stand against evil. The yoke of oppression is not lifted by prayer alone. God is our shepherd and we are his sheep. As long as there are wolves about, God will use some of us as sheep dogs to defend the rest of us. These stories are about people like that and the forces they fight against. The stories describe violence because it occurs in the real world and it is active in the lives of all people whether they recognize it or not.

To my non-Christian readers –
The Crossfire series include depictions of spiritual warfare and spiritual activity with which the non-Christian reader may not be familiar. These stories describe the realms and activities of both God and Satan because they're real and active in the lives of all people whether they recognize it or not.

Steve Thompson

CHAPTER ONE

As Mark Connelly walked out of the Chamberlain food plant in Tymeria he could sense an undercurrent of trouble. Even though there were a lot of people using the street they were much quieter than normal. He knew that standing six foot two and looking like a poster of the ideal American Marine recruit, caused him to stand out in the Zyngolan crowd like an English double-decker bus in traffic. Having a physique which was half NFL football player and half sprinter was normally effective in keeping people from confronting him. Today looked like it was going to be an exception.

He watched five young men, who, although separated, shifted their positions around Mark as he walked back towards his hotel. He noticed also that they were stopping people, whispering to them and pointing him out to them. Many of those people started walking after him.

He thought that it would be prudent to turn into a shop selling meat and get out of sight. But, as he headed for the shop the owner shut and locked the door in his face, this was another bad sign.

The number of people moving along with him had grown to about twenty when one of the young men pointed at him and yelled something that included "Infidel and Spy". Mark broke into a sprint and outdistanced the group and cut around a corner to his left. He double-timed it to the next alley and cut down it before any of the crowd came around the first corner.

He knew it would only be a matter of minutes until they found him again. The hue and cry was growing and there were more people being added to the lynch mob by the second. Mark thought, "This country needs more nightlife, they'll riot just for something to do." He cut through a small marketplace and picked up six or seven more people chasing him yelling and screaming. He heard the same sounds on both sides of him as well as behind. He remembered the city layout and realized that he was being herded into a slum area where everyone would be glad to take their frustrations out on an infidel foreigner.

He saw a woman at the next corner. Even though she was dressed in an all-covering black burka and veil he recognized her. He stopped near where she was standing, seeming not to notice her. She didn't look at him either.

Mark said quietly, "This setup has been well thought out and is just about to close in on me. Get away and get help."

His wife said back to him, "Don't let them kill you. Find a Zulam and ask for asylum. I'll keep track of you, Go!" She slowly walked away from the man she loved more than her own life.

Spotting a Zultarian mosque he sprinted down the block and up the steps. He met one of the teachers at the top of the steps. He asked for asylum but the man either didn't want to help him or simply didn't understand English.

The mob saw him on the steps and came surging up to where Mark was standing. One of the original five young men was in the lead of the herd of people all screaming and shaking their fists at Mark. The young man ignored the Zulam and swung a fist at Mark's face.

Mark blocked the punch and pushed the punk away. But that just made the mob madder and they came at him all at once. Fists flew and feet kicked and Mark went down under the weight of so many bodies. He curled himself into a ball and deflected much of the punishment. But he couldn't deflect all of it. A shoe slammed into the side of his head and he lost much of his coordination. The mob just screamed louder and tried to inflict as much punishment on him as possible.

A rock hit him in the ribs and sent a flare of pain through his side. Someone was trying to ram his head into the cobblestone steps and a dozen fists kept hitting him. He tasted blood and knew if it kept up he wasn't going to make it out of this alive. He prayed that God would send him help.

Suddenly the attack slackened and then quit. Mark shook his head and looked out of the one eye that wasn't swelling shut to see the local police forcing everybody back from him. He saw that a lot of the mob was quickly melting back into the houses because they didn't want to draw the attention of the security force. No one offered to help him up though, and as he slowly got up to a kneeling position, one of the security forces grabbed his arms and pinned them behind his back. Shackles were locked onto his wrists and he was forcibly jerked to his feet. The officer in charge had his men frog-march Mark to a waiting security car and had him stuffed into the back. The pain of sitting on his manacled hands was minimal after the beating he had taken.

Mark sat with his head down as the car started off with a jerk and pulled into the street. Out of the side window Mark saw Sarah walking to a car with a driver holding the rear door open. He kept his face unmoving but inside he had a secret smile. He took a quick inventory of himself and listed the bumps and bruises he had received from the mob. His lower lip was cut and bleeding on his dress shirt. He had several cuts on his head that hurt but weren't serious. The rock to the ribs may have cracked one but he wasn't sure about that. His left eye had gotten hit and was swollen mostly shut and his $1400 suit was in tatters.

The car drove into a walled compound through a gate that was closed behind them. They stopped in front of a large building and Mark was hauled out and half-carried up the stairs to the top where the entrance was located. He managed to glance around and looked for Sarah but couldn't see her. It didn't matter, she was out there somewhere and she now knew where he was. Then he was hauled roughly into the building and down a tiled hall to an ornate door leading to the Commander's office. Once inside, the two men moving him shoved him into a chair and stood on either side of him.

The Commander looked up from his paperwork and studied Mark. "Who are you?" He asked.

Mark cleared his throat. "My name is Mark Connelly. I'm an American Security Consultant working for the Chamberlain Corporation."

The Commander steepled his fingers and looked at Mark over his fingers. "Why were you involved in this riot?"

Mark shook his head. "I have no idea. I finished my report to the plant manager here in Tymeria and was walking back to my hotel. These young men started agitating a crowd and calling me an infidel and a spy. They chased me and I ran. They caught me and beat me. End of story."

The Commander almost sneered as he said, "I see. Well Mr. Connelly, I will need to investigate your story. You will remain here until I am satisfied with the results of that investigation." He made a motion with his fingers and the two men hauled Mark out of his chair.

Mark said, "I am the innocent party here. Could I get some medical aid?"

The Commander smiled, "Of course, Mr. Connelly. I will have a medical technician sent to your, ah, "room". And, I will be the one who decides if you are the innocent party or not. Half of your story doesn't shed a bad light on the people that attacked you, you know. You are an infidel so they had that part right. It's the spy part I need to look into carefully."

Mark glowered as well as a one-eyed person could glower and asked him, "How long will this take?"

The Commander smiled even bigger. "It will take just as long as it takes." The men yanked Mark around and hauled him out of the office. They took him down to the level below and shoved him into a cell. They locked the door and motioned him to back up to the bars. He did and they removed the manacles from his wrists. He stepped away from the bars before they hit him to make him move. He rubbed his wrists and sat down on the ratty bunk and waited.

CHAPTER TWO

Abdullah Hami was serenely calm and silent to his followers. He was an excellent example of a Zulam, a teacher. Even though he had just been given a tremendous gift to further his studies and work, he gave praise to Zultar and set the gift aside for more prayer at a later time. The funds he had just received were worth millions of U.S. dollars but it seemed inconsequential to the teacher. His followers were very impressed and determined to learn to be even more like him.

Hami considered himself a great actor, not merely a good actor, but a great one. He felt he was possibly one of the greatest actors ever. He maintained his character on the outside while on the inside he was doing cartwheels of joy with the full funding of his operations. He gave thanks to Zultar on the inside too, but it was more of a conspiratorial wink in the direction of his god rather than worship. Zultar had already told Abdullah that he was going to get this money, and when. But until it was in his hands he wasn't completely sure that it would really happen. Zultar was capricious and nobody knew if he would really do what he told you he would do.

Now he could expand his operations into the hundreds of thousands of Zultarian warriors bringing Jihad to the Jews and Christians in the world. At least he could do that as soon as he took care of the matter of the pesky American efforts in Zyngola.

Valach had been very specific in his directions for a sub-god. He had specified people to be secured and held specific ways, very odd but doable. All Abdullah had to do was secure the capture and containment of five Americans that would be present in Zyngola in the next few weeks and Valach would allow him to concentrate on creating more Jihad warrior cells and driving the infidels out of Africa and the middle East. Eventually his warrior cells would lead the infidels to their death!

Abdullah Hami had been blessed by Zultar since his birth. He had been raised in Palestine to worship Zultar

5

above all other activities. His parents had distorted Zultarian scriptures concerning infidels so that he grew into a teenager having love and respect for all mankind. His life view changed radically when a Jewish raid into Palestine to hunt terrorists had resulted in the death of his whole family with the divine exception of himself. A missile fired from an Israeli helicopter had gone astray and impacted in the front of his home where his mother, father, and two sisters were praying. They had all been killed instantly. He had been asked to deliver a meal to an invalid neighbor just before the attack and thus had been spared. He now knew that Zultar was punishing his parents for not following the Holy Scriptures pertaining to the death of all infidels. He didn't understand why his young sisters had to die at the same time. It really didn't matter anymore. That was over fifteen years ago. Since then, he had traveled far down the path of death and destruction of the infidels that had killed everyone he had loved that afternoon.

He remembered that horrible day as he stood there staring at the blackened and shredded bodies of his family in the rubble of the only home he had ever known, he swore an oath of vengeance against the Jewish nation and all other infidels at the same time.

That evening Zultar's voice had roared in Abdullah's mind. His god was mad that his parents had to die because they loved everyone, even the infidels. Zultar had then told Abdullah to listen to Valach, a lesser god of vengeance.

Valach had commiserated with Abdullah about his family, redirecting his pain and fanning the flame of vengeance into an all-consuming fire of anger. Valach had told him that in the years to come, Abdullah would be blessed because of his loss and Zultar would help him to avenge his family many times over. But to do this, he would have to be faithful to not only Zultar, but Valach also. In his pain and loss he agreed readily to the voice in his mind. His first assignment was to learn the The'an, Holy Zultarian scriptures, and become a teacher of the true faith. He especially wanted to teach the The'anic scriptures involving the elimination of all infidels.

Over the years he had become knowledgeable and had been elevated rapidly to his present position of Zulam. Actually there are many meanings for the title. His title of

Zulam was out of respect for his accomplishments for the faith and his detailed knowledge of scriptures in the The'an. The few that wanted to argue reasonableness and accommodation with infidels were silenced by Valach or by Adullah's followers. There is no room for wishy-washy Zultarians. The The'an was precise in its definitions. You were a Zultarian, you were becoming a Zultarian, or you were to die. Simple, just as the Prophet Blemian had written them hundreds of years before.

Abdullah's secret Jihad training center had proven Valach's teachings and had allowed Abdullah to train a small cadre of followers to repeatedly attack infidels in their homes at night without any reprisals or even suspicion that the attacks were taking place. The results had been heartwarming also. All of the infidels attacked had suffered greatly, most had died. And, no one was the wiser.

CHAPTER THREE

As the victory celebration party continued out on his side lawn, Jack Malone and his wife Laura sat by themselves and prayed together in consideration of the request from Victor Chamberlain to investigate the work interruptions at his plant in Zyngola.

After listening to the Lord for direction, Jack said quietly to Laura, "I feel led to help him with this investigation. What did God's Spirit give you?"

Laura thought for a few seconds. "We need to proceed with great caution on this because it is so volatile. Most of the people that follow the Zultarian faith are decent, law-abiding, friendly people who just want to live in peace. As usual, it's the radical fringes that generate the bad image that the press loves to publish. Of course, we have that problem right here at home in Christianity."

Then Victor brought up a different matter. "Jack, both you and David might need to give me advice on something. The food processing company was involved in some shady dealings under the men that stole it from me. I have done what I could to make amends to those hurt by these things. But, I have run into something that causes me concern. My processing plant in Zyngola was sold, illegally of course, and the money used for things I don't wish to know about. I have repurchased it at a considerably higher cost from the Zyngolian people that unknowingly bought it from the usurpers. The problem is that the local people now say that the facility is theirs regardless of who bought it or pays for it. They won't let anybody but their people enter the plant."

David was slowly nodding his head. "Exactly where is the facility located in Zyngola?"

Victor made a small face, "It is in the north, just north of Tymeria."

David looked at Victor for a few seconds. Then he included everyone in the information he had on the area, "The Republic of Zyngola is in Sub-Saharan Africa. It has approximately 21 million people in a country that is 3.5

million square Kilometers in area. The literacy rate for men is about 40%. If you count the women also, it drops to 23%. The country is 99% Zultarian and that is the basis for your problem.

The Zultarian faith instructs its adherents that once a place is owned by a Zultarian it is forever Zultarian, regardless of the governmental decrees or who owns it on paper. There is no room for negotiation. 'Once Zultarian, forever Zultarian' your plant, Victor, was owned, even if illegally, by Zultarians. Their faith now says it, and the land it is on is theirs forever. I take it you have appealed to the President and the Minister of Foreign Affairs?"

Victor frowned, "Yes, we did. Their position is that they don't want to rile the people because of the delicate balance over the revolt by the rebels in south Zyngola. So, there's nothing they will do to convince these people to let me staff the facility. The really sad part is that they are hurting their own people. Twenty percent of the output of the Zyngola facility went to the indigent of Zyngola free of charge."

Jack asked Victor. "What are you asking of us?"

Victor shook his head, "I don't know. I was hoping that there would be something you can suggest. I don't want to give up the plant, but I will if there is no other way."

David commented to Jack, "If you're thinking of getting involved, remember another one of the Zultarian faith's teachings. You are a Zultarian or you must die. This is similar to other teachings in that part of the world. The Jewish plus the Christian population of Zyngola is only 1% and it is one of the most persecuted groups in the world. Also, the Zultarian faith allows its members to enter into and sign agreements and pacts with non-Zultarians, but, since they are not of their faith, then the Zultarian doesn't have to honor what he has agreed to or signed. They don't give the other party the same rights of course."

Laura added, "We need to ask Mark and Sarah if they want to be part of this."

Victor looked up with a distressed look on his face, "Oh, I'm so sorry. I forgot to tell you that I hired Mark's company to look into security at that plant. Since I can't get my people into it, I needed to see if they could suggest steps to protect the plant while it is empty. I don't want it stripped and destroyed. I actually have a small staff inside the facility which includes a plant manager. I believe that Mark and Sarah decided to go to Tymeria to look into the situation this week."

Jack smiled, "Well then, I can't think of anybody that could scope out the problems and solutions better. Mark's security and anti-terrorism capabilities matched with Sarah's training in that area of the world are first class. We need to call them and see what the situation is and what we can do to help."

Victor smiled and said, "Great! After hearing about your problems here in Denver with the criminal element I could really use your experience. I don't think I'm capable of handling confrontational politics."

David sat there considering all of the options. He was very concerned because that area of the world was exceedingly confrontational on all levels.

CHAPTER FOUR

Mark rested and let his body heal as best it could. The "medical tech" had never shown up and Mark had really not expected one to appear. This whole setup stank of persecution and he knew that he was obviously a prisoner of religious politics.

He had examined his "room" carefully and found it to be just a ratty old cell. No cameras, no microphones, no room service, no mint on the pillow. "Oh! That's right; I don't even have a pillow."

He wondered if they would remember to feed him in the next few days. They hadn't even searched him when they brought him in. That was probably because of his tattered shape. He didn't have a wallet and he wasn't carrying any money. The arresting officer had taken his passport as soon as he was handcuffed on the stairs.

He casually checked his belt and felt the two lock picks hidden there. If he got the chance he'd open this cage and have another talk with the Commander. He was thinking these thoughts as two large security men came down the corridor and stopped at his "room". Mark stood up and faced the door.

They unlocked the door and entered the cell. They were both prime specimens of African-Arab manhood and very muscular. They both had thin leather gloves on.

The one with the worse scowl stood in front of Mark and sized up the American. "We're here to provide you with an education." To emphasize his intentions he smacked one fist into the other hand and grinned.

The other man had circled around behind Mark and now grabbed him in a bear hug from the back by wrapping his arms around Mark's chest. The man in front stepped up to Mark and delivered a strong underhand punch to the stomach.

Mark tightened up the muscles in his abdomen and rode out the punch, but, he acted like he had been hurt and bent forward. This pulled the man behind him forward and down. Mark then quickly reversed his motion and slammed the back of his head into the face of the man behind him. The satisfying "crunch" told of a broken nose and the arms let him go.

Mark then drove his own punch into the abdomen of the man in front of him. Mark's martial arts training and massive muscles in his arms put twice as much punch into his attacker than Mark had received from him. The man's face lost its color and he bent forward holding his stomach. Mark grabbed him by the back of his head and pulled downward as he brought his left knee up. This smashed the man's teeth resulting in several of them falling to the floor. The blow had also broken the man's nose and flipped him out of the cell to fall backward to the floor unconscious. Mark then bent at the waist and executed a rear mule kick to the second man's chest. Mark had put all of his two hundred plus pounds into the rear kick and the man flew across the cell to smash into the wall of the cell. He slid down the wall leaving a trail of blood and he fell bonelessly without resisting the fall.

Mark quickly dragged the first man back into the cell. This man was bleeding from his mouth and what was left of his flattened nose. He was moaning and thrashing about. It wouldn't do to have him regain consciousness too soon. Mark used the hair on the man's head to raise his head up about six inches from the floor and then Mark slammed it back down onto the concrete. The man quit his moaning and decided to sleep for a while.

Checking the second man, Mark found him also sleeping satisfactorily. Mark took the gloves from the larger man and put them on. He helped himself to the identification badge whose picture looked the most like himself except for the color and the blood on his shirt. He took the shirt off of the larger man. It was a tight fit but it wasn't covered in blood. He patted the two bodies down and didn't find anything else of interest except the keys to the cell and cell block. He stepped out of the cell and shut and locked the two sleeping beauties inside. Just to give the whole place trouble he broke the key off in the lock. He then walked to the end of the cell block, unlocked the door at the end of the hall, dropped the keys in a handy disposal bin, and let himself out.

Remembering the path to his cell, he retraced it and came to the door marked "Commander". Just as he was about to open the door, he heard a voice inside the office coming closer to the door and he quickly stepped to the side of the door frame. Checking the hall both ways he didn't see anyone else in the hall.

The door opened and the Captain in charge of his arrest at the mosque stepped out and shut the door behind him. As he stepped away from the door Mark looped his arm around the man's neck and yanked him back to the wall. The man struggled for a short while and then grew limp in Mark's choke hold. Mark reached around the man and took his pistol out of the holster. Then he reached around him with his free hand and opened the Commander's door. Stepping inside and closing the door he heard the Commander say, "Captain?"

Mark threw the Captain to one side and aimed the pistol at the Commander. "Don't get stupid! Keep your hands up and move away from your desk. You signal for help and you get to meet Zultar right now."

The Commander held his hands up and backed away from his desk as Mark approached. He smiled a wry smile. "Well, it seems that the spy part was true also."

Mark moved close to the man and smiled an icy smile, "Not even close. You have no idea who, or what, I am. Now, I want to know several things and your answers will determine the amount of damage you sustain before I leave. Be assured that I will discuss you and your little band of bullies with a special group with whom I am associated. They should pay you a visit, very soon."

The Commander blanched. "What do you mean?"

Mark moved around the desk and told the Commander to sit in the "guest" chair. Mark then sat in the Commander's chair with the automatic still trained on the man's chest. "I'll ask the questions. First, who set me up?"

As he talked, Mark opened the drawers in the desk. In the first drawer he found his passport and an ornamental knife. Mark put the passport into his pocket and then he took the knife out of the sheath. He got up and walked over to the Commander. Holding the knife to the Commander's throat he put the pistol into his belt at his back.

Looking the man in the eyes, he gestured with the knife. "If you are not completely cooperative or if your answers are incorrect, I will start taking fingers, then toes, then limbs." He reached out so quickly the other man did not have time to move. Mark used his left hand as he grabbed the man's right wrist and held that hand tightly down to the wooden arm of the chair. Mark then put the knife between the Commander's ring finger and little finger with the sharp edge against the little finger. A little blood ran down the knife blade and dropped onto the Commander's pants leg. Just a few bright red drops.

The Commander instinctively knew that this man wasn't bluffing. He would carve him up and leave him a cripple for life or take his life without anger, just efficiently. As the reality of the situation became crystal clear to him, he was filled with fear. He looked Mark in the face and started answering the questions truthfully.

Twenty minutes later he walked out of the building with Mark. The Commander still retained all his digits and limbs and was escorting "Mr. Connelly" back to his hotel a free and released man. The Commander had passionately implicated a dozen of his peers and bosses and Mark believed the Zultarian was telling him the truth.

Mark had explained that he wasn't interested in the Commander other than to get the charges dropped and to take care of the damaged goods in the "room" he had occupied with no questions asked or other problems.

Mark assured the Commander that the organization he represented would leave him alone, only if he forgot about Mark and did not bother him again. They parted company at the corner of the street in front of Mark's hotel. The Commander did not look back and headed for home. His home was the only place he knew of where he could have an illegal alcoholic drink and forget Mark and everything that had happened involving him. He was quite sure he didn't want a visit from Mark's "special group".

As the Commander walked he used his cell phone to issue orders concerning the sleeping Captain in his office and the "damaged goods" in the cell. He did not explain what had happened but his fear was communicated as anger to the man the orders were given to and there was no tolerance for questions or deviations from his orders. He then prayed that Zultar would forgive him for his actions today.

CHAPTER FIVE

Mark carefully checked his room for any signs that it had been searched or for any listening or video devices. His equipment was as he left it and he cleared the room without any sign of video, recording, or eavesdropping gear.

He had been back almost an hour when a coded knock came at the door and he checked it and opened it up to let Sarah into the room. His wife gave him a fierce hug and kissed him. She then held him out at arm's length and spun him around to see if there was any major damage other than the swollen left eye. Not finding anything she passionately kissed him again. Stepping back she said, "You were in and out of there so fast I didn't have time to set up an escape." She grinned at the slight smile on his face. "How many of them did you have to damage?"

He raised an eyebrow, "Three wounded, one scared."

Sarah smiled, "Oh, and do we have to "get out of town" right now?"

Mark laughed, "No we don't. But we are leaving anyway in about an hour to regroup and get some reinforcements before we come back. I got some very interesting information from one of their officers which we'll discuss after we're out of Zyngola. Help me pack and get a car for a trip to the airport."

Six hours later as the plane they interconnected to in Cairo flew towards France, Mark and Sarah were seated in two first-class seats and he filled her in on the events after his entering the security building. He then told her what the Commander had revealed. "It's funny in a bizarre way. I was not a specific target for this oppression and persecution. I just happened to come out of the food plant right after the order was issued from a Zulam to find, and harass Christians or Jews." He looked at Sarah with compassion because he knew that her people suffered this all the time, all over the world.

Arranging his thoughts carefully, he continued. "As I am sure you know, Zyngola is renowned for its civil rights violations and persecution of all forms of people, especially the Jews and Christians because of the overwhelming Zultarian population. I would think that most Jews would be intelligent enough to stay out of there. I understand that the Zultarians believe unless you are a Zultarian you are an infidel. Their version of the connotation means pretty much the same thing that Hitler called the Jews during World War II."

"We, or any non-Zultarians are characterized as a lower life form by the ruling council and the lunatic fringe that runs the country and it doesn't really matter what happens to us or what is done to us. After having been with Jack and Laura for a while, I see this whole thing as a satanic policy to turn one group of people against another group. No matter who loses, Satan wins."

Sarah was slowly nodding her head, "Yes, this has been a principle in the Middle East since Abraham's time. It seems that Christians and Jews are treated the same, at least here. We're sport to be taunted, hunted, and destroyed. This has always been and still remains intolerable. This is the same emotion I had when I was Jewish and working for the Mossad. Even now as a Messianic Jew I am disgusted by the concept."

Mark agreed. "As Jack would say, "we live in a fallen world that will only get worse until Yahshua returns". But, even with this problem, we have a job to do and we need to come up with a plan to counteract the intolerance and persecution affecting Victor's plant and its operations."

Sarah stared at her husband for a while with a small smile. "Do you realize that what you're proposing is exactly what the Israelis have been attempting to do for the last century without success?"

Mark took that thought into consideration and it caused him to regroup mentally. After adding in the effects of the cultural heritages of the Jewish and Arab and African races he agreed that the problem was outside his scope to solve. He knew that God would have to provide the answer. Mark realized that he was learning to lean on God for the proper direction rather than ask for God's help to do what he thought was right. He decided they needed more brain power on this problem than the two of them could supply.

"We should call the team together." He said as he reached for the Air Phone in his armrest.

The phone rang at Castle Malone and it was answered by Laura. "Hi Mark. We were just about to call you."

Mark felt the unction of the Spirit of God and discerned the connection. He asked her, "Oh, and why were you going to call us?"

Laura said, "Hold on a moment, here's Jack."

Jack listened to her and spoke to Mark. "Victor asked Laura and I to help him with the problem that he is having with the local population in Zyngola. He explained to us that he already had you working on the security of his plant there and we thought that you might have some insight we could use to start our investigation."

Mark laughed, "Do I have some insight? Yeah, I have gotten a good look at the problem, at least with one eye. You could say that. We're on a flight to Paris right now and want to get together with you two, Minister Throman, David Zahavy and Gary Eisenthal if at all possible. We need a Crossfire Team war council as soon as possible."

Jack digested the news for a minute. "Okay. When will you be here? I'll try to arrange for the others to be here."

Mark looked at their flight connections. "We will be in Paris in about two hours. I've already booked a private jet to Denver International Airport that will take about sixteen hours. It's two p.m. in Denver right now so make the meeting for around noon tomorrow and that way we can spend a couple of hours kicking this around first. Oh! Yeah, I guess that we ought to get Victor in on this too seeing that it is his plant that is in contention."

Jack looked at the billionaire sitting across from him. "I think that can be arranged."

After their conversation with Mark, Jack explained their request to David and Victor. "From the way Mark sounded I think their information may well be crucial in determining how we should tackle the whole problem."

Victor raised a finger. "If this is going to cause too much trouble, I can just sell it back to the original buyers and let them handle it on their own."

Jack considered everything that had happened so far. "I would think that the best course would be to wait until we hear what the Connelly's have to say before we decide on any actions."

David agreed, "The situation in the northern part of Zyngola is very unstable and could make our involvement completely moot at any time. I want to talk to my people and see if there have been any new events or trends going on there that would have a bearing on our involvement."

Jack pointed to a phone in the living room. "Use that one. It is capable of handling scrambled calls. Just push 7777 before dialing your number."

Victor went back out to the party and David left to make his phone call. Jack looked at Laura and suggested that they again pray about their involvement and what course of action the Lord would want them to take.

Retiring to their bedroom upstairs, Laura went to her favorite prayer place which was an overstuffed divan. Jack knelt by the side of their bed and they sought the Lord.

CHAPTER SIX

As Jack relaxed into his communion with the Lord he felt a familiar heaviness settle on him that was his way of feeling the presence of God's Spirit. He continued to praise and worship Yahshua and even though he was resting his head on his hands on his bed, with his eyes shut, a stunning vista opened up before him. Visually it was breathtaking. He was hurtling over the surface of an ocean at a great speed. His travel was away from the sun and the colors of the ocean and sky were brilliant and vibrant. He realized that he was slowing down as an island appeared before him on the horizon. It was a beautiful sight. The white sands were contrasted with the dark green foliage of the trees. The lone mountain peak stood tall in gray granite, towering over the little piece of land.

As he came to the island his speed decreased even more and he noticed that his path led to a point halfway up the mountainside. Closer still he realized that the island was idyllic in that everything was working together in perfect order and that there wasn't a single thing out of place. He couldn't have named all the things that made up this impression but he knew that he knew that this was a sign of the presence of the Lord of the Universe.

His flight ended on a large, flat area. He was able to shift his view from the mountain to the sea and looked out from the island. The wind sang a beautiful harmony to his spirit as it flowed over his body. The feeling of peace was so overpowering he could not worry about anything or even care if he ever left the ledge on the side of the mountain.

He did not know how long he rested in this state of bliss. He could feel every muscle, sinew, nerve, and fiber of his being aligning with some cosmic standard of correctness and his thinking became crystal clear. The refreshing continued into the evening and even as darkness fell over the island.

Jack knew he had business he had to take care of but the peace in his spirit was so great he wasn't worried about it. He knew it would be taken care of in the proper time and the proper order. He then realized that there was a glow behind him that was growing in intensity. He felt no fear or dread, only peace. He turned around and saw the angel Caleb floating near him. "Hello Caleb." was Jack's only comment.

Caleb tipped his head to the side and studied Jack for a few seconds. "How are you Jack?" came as a solid voice in Jack's head.

Jack continued to speak aloud although he doubted that it was needed. "I'm fine Caleb, but I have some concerns and need direction from the Lord almighty."

Caleb floated closer to Jack. "Concerning your involvement in Zyngola, right?"

Jack nodded and this seemed to be sufficient for the angel.

Caleb was about to answer when a strange thing occurred. A single, red spot appeared on the angel's right temple for a split second. It came and went so fast Jack wasn't sure he saw it.

Caleb spoke, "Before we cover that, I am concerned that the security and concealment of the crucifixion nail are no longer acceptable. You need to move it to a better place of security."

Jack was a little confused and wanted to clarify this direction. "Caleb, you told me just a little while ago that the nail was as secure as it could be. Now you are telling me that it isn't safe?"

Caleb hung there for a few seconds, "Jack, believe me when I tell you that new things have been happening and the nail isn't safe anymore. But, we can discuss that later. I want you to look at the rock to your right side."

Jack looked down at the indicated rock. There was a beautiful golden sword laying there. It was so beautiful that it caused an ache in Jack's soul to take it up and keep it forever. He started to reach for the sword when he suddenly saw a festering wound on the handle of the sword. He pulled his hand back and realized that things just weren't right. He turned to the angel and asked him, "In whose name do you declare the truth about yourself and this sword?"

Caleb frowned and acted hurt. "Jack, we've been through too much for you to doubt me."

Jack repeated, "In whose name do you confess that you are an angel from Yahveh, God and creator of the universe?"

Caleb was silent. Jack knew then that this wasn't an angel of the Lord. "I ask God to bind you and I ask Yahshua to have his Holy angels cast you into the abyss to never return."

The image of Caleb shifted and blurred. The evil visage of a demon showed for a brief second and then it was gone with a faintly heard scream of rage and frustration that seemed to be moving away.

Jack stood on the ledge in the night and waited for the next event to occur. It was another glow and another Caleb that approached. Jack immediately tested the spirit. "In whose name do you confess the truth that you are an angel of Yahveh, the most high God?"

The Caleb image smiled and spoke, "The Lord Yahshua the Christ of Nazareth who came in the flesh. He is my Lord and Master as he is yours, Jack. I am so glad that you were able to see through the imposter. The Lord heard your prayers and I was sent. I was delayed by battle for a while, trying to reach you. I was victorious but at the cost of leaving you to be deceived by the enemy."

Caleb continued, "The enemy is aware of our relationship as they are of the one between Laura and Rose. But there is little they can do to interfere except to try to cause you to sin. The demon knew of your passion for edged weapons and he was attempting to cause your desire for the sword to make it an idol. But your wife's prayer coverage for you fought with his efforts to deceive you. That is why you saw the spot on the demon's head and the wound on the sword. Her prayers undermined the demon's concentration and abilities. Your response was correct to send him to the pit forever and I doubt that they will mount such an effort again."

Jack indicated the island and asked, "Then tell me, is this vision really from God or is it from the enemy?"

Caleb nodded slowly, "Your discernment grows every day. This vision and island is the Lord's and the enemy only intruded on it temporarily at a large cost to them. It was meant as a place pleasing for you to meet with me so that I can help you understand God's will concerning the

Zultarian deception and the overall situation. Listen now to the word of the Lord!"

"Long have the followers of this pagan moon god rejected me as they follow the teachings of Blemian who himself rejected me for self love and worship of his own greatness. In a season soon to come I will show them the true way. Most of these deceived ones are seeking me and are trying to live their love for me, but have been deceived by an idolatrous teaching that is abhorrent to me. Now there are certain followers of Zultar who are even more deceived by the evil one. He has put them to planning a great infamy in the name of their moon god which I will not allow. I have chosen you to stop this evil in My Name. Though many dangers face you and those with you, do not be afraid, nor fear death, for I will be with you always."

Jack stood there in the glow of Caleb's light and considered the mission that the Lord had just given him. Looking up at Caleb he asked, "What is this great infamy that we are to stop?"

Caleb seemed to look at a great distance for a short time and then refocused on Jack. "The answer to that question is waiting for you in Africa. I see many things that are to be, but I do not know the actual disaster that they are making. I can tell you that the evil one has placed this operation almost completely under the direction of a major demonic force named Valach who deceives human minds through their worship of Zultar. I can tell you that Valach is aware of you and your team and that you need to be on your guard against his efforts."

Jack slowly turned around and stared out over the darkened ocean. It was still very peaceful on the island but he could sense storm clouds headed his way. He remembered when he didn't know Yahveh God or Yahshua and life seemed so much simpler. Tracking that thought he remembered the feeling he had in a men's store in Denver when his walk with the Lord began. Then he felt that he was poised over the vastness of a huge, unseen abyss and the winds blowing over it were suddenly affecting his life. This time he knew what the abyss was and on which side he was fighting. Shaking his head he realized how far he had traveled since those days. It was obvious that there was still a long path ahead of him and Laura and their friends. He said quietly, "Thank you Caleb."

Caleb's voice was full of admiration. "You are most welcome, but, it is I who Thank you." The glow behind him faded, followed by the island and the sea. Jack looked up from where he was praying at the side of his bed and looked to see Laura watching him intently. Jack got up and walked over to her chair. "Did you get any advice from God?"

She nodded, "Yes, but I think your revelation is going to be far more interesting than mine.

After Jack recounted his meeting with the fake and real Caleb's he knelt down next to Laura and pulled her into his embrace. He hugged her tightly. "Thank you for your constant prayer coverage for me. That is the only thing that kept them from fooling me."

Laura patted his hand, "You're welcome. I just love you so much I keep asking the Lord to protect you and keep you safe for me." She looked up at him and asked, "What is our plan? It seems obvious that we are going to go to Zyngola pretty soon."

Jack let her go and sat down next to her. "I really don't know. The Lord's words, *I and those with me will face great dangers"* bothers me. I know you have become a warrior for the Lord and I have great confidence in your abilities. But I'm still leery of leading you into harm's way."

Laura smiled at her husband's gallantry. "I know you want to care for me but where does our protection come from?"

Jack nodded, "Psalms 91, *I will say to the Lord, You are my place of safety and protection..."* I want to wait until we have the team meeting with Mark and Sarah tomorrow and see what they have to tell us. Then maybe we will have some idea how to proceed with this assignment."

CHAPTER SEVEN

At noon the next day, the strategy meeting of the Crossfire Team was held in the Malone's home which had become known as "Castle Malone" due to the NovaStar Home Defense System and the defensive construction of the dwelling.

Jack's six-foot, four-inch frame had filled out over the last three battlegrounds and his blonde hair had been shortened and had darkened a little. Gray-green eyes were still the dominant feature of his strong, chiseled face. Normally warm and caring, Jack's eyes would turn ice-cold when evil or insanity threatened.

Laura's crown of ash-blonde hair was slightly longer than Jack's and four inches closer to the ground. Standing at an even six foot tall, she noticed that she hadn't lost any weight in her world travels and combat with the forces of darkness and terrorism. But it had moved around on her frame somewhat. Her waist was as small as it was when she was in high school but her upper body, especially her arms, had filled out. She was quite sure that was the result of packing equipment through deserts, forests, jungles, and ice fields. Not to mention carrying and using a variety of assault rifles and grenade launchers. There also were the various trainings that her husband insisted on every day. The martial arts training from Jack, the combat training from Mark, and, of course, spy world training from Sarah. Laura noticed that her legs had become leaner but stronger and still had the curves of youth. Laura spent as much time as possible keeping her skin soft and moisturized but sometimes she was hard-pressed just to find any cosmetics in this high-speed world. Still, she tried.

Mark Connelly stood next to Jack discussing the events of the last few days. He outweighed Jack by thirty pounds and none of it was fat. His physique was what the young people called "buff". His black hair hadn't started to thin or turn gray and was an unruly mop most of the time. His good looks were strangely at odds to his fighting abilities. His mind was very focused and he seemed to be constantly alert. At six-foot, two-inches he was only slightly shorter than Jack and the two of them made a dangerous combination.

Sarah Connelly was a darker version of Laura but with the same twinkle in her eye that made people consider her "fun". But as an ex-Mossad field agent and assassin her idea of "fun" would cause most people to blanch. Her new marriage to Mark was literally a match made in heaven. This combination was also one that a person would be smart not to go up against.

The other members of the team included Minister Alan Throman, an elderly Christian pastor whose active life-style belied his eighty-plus years of age. His hair was white and his frame was dwarfed by the other men present but his presence was notable by the purposeful attitude he exhibited. He relaxed in one of the living room chairs and watched the other people and their interactions with interest.

Tastefully-dressed, David Zahavy added class to the mostly casual crowd. At five-foot, eleven inches tall he fit in well with this crowd. His thinning brown hair was still full enough to require combing but he liked it short which made it look thinner. He still managed to arrange field assignments for himself which kept his mind and abilities at a level of the people he normally managed. His position as one of the lead control agents of the Israeli Mossad had been instrumental in the effectiveness of the Crossfire Team in past assignments. He had received permission from the Mossad to become an attached member of the team after their success in combating terrorism in Israel. His ability to cut through to the core of complicated problems was a major asset to the team's capabilities.

Stan and Debbie Hargrove sat next to each other on one of the sofas. Stan was a "retired" police captain from the Salt Lake City Police department. His wife was an on-leave, CIA assassin, a fact that Stan had not realized until the President of the United States revealed her clandestine occupation to him. Stan stood five-foot, ten inches tall and was similar in build to most policemen, minus the doughnut-fueled waistline. A good-natured man, he was capable of facing down the meanest of bad guys without a qualm. Debbie was a petite, non-descript woman that could blend in anywhere with a housewife's charm. She had left her brown hair shoulder-length with a flip. A person would never expect her to be what her government job required her to be.

Stan and Debbie had gone to work for Mark's Security Company after leaving the Utah area. They were a major asset to the team in their ability to dig out information and do the hard leg-work needed by the team. Debbie's exceptional skill with a rifle was matched by her ability with the computer.

The last member of the team was a large man, six-foot two, who looked like a retired wrestler in build. His graying hair and beard made him look more genteel and worldly. Jim Grady was, like Stan, a retired policeman and enjoyed talking and working with Stan when they were together on team business. Jim's police work had been for the City of Denver, Colorado. The fact that Jim Grady was also an eighth-level black belt instructor in martial arts wasn't obvious until needed. He was also the Sensei that had trained both Jack and Mark in years past.

Although not an active member of the team, a tall, good-looking African-American man, Victor Chamberlain, was also present. He had become a good friend, benefactor, and sponsor of the Crossfire team after they had rescued him from captivity on his own island.

The fact that he was one of richest men in the world had become secondary to his new goals in life. He had found Yahshua when he had nowhere else to turn. He was now on a mission to see what he could do with his wealth that would give glory to God. He had also found that he could use his organizational and creative talents to help the team in their battles with the dark world of evil.

Jack called everyone together and explained the situation facing the team concerning Victor's food processing plant in Zyngola in general terms and then turned the meeting over to Mark to explain the local conditions and prevailing attitudes in the area of the processing plant.

Mark put his questions concerning how to change the local hatred towards Christians to Minister Throman.

Alan started his discussion with a history of Zultar. "The word Zultar is an Arabic word for "god", meaning, 'the god Zultar'. Zultar is purely an Arabic term used exclusively in reference to a specific Arabic deity. "

He looked and saw that everyone was paying attention to his presentation. "Most people are not aware that the name Zultar is a pre-Zultarian name which corresponds to the Babylonian Bel. He was one of the Meccan deities. The Arabs, living in this part of Africa, before the time of Blemian, accepted and worshiped, after a fashion, a supreme god called Zultar. The name Zultar is also evident in archaeological and literary remains of pre-Zultarian Africa.

The Minister took a sip of his water and continued, "According to Middle Eastern scholars, both in pre-Zultarian times, Zultar-worship, as well as the worship of Baal, were astral religions in that they involved the worship of the sun, the moon, and the stars. The name Zultar was used as the *personal* name of one of the moon gods, in addition to the other titles that could be given to him. "Zultar, the moon god was considered a "high" god. That is, he was viewed as being at the top of the pantheon of African deities" "Along with Zultar, however, the Arabs and Africans in this part of Africa worshipped a host of lesser gods".

Sitting down, the elderly man warmed to his history lesson. "It is a well-known fact, archaeological speaking, that the crescent moon was the symbol of worship of the moon god in Arabia, Africa, and throughout the Middle East in pre-Zultarian times. Archaeologists have excavated numerous statues and hieroglyphic inscriptions in which a crescent moon was seated on the top of the head of the deity to symbolize the worship of the moon-god. Now this is very similar to other Arabic and African religions. Interestingly, while the moon was generally worshipped as a female deity in the Ancient Near East, the Arabs in this part of the world viewed it as a male deity. The worship of stellar deities, instead of Yahveh, was always a temptation faced by the Israelites. The Zyngolic tribe into which Blemian was born was particularly devoted to Zultar, the moon god, and especially since he was viewed as an intercessor for the people.

Switching to the subject of the creator of the Zultarian movement, Blemian, the Minister laid out details that the team needed to know to understand the origins of the religion. "Blemian lived in the Eighth Century and had become embittered towards the Jewish race and their upstart off-spring the Christians. He started a new religion he called Zultharism based on the moon-god Zultar. Since most of the people in the area that was to become Zyngola eleven centuries later already worshiped the moon-god Zultar, Blemian convinced the other African-Arabs to eschew the lesser gods and worship only Zultar as the supreme god. His movement swelled for two hundred years until it ran, headlong, into the Muslim/Allah onslaught. Most other religions were absorbed or destroyed by the followers of Islam. But, Zultarism wasn't absorbed. It went underground in the face of an unbeatable opposing force. It stayed underground and gained members as a secret society until the late nineteenth century. Many Zultarians feign allegiance to Islam to survive. But, their hearts were pledged to Zultar and they continued a double life until Zyngola was formed by international law in the mid-twentieth century."

Taking another drink the Minister continued his lecture to his interested audience. "Blemian had laid down the laws in his version of the scriptures which he called the The'an. Now consider that the literal Arabic name of Blemian's father was Abd-Zultar. His uncle's name was Mulha-Zultar. These names reveal the personal devotion that Blemian's pagan family had to the worship of Zultar, the only moon god in Africa that could compete with Allah of the Muslims."

"History proves conclusively that before Zultarism came into existence, the faithful in the Kingdom of Kush worshipped the moon-god Zultar. We have also seen that it was a matter of common practice to use the name of the moon-god in personal names in Blemian's tribe. That Zultar was a pagan deity in pre-Zultarian times is incontestable. So, why was Blemian's God named after a pagan deity in his own tribe?"

"It is an undeniable fact that a Zultar idol was set up at Kush along with all the other Arabic-African idols of the time. The pagans prayed towards Kush because that is where their gods were stationed. It made sense to them to face in the direction of their god and pray since that is where he was. Since the idol of their moon god, Zultar, was at Kush, they prayed towards Kush. An entire nation-tribe of African Arabs was involved in moon-worship. Therefore, you can see, in part, the early success Zultarism had amongst African-Arab groups that had traditionally worshipped the moon-gods. Also, you can see that the use of the crescent moon as the symbol of Zultarism, and which appears on the flag of Zyngola, Africa, and surmounts Zyngolan minarets and mosque roofs, is a throwback to the days when Zultar was worshipped as the moon-god in Kush. "

"Educated Zultarians, including the ones in Zyngola, understand these facts only too well - better, in fact, than most Christians. "

The reason for this lengthily diatribe is to show you the validity of the argument that the worship of Zultarism is based on a pagan god and is misleading millions of people. The sad fact is that the upper level of the educated African-Arabs knows the truth but many of them use the "gospel" of Zultarism to control masses of people. They use the believers in this "religion" to eliminate others that do not fall under their control. You are facing a major move of the enemy, but the fact is that most Zultarians believe in peace and love and should not be targeted or eliminated. Yahveh God wants all men to renounce false religions and turn to Him and be saved. To change the attitudes of the people around this production plant would require re-education of all Zultarians. I'm afraid that is an effort only God could accomplish." He waved his hand as if to say "Okay, I'm done."

CHAPTER EIGHT

As Minister Throman sat down, David Zahavy stood up. His knowledge of the political climate and the clash between the Zultarians and the rest of the world, especially the Jewish race was encyclopedic. But to focus the discussion on the matter at hand, he picked out the pertinent points that he knew would benefit the team.

"Personally I don't think we have much chance in changing the attitudes of the population of that area. They are solidly anti-anything except Zultarians. Therefore, if you are determined to keep the plant, I suggest we concentrate on solidifying the surrounding area."

He looked at the owner. "Victor, my recommendation is that you go through Zyngolan middle men and buy up everything in a ten to twenty block area around your plant. Your finances would allow you to meet any reasonable demands. Do this all secretively so that the ruling council in Tymeria doesn't get wind of it until it is done. Use all of your contacts and whatever influence the team has with the United States and Israeli governments to put pressure on the government there to cede the area to you so that no one can dispute it legally. They are extremely needy in that part of the world. Your initial investment and monthly fees in U.S. dollars will cause many in the government to set aside their religious preferences to acquire your money to further their own aims. This I can assure you will work."

"Then we build a security wall around the complete area and build a mini-city for your workers. In other words, create an independent operation that will allow your people to work and function without interference during normal operations. Include a helipad so that you can transfer workers and staff to and from the airport without having to travel through the city. There would be a lot of resistance to begin with, but over time your generosity to the locals with your free food program and a free-market zone for your people to procure local items would set up a lucrative sub-culture that would be very beneficial to the population. This will cause the local people to want to keep the status-quo and not demonstrate or attack you. Eventually your plant would become a part of the economy and be accepted."

David walked back to his seat. Turning around he added a comment. "Don't use local people for any internal work including cleaning, construction, or services or you will end up with the same situation we are faced with in Israel." He sat down and arranged the crease on his trouser leg.

Laura stood up and suggested that the entire team pray and ask God what He wanted them to do since they were faced with such resistance and violence, including the Zultarian insistence that the land belonged to them forever, that to forcibly insert the plant could lead to a variety of possible ends that none of them there could foresee."

Everyone agreed with her and Jack asked the Minister to lead the prayer. Anyone that received anything from the Lord should add their comments. Debbie Hargrove suggested that they have a time of praise and worship first to set their hearts and minds into the proper mode for seeking the Lord.

She had her guitar and began playing Christian songs that the majority of the people there knew and could sing along with as they worshiped. The ones that didn't know the words picked up on them quickly and the praise flowed together as one voice to God. As they sang and praised the Lord, a peaceful heaviness settled on the group. After a while the singing came to an end and Alan Throman started praying that Jesus would give them direction in the matters at hand. He knew that the Lord knew what they were going to ask before they asked it. So he didn't elaborate or get really specific, just asked for wisdom and direction.

Jack remembered the words of the Lord that Caleb had given him on the island in the spirit. "*Now there are certain followers of Zultar who are even more deceived by the evil one. He has put them to planning a great infamy in the name of their moon god which I will not allow. I have chosen you to stop this evil in My Name. Though many dangers face you and those with you, do not be afraid, nor fear death, for I will be with you always.*" He had a sudden clarity of understanding which he identified as a revelation from God. He spoke forth the revelation into the spirits of the rest of the team.

"This 'great infamy' that the Lord has spoken of is the reason that Victor's plant is under duress. The plant problem is actually a side issue which will be resolved when we have dealt with the true issue that God wants us to eliminate. We are being called to operate as God's agents on Earth to confront and destroy this evil. Our answers will be found in Zyngola but will be fraught with danger and peril for each of us. The battle is the Lord's and we are His warriors. We will be victorious in this confrontation with Satan's agents if we walk in God's will and his protection. I thank you Yahshua for your insight and your faith in us. We pray in agreement for your wisdom and protection as we strive to serve you. Place the full armor of God on each of us and send your angels with us to the battle. We pray all things in your name, Lord Yahshua, the Christ of Nazareth who came in the flesh."

Mark and Sarah glanced at each other and Mark stood up. "I have no knowledge of what we are up against in the spirit, but Sarah and I can prepare the team for any human combat that the enemy throws against us. We need to figure out who should go, when they should go, and what we are going to do." He looked to Jack for input.

Jack had continued to pray about the same questions and felt he had some answers. Standing up he clapped Mark on the shoulder and addressed the group. "I feel that we don't have to have a well-defined agenda for the following reasons. We don't know what the enemy is attempting to do so we can't focus our actions yet. We do know that through the demon "Valach" they are aware of us. Therefore if we simply show up in their part of the world they should take the initiative and come against us. That should give us the leads we need to move against them until we have sufficient information to determine our course of action."

Mark smiled, "But of course, this gives them the first strike which will be a large advantage for them."

Jack nodded his agreement with that thought. "True, but we aren't novices at this game anymore. We can manage our vulnerabilities so that they take the one we want them to. If we plan it right we should be able to turn the tables on them."

Mark thought about that for a few seconds. "I like that idea. It will definitely bring them out into the open and we should get a handle on who the enemy is, and perhaps, what they are doing."

David had been following their discussion closely. "I think I have an idea on how we can enter Tymeria without being watched like hawks and this should give us an edge on arrangements and setup. Israel has been using Greece as a middleman to allow us to get agents into Zyngola and I think we can get entry visas as part of an entertainment group."

Laura laughed, "What are you going to bill us as? The dancing Crossfire Team?"

After the laughing settled down David agreed that they needed a legitimate cover. He asked, "How about your step-sister? She performed in Tel Aviv during the poisonings?"

Jack said, "You mean Christi Steel?"

David nodded, "Yes, she is a legitimate entertainment act with publicity and fans and everything we need to disguise our presence."

Jack said, "But she is a Christian singer. Wouldn't they refuse her entry because of that?"

David shook his head, "No, because she is classified as a singing act, not as a Christian singing act."

Laura frowned somewhat, "David, you have been doing some homework on this haven't you?"

David laughed, "Well, yes. I was looking for any angle to get us into the country that wouldn't compromise us or connect us directly with Victor's operation."

Mark asked, "How much danger will she be in?"

David thought for a minute. "I don't see that she will be in much danger. We could act as her entourage and she could deny anything if we were discovered. Anyway, I just want to use her cover to get into the country. As soon as we are in and out of sight, we'll slip away from her and her association with us will end."

Laura shook her head, "Like the last time she came to Israel? She wasn't going to be involved then either."

David said, "Well, I think she would be only slightly involved, if at all. But if you have a better way, I'll be willing to listen to it.

It quickly became obvious that David had done his homework. There didn't seem to be a better solution as to how to get into the country without sending up flags all over the Zyngolan government and the rest of the Zultarian world.

Jack made the call to Christi. She wasn't available but he left a message for her to call him back as soon as possible. Basing their operation on the fact that they should be able to convince the rising singing star to help them they began to build scenarios and equipment packaging on the basis of being an entourage to her group. It wasn't easy considering the amount of firepower they were planning on getting into the radical Zultarian country.

CHAPTER NINE

The planning was winding down when Christi called back. Jack explained the entire situation to her so that she could make a reasonably informed decision. She checked her bookings calendar and then used a second line to talk to her agent. Coming back on line with Jack she said that it would be possible if David could get someone in Zyngola to sponsor her concert. She said that she would keep it country and light rock with an imbedded Christian message. But first, she needed to pray to see if God wanted her to do it or not.

God indeed wanted her to do it and had arranged the cancellation of another concert to give her the time to do it. She realized that in the first five minutes of prayer. Then she prayed that the Lord would give her a significant part to play this time in helping the team to succeed. Since she was praying in God's will, she was sure that God would grant her prayer.

Jack got Christi's confirmation at one p.m. and David's organization had a sponsor for her by two p.m. with a scheduled concert in Tymeria the next week. Working with David she supplied the names of her band and the road people that were needed to make the concert a reality. David added seven pseudonyms to the list and forwarded it on to the Zyngolan government for approval. Visas and other documentation were already on their way from Israel for the team.

Mark, Sarah, and David had altered some sound and stage equipment to allow for secreting seven Armitage Arms M16Z "Snakes" so that they would pass customs. The Snake is a heavily customized M16 used by American Special Forces units. It is a very compact rifle that features a high-recoil absorption stock, under barrel mounted high-intensity xenon flashlight; and a unique mechanism that allows the shooter the option of unsuppressed or suppressed fire via an integral barrel silencer at the flip of a switch.

Additionally, these assault rifles were equipped with custom Nikon-Zeiss MT-12 variable magnification optical scopes with lowlight and passive IR capabilities and an M109, 40mm grenade launcher. This allowed the team to have volume firepower in an extremely compact design and still retain the ability to do sniper work out to four hundred yards. The ammunition was standard .223 caliber rounds used by half the world.

David also arranged to have handguns and other weapons of smaller size smuggled into the Zyngolan nation prior to the team's arrival. David had to return to Israel to attend to some critical business so the team that was going to Zyngola consisted of Jack, Laura, Mark, Sarah, Stan, Debbie, and Sensei Grady,

Since Christi was based out of Denver, it was an easy arrangement for them to join her band for the trip to Tymeria three days later.

Like all airline trips it was long, tiring, and occasionally frustrating. The team weathered the trip quietly and by the time they passed through customs they were glad to escape the airport restrictions and climb into an aging minibus for the ride to their hotel.

As they rode along, Mark mentioned that it seemed like they made it into the city without attracting any undue attention. Their plan was to get situated, then slip away from Christi's group quietly. David had given them the address of a safe-house they could use for a short time. They would then set about dangling some attractive bait and see what bit.

It was a good plan. Unfortunately, like most plans it went awry almost as soon as the bus reached the hotel. As they started to disembark from the bus there was a disturbance in the crowd on the sidewalk. Jack, Mark and Jim had already gotten off and started for the hotel when a contingent of Zyngolan police came around the corner and made a dash for the bus.

Jack started back to help the others when Jim Grady stopped him and shook his head. "We need to slip away now! We can't help them if we get arrested too."

Mark agreed with him, so they slid slowly back into the entrance to an alley. Watching from the alley they saw the police take everyone, including the Zyngolan driver, into custody and march them off to a security van. Mark saw Sarah wink as she was herded past the end of the bus. So, at least she was aware that they were still free and why they didn't come back.

Quickly moving away from the scene of the arrests, the three men conferred as they walked and decided that they needed to get out of sight as soon as possible. They were still dressed in western clothing and were obviously strangers.

Mark had memorized the address of the safe house and had a mental map of the city in his mind. He steered the three of them to the right place and they carefully observed the building. It was a three story apartment. Their rooms were on the ground floor and seemed to be empty and Mark couldn't detect anyone watching the place. They walked into the foyer and down a shabby hall. In the dim light of a single bulb he found the key where it was supposed to be, in a crack at the top of the door.

Jack felt that there were eyes watching them but couldn't discern if they were physical eyes or spiritual eyes. Mark opened the door and they quietly entered and shut the door. Checking the place out, Mark found an audio bug hidden under a lamp. Other than that the place was clean. Mark examined the listening device and felt pretty sure that it was Israeli and not Zyngolian. He clipped the wires anyway.

The three men sat down at the small kitchen table and took stock of their situation. It wasn't good. They had no weapons, no supplies other than what they could find in the safe house. Four members of the team were in the hands of the Zultarian government, along with Christi and her band. Jim Grady added, "Don't forget the Zyngolan driver of the bus too."

Both of the other men looked at him with an obvious lack of understanding as to why that was important. Jim elaborated, "Either the driver was in on the trap and they took him in to make him look innocent or they were just ordered to get everyone on the bus. I would suspect the latter. That means, whatever information they have is probably with someone else than the arresting party. More than likely the key player will be in on any interrogation. It is at that time they will discover that we are missing and start their dragnet to find us. They know we came into the airport and went through customs, but they don't know when we got off the bus. It is probable that one of the band members will tell them that we got off at the hotel."

Using his years as a policeman, Jim followed the probable course of the investigation and tracking that Zyngolian police would do to find them. "Starting at the hotel they will use bribery or intimidation to get anyone in the area to identify pictures of us and tell where they saw us go. They probably have informants all over the city also. I doubt that it will take them more than a couple of hours to track us to this building."

Jack mentioned the eyes he felt as they entered the room. "If the enemy is using spiritual tracking they may be here even sooner than that. We need to determine the right course of action and act on it real soon."

Mark was thinking of the option when there was a quiet tapping at the front door to the apartment. The three men exchanged looks and moved to the door. There were no windows or peepholes to forewarn them, so Jack and Jim moved to each side of the door and Mark carefully opened it with his foot planted so that if they shoved the door it wouldn't open all the way.

Standing in the doorway was a nondescript young man with three heavy canvas bags sitting on the floor beside him. He was about five-foot, eight inches tall with brown hair and a small build. He had penetrating brown eyes which took in the apartment and Mark in a glance. He said, in good English and quietly, "David sent these to you." Mark reached out and grabbed two of the bags and ushered the young man into the apartment carrying the other one.

The man quickly sized up Jack and Jim and shut the door. "You must get out of here in the next twenty minutes. The government agents are heading this way as I speak!" His urgency couldn't be denied and it added to the concern the three men already had about their situation.

Mark pointed at the bags, "Jack, Jim, unload these and see what we have." He turned to the young man and stuck out his hand. "Thank you for risking your cover to come here and warn us. I'm Mark Connelly. Did David give you any other instructions?"

The man flicked a quick glance at the one window and the door to the apartment. "I'm Hiram with the Mossad. Commander Zahavy told me to help you any way I could. I've got another place the police aren't aware of that you can use as a base and we can get there in ten minutes if we hurry."

Jack and Jim had inventoried the bags and told Mark, "Handguns, knives, grenades, ammo, and other fun toys."

Mark zipped up one of the bags, picked it up, and said, "Let's go!"

They left the apartment and Hiram led them out a back door into an alley where an old car sat. It was so beat up and repaired with anything available it was impossible to tell what make it was, or what the original color had been. Putting the bags on the floor in back, the four men got in and drove away from the building. The car was originally a 1959 Chevrolet and very large inside. Jack and Mark sat on the floor in back and kept out of sight to make it look like there were only two people in the car.

A few minutes later they stopped and Hiram got out. He came back and drove a short distance and got out again and closed the gate he had just driven through. They pulled into a garage and he got out and closed the garage door and turned on a dim light. The four men went into the house and put the bags on the kitchen floor. Hiram checked the security indicators and got a clean bill of health for the house. "I'm going to check in now with Tel Aviv. I assume that you'll want to talk to the Commander?"

Mark nodded and went with Hiram to a small closet that turned into an entrance to a secret room with the communications gear on all walls. Hiram talked in Hebrew to his controller and then got up and motioned Mark to sit in the chair. Mark sat down and picked up the handset. A few seconds later David Zahavy said "Hello?"

Mark greeted him and explained their situation. David told them to stay there for the time being while he checked out the situation concerning the other members of their group. Mark agreed and hung up.

Mark called his headquarters and brought his dispatcher, Randall McDuff up to date on the arrest of Sarah and the others. He also described the pursuit they were going through at the moment.

Jack sat in the tastefully decorated living room and started praying for God to protect them all, especially his wife, Sarah, and his step-sister.

CHAPTER TEN

As the police quickly surrounded the bus and blocked the exit. Sarah looked out the window and saw her husband, Jack, and the Sensei move into the alley next to the hotel.

A Sergeant got on the bus and told them, in somewhat broken English, that they were all under arrest for crimes against the state. Christi argued that they were there to put on a concert and showed the man her visa. He took it and then demanded all of their papers. Then he had them get off the bus one by one and had them handcuffed and led to a waiting security van.

As Sarah was being led away she made eye contact with Mark and she winked. "That should let him know that we're aware of their escape." she thought. The police crowded Sarah, Laura, Christi, Stan and Debbie Hargrove, the five band members, and eight other supporting personnel, and the bus driver into the van. Two of the officers got into the back of the van with the prisoners and the doors were shut.

The van driver complained in Hindi about his bus being left in front of the hotel with the keys in it. One of the police yelled at him to shut up in the same tongue. There was no more conversation for the duration of the ride, which, blessedly, was short.

They were unloaded at the back door of a police station and taken to a row of cells. The police took off the handcuffs and pushed six people into three separate cells. Then they were alone. Sarah, Laura, and Christi were in one cell and they conferred quietly.

Christi looked around to see if there was anyone listening and was about to speak when she saw Sarah shake her head and point to her ear. There were probably listening devices somewhere and it wouldn't be smart to break their cover at this time. Christi nodded, "I've never been treated like this!" She said in a loud voice. "Who do they think they are? I'm going to complain to my sponsor when I see him." Then she mouthed silently, "What do we do?"

Sarah affected a somewhat southern American accent. "Now don't you worry Miss Steele. I'm sure it's just some kind of awful mix-up and they will get it straightened out before long. They just have us mixed up with somebody else, that's all." Sarah rolled her eyes at the same time to indicate that her comments had no validity whatsoever.

Sarah was sure that the police knew exactly who they were. She smiled to herself because she knew that they were going to be really upset when they found out that they didn't have the guys.

After about an hour the door to the station opened and several swarthy types came in with a police officer. The tallest one was dressed like a Zulam and had a clipboard in his hands. He went to the first cell and looked at the six band members and Stan Hargrove. He said something to the police officer who came over and unlocked the cell door. The officer motioned the six people out of the cell and walked them over to the outside door they had been led into the station originally. He opened the door and said, "You are free to go, so go."

Stan started to argue with the man about the others but stopped when the officer took a short nightstick out of his belt. The officer would not listen to any argument with his directions. So Stan and the others left and the officer closed the door.

The man with the clipboard had moved to the second cell and looked from the clipboard to the occupants of the cell. These six were ArchAngel Fire employees and not aware of anything else. They were also released.

The man came to the cell with Sarah, Laura, Christi, Debbie Hargrove and two more band employees. He compared the people with what had to be pictures on the clipboard several times. Then he calmly spoke to the officer. The officer opened the door to the cell and Sarah's hopes went up.

The officer pointed to the employees and Debbie and motioned them out of the cell. He escorted them to the outside and returned. The other men left the cell block and the officer handcuffed the three women and marched them into the station proper and to an interrogation room. They were shackled to chairs and then he and his fellow officer left them alone again.

Although they couldn't understand the conversation being held outside the door between the Zulam and the police officer in charge, it was obvious that the Zulam was unhappy and the officer was getting a real dressing down. Things were quiet for a while and then the Zulam returned to the room alone.

He casually looked at the three women and it was quite apparent that his inspection wasn't completely impersonal. The three of them didn't flinch and look away from his salacious appraisal. Sarah had an idea of what was about to transpire and she was praying silently that God would give them all the ability to endure.

The Zulam sat down in a chair across the table from them and stared at each one for a few minutes. He tapped his fingers on the clipboard in front of him. Nothing was said for several minutes. Then he spoke in Arabic and got no response. Then he spoke to them in Hindi. Still he got no response. Sarah readily understood both languages but pretended she didn't understand either.

There are over 120 languages spoken in the area of Zyngola with the majority of people in the cities speaking standard Arabic and in some cases, English.

Finally, he got up and went to the door and opened it. He called out in Arabic and asked for a translator. Actually, Abdullah spoke fairly good English but he didn't let anyone know that fact.

A few minutes later a low-ranking police officer came in and sat down to interpret. Speaking through the interpreter Abdullah Hami asked them their names. Christi spoke up. "I'm Christi Steele." Tipping her head to the left towards Laura she continued, "This is Mrs. Thornton my seamstress. Tipping her head the other way since her hands were secured to the chair, she indicated Sarah. "This is Mrs. Carter." She used the pseudonyms that David had given them.

Abdullah stared at her for a few seconds. Then he addressed Sarah. "Mrs. Connelly, why have you come to Zyngola?" Sarah didn't miss a beat and she kept her eyes locked on Abdullah's. "My name is Sarah Carter and I want to know by what right you have arrested Miss Steele and us."

Looking at his clipboard he spoke again and the interpreter spoke to Laura, "Mrs. Malone, where is your husband?"

It was obvious that he wasn't interested in the phony names or their story. He knew who they were and the only place he could know that was from the enemy of all mankind. Laura didn't answer him but started praying silently for an intervention of the heavenly kind.

Abdullah shook his head. Sending the interpreter out he called the officer he originally berated back into the room. They spoke in rapid Arabic for several minutes. Then the officer called in two other officers and they unshackled the women from the chairs and marched them out of the room and back to their cell.

When they were alone, Sarah pulled them both close to her and told them what had transpired in the last conversations. "The Zulam told the officer that we needed persuading so that we would be more compliant. I would assume they mean sexual persuasion. In that case we need to take as many of them out as we can. I for one will not stand for anybody raping me! Be ready."

A few minutes later three men entered the cell block and smiled at the women in the cell. They weren't policemen, just thugs. They started talking to the women in Arabic. Then one of them produced a key and unlocked the cell door. He stepped in and grabbed Christi by the arm to lead her out of the cell. Christi reached up and over with her other hand and broke the little finger on his hand by bending it backwards.

The man screamed in pain and turned to strike her in the face with his other hand. Christi stepped into him and simultaneously kneed him in the groin and drove a palm-heel strike to his chin with her right hand. Her knee hit first and he jerked forward and down with the new pain. True to her training, Christi drove the palm heel strike as hard and as high as she could. This resulted in straightening the man up and propelling him out of the cell with teeth and blood flying. His body described a short arc and slammed as if boneless to the floor on his back. He was thoroughly unconscious. Even though her whole right arm was numb from the palm heel strike, Christi stepped out of the cell followed by Sarah and Laura.

The other two men stood there dumbfounded. These were women! Women were docile and did what they were told. Before they could begin to understand the different attitudes western women had, Sarah stepped between them and set their minds at ease. Using her right elbow she struck the man on the right in the temple, which caused him to collapse under the assault. He was dead before he hit the floor. She continued with a full knuckle punch to the throat of the third man, crushing his larynx. She then re-centered herself and struck him in the forehead with a left hand palm heel strike that knocked him over and out. It didn't matter because he was choking to death anyway. This way he just did it more quietly.

The door to the police station slammed open and three officers entered with handguns drawn and pointed at the women. The officer that was in charge of their case walked in and looked at the two dead men and the one that was definitely out of service. He looked at the women and called in two other officers who moved around the women so as to not block the line of fire. Each of the women was handcuffed and leg shackled and then a chain was connected between the handcuffs and the leg shackles. There was little they could do at this point.

But, the officer had been shaken by the elimination of the three thugs he had sent in to "subdue" these women. He secretly admired the way they had defended themselves, but it would be wrong to let anyone else know that. He ordered them to be taken out and placed in a van. The three women shuffled slowly out of the station and were lifted, none too gently into the van. The doors were shut and it was dark inside the unlit van body. Laura quipped, "Well, our odds of survival haven't gotten any better, but I feel good."

Christi chuckled softly. Then she asked Sarah, "How do we fend off unwanted male attention trussed up like this?"

Sarah relaxed as best as possible considering that her hands were cuffed behind her and she had to sit on the chain between the handcuffs and the leg shackles. "We don't have to worry for a while. They are taking us to a remote base up north because they are worried that Jack and Mark will try to break us out of the jail. The Sergeant told the others that if they were as lethal as we were, then he didn't want to meet them. Apparently, our interrogation will continue in a place where there is no hope of rescue."

Laura spoke up in the dark. "There is always hope with the Lord." She started praying quietly. Christi joined her in prayer. Sarah listened and let the worship envelop her as she considered possibilities.

CHAPTER ELEVEN

The three women were pulled out of the van and unceremoniously dumped on the ground. The police took off their handcuffs and shackles and threw them in the van and shut the doors. The leader told the lone man with a rifle that the women were his problem now. The three women watched silently as the van pulled away and headed back to the city.

The lone guard kept his rifle pointed at them but didn't do anything else. Soon aircraft engines could be heard approaching them. Sarah looked around and saw a twin-engine turboprop aircraft coming in to land on the flat land behind them. Sarah knew this aircraft. It was an Antonov An-24 "Coke" transport. It was a fifty-year old plane which normally had a crew of two to five and could hold up to fifty passengers. In its heyday it could cruise at 500 knots per hour and had a range of a couple of thousand kilometers.

The plane landed and taxied to the location where the guard was standing. He motioned with his rifle and the three women stood up. The door on the right side of the aircraft was let down and the crew man motioned them onboard with his pistol. The pilot had not shut down the starboard engine and the wind blast tore at their hair and clothes as they climbed into the body of the plane.

The crew man made them sit in the first row of seats and held them at gun point while the pilot came back to handcuff each one of them by the right wrist to the arm of the chair they were sitting in. Sarah risked some exposure by asking the pilot, in Arabic, if she could use the bathroom.

After thinking about it, the pilot unlocked the handcuffs and had the other crew man take Sarah back to the small bathroom in the back of the plane. The crew man wouldn't let her shut the door but did turn away as she used the facilities.

While he wasn't looking, she reached down into her shoe and slid out a small key. She kept the key in her left hand as she was escorted back to her seat and handcuffed in place.

The crew man holstered his handgun and sat down on the other side of the aisle. These were only women anyway. He bounced along with them as the plane tore over the field and then lifted into the air.

Pretending to sleep, Sarah kept an eye on their guard. After thirty minutes he dozed off. She didn't have to worry about his hearing anything because of the racket the plane made. When his head dropped to his chest, she took the key and unlocked her handcuff. Watching the pilot through the open cockpit door, she gave the key to Laura. She carefully stood up and waited until the pilot was busy with a change in direction and she stepped across the aisle. Rotating to her left she side kicked the sleeping man in the head with her right foot. There was an audible "crack" and the man's head hung unnaturally to the side. He wasn't going to wake up ever again. Some of the deadliest agents in the world had extensively trained Sarah.

Sarah took the handgun out of the man's holster and checked to make sure there was a round in the chamber. Seeing that the other two women were free from their handcuffs, she got up and walked to the cockpit door.

As she got to the door, the pilot turned suddenly to his right and fired a handgun with his left hand. Fortunately, he was right handed and not a very good shot with his left. Sarah was a much better shot, and she didn't miss from that range. The pilot slumped forward onto the controls and the plane began to dive.

Dropping the handgun, she leaped forward and pulled the dead pilot off of the steering yoke and pulled back on the yoke. The plane stopped diving and leveled out. Sarah waved the other women into the cabin. She looked at Laura and asked, "Can you fly this?"

Laura shook her head and so did Christi. Sarah told Laura to unbuckle the seat/shoulder belt on the pilot. She reached over to her right and grabbed the co-pilot's control yoke and sat down in that seat.

Laura and Christi were able to unbuckle the dead pilot and drag his body back into the rear of the passenger compartment. Sarah then changed places to the command seat. The pilot had leaked some blood on the seat and the window next to it but Sarah didn't have time to worry about neatness. She had much more experience flying than Laura or Christi but only by two hours. And those were in a different airplane, and while it was in flight. She had never taken off or landed anything.

Settling down she put the pilot's seat/shoulder straps on and inventoried the instrument panel. She knew the basic instruments like the eight-ball which told her the attitude of the airplane. She was in level flight so far. Her eyes traveled to the fuel gauges and she saw that they had at least fifty percent of the fuel the plane could hold. Then she checked her heading and saw that they were heading in a south-southeastern direction on a magnetic compass heading of 145 degrees. She slowly depressed the left aileron pedal and turned the control wheel to the left. The plane banked to the left and came back around to a heading of 325 degrees which would take them back in the direction of Tymeria. She leveled the flight out and started decreasing the altitude which she saw was eight thousand feet.

There was a little voice trying to tell her something and she couldn't tell what it was. It kept chattering at her until she realized that it was coming from the pilot's headset which had flown off his head when he was shot. She had forgotten to put it on. Picking it up with one hand and putting it on, she heard a voice in Arabic demanding that she answer.

Even though she could speak the language Sarah knew that she couldn't fool whoever was on the other end so she didn't talk but pushed the button on the side of the microphone several times. This would give them a non-committal response that could indicate radio trouble.

The voice on the other end tried to get her to talk for a few minutes and she continued to press the button and rub her fingers over the microphone that made it sound like static. This worked for almost ten minutes until the voice demanded that the plane descend and land at some airfield near them.

Hoping to drop below whatever radar they had, Sarah kept descending until she was only fifteen hundred feet over a small mountain range and could make out the individual trees on the hillsides.

The air traffic controller had stopped demanding compliance and issued a final warning for her to turn to the right. She ignored his demands and took the headset off. Yelling back to the other women she told them to sit down and strap in. She knew two things for certain. She hadn't gotten below the radar and she didn't know how to land this thing. So they knew where the plane was and she couldn't take a chance of getting too low and risking a collision with the ground. This was not a situation that would last forever but she milked it for all it was worth.

Seeing a bright flare of light ahead of her and to the left, she banked the plane away and down to avoid what she was sure was going to be bad news. Just before it got to them she was able to identify an SA-2 Guideline surface-to-air missile. Pulling back on the throttles the Antonov shuttered and dropped like a rock. The missile tried to adjust but was operating at its minimum altitude to begin with. It exploded just above and slightly behind the airplane rather than hitting it directly.

Not that it made a lot of difference to Sarah. She basically lost steering control and most of her vertical control. The back of the plane was on fire and they were hurtling towards the earth at a great rate. She pulled on the throttles but the engines didn't respond. She saw the ground rushing up and she pulled back hard on the control yoke. The plane struggled to respond and did come back to an almost level flight position. But it was too little, too late. Running out of altitude Sarah saw the ground coming up to meet the plane. She flicked the main power switch to off and shut off the fuel to the engines. They had time to slow, cough, and sputter once before they just cleared the top of a ridge. Then the plane struck the ground on the downhill slope after the ridge and started slamming into trees, rocks, and bushes. The plane was slowing but completely disassembling around her. The noise was immense as the passengers were slammed one way and then the other. They lost both wings on two large trees and the cockpit filled with flying glass, dirt, and debris. The plane slid in between two big rocks and Sarah was suddenly slammed forward in the seat. At that point everything went to silence and black.

CHAPTER TWELVE

Sarah lifted her head slowly from the wheel on the top of the steering yoke. She instinctively ran a quick check of her body before moving any farther. She felt like she had been hit and run over by a truck. Every muscle and nerve was screaming at her. She put them on hold for the moment while she carefully moved her fingers one at a time. "Ten, that's good," That was followed by a careful check of her hands and arms. Then she checked her toes, feet, ankles, legs and knees. She thought, "So far, so good." She slowly sat back into the pilot's seat and rested. She wanted to rest for a lot longer but her training had been thorough. She opened her eyes and moved them around. They seemed to work. They showed her a close-up of a bunch of pine needles and small limbs forced into the cockpit a short distance. Sarah moved her neck and checked the operation there, "Pain but, not insurmountable." She rotated it and that also worked.

She realized that she was in much better shape than she could have hoped for after the crash. The seat restraints had done a good job but she realized it was God that kept her from dying. She wiggled her backside and decided that part of her anatomy was functional. Then she attended to the various aches and pains that were crying for attention. Somewhat wrenched left shoulder, both knees banged against the dash. Her right hand ached and the wrist didn't like to flex but it would work as requested. The raging headache could be a sign of a concussion or just her brain's outrage at being slammed around. She needed a rest room and was surprised that hadn't taken care of itself during the crash.

Unbuckling her safety harness she levered herself out of the seat and bent below the smashed switch panel hanging from its wires in the ceiling. Even though none of the wires sparked when they moved, it made her think "Oh, yeah". Turning around again she found the main power switch and checked to see that she had switched it off before the impact. She was glad that she accomplished that much.

Exiting the cockpit she surveyed the mangled passenger compartment which was easy because from the third row of seats back there was no airplane. The crash had ripped the back end off of the airframe and left a handy opening for getting out of the plane. She noticed that the pilot and crewman, who hadn't managed to survive the flight let alone the landing, had left with the back of the plane.

Sarah was glad to see Laura lying among a jumble of seats on the right side of the remaining passenger compartment. Sarah pulled one loose seat away from the blonde and checked her vital signs. She was breathing and her heart rate was near normal. But she was unconscious. Sarah was about to unbuckle Laura's seat belt when she heard a voice.

"Can I do anything to help?"

Looking over her shoulder she saw Christi kneeling on another seat. "Hi, I'm glad that you made it through my rather poor landing."

Christi smiled and looked around the wreckage, "I've been in a couple of arenas that looked worse than this after a concert. I thought you did great considering you were missing most of the back end of the plane."

Sarah smiled her thanks, "Let's get Laura out of here."

The two women got Laura out of her seat belt and carried her through the hole in the back of the plane. Looking around Christi saw a grassy glen about one hundred feet from the wreckage. Since they could smell aviation fuel they carried her up the hill and under the trees.

Checking Laura over, Sarah told Christi to stay with her while she got the medical kit from the plane.

Sarah came back loaded down in a few minutes. "I also found some backpacks, two rifles, a handgun, and some emergency rations. I figure since we aren't going to fly out of here we might need some supplies.

Christi looked back the way they had come during the flight. "Do you think they'll come after us?"

Sarah frowned, "If they are halfway competent they will."

Laura moaned, coughed, and tried to sit up. Christi put her arms around her and told her it was all right and to stay down for a bit. Laura looked around and up at Sarah. "Did we crash?

Sarah smiled at her, "That's a polite way to say it. Are you all right?

Laura slowly sat up and took a deep breath. "I think so". She spotted what was left of the airplane. "Oh God, did we live through that?"

Christi laughed, "I hope so, and I still have a lot of songs to sing."

Sarah put her arm under Laura's shoulders. "Come on; let's see if you can walk."

Although she had to shake out some aches and stiffness Laura was able to move around all right. She looked at Sarah, "Okay, what's our plan?"

Sarah hadn't forgotten how to land on her feet in dangerous situations. "We divide up the load and head for those two peaks due west." She pulled out the map she had grabbed from the cockpit. She looked back at the wreck and the swath of trees knocked down during the landing portion of their last flight. "I don't know how we can hide the crash track or the wreck before they find it, so we need to send them off on the wrong track to buy us some time."

They looked for the easiest way to the south from the wreck. Finding a game trail, Sarah had them stomp their way out of the wreck and to the trail. They continued down the trail for a quarter of mile until they found a stream and lots of rocks. Sarah showed them how to leave the trail without leaving any marks. They used a lot of rocks before they got into the trees. Then they worked their way back to the area of the wreck where they had hidden their backpacks. Putting one of the backpacks on, Sarah took one of the rifles and gave the other one to Laura. She gave Christi the handgun and warned her not to use it until an enemy was very close.

Careful not to leave any signs like footprints or broken twigs, they left the wreck and headed down a shallow grade towards the same stream they had run into further down the mountain. Crossing the stream they kept their steps to the rocks and then slipped back under the trees as they started up the next hillside. Sarah brought up the rear and watched for any traces of their passing. She found some and she fixed them as they went along. She knew there was no time to teach field craft to either of the other two at this time. She'd just have to do it for all three of them. Although she had to admit, they were doing a good job for their first time.

They crested the next ridge and started down the other side. At this point Sarah moved to the front and they started moving quickly regardless of any tracks they might leave. Sarah knew that the enemy wouldn't search two hills away for signs of their passage until long after it was too late to catch them.

After three more ridges and valleys Sarah called a rest break. She checked Laura and Christi to see how they were holding up. She was pleasantly surprised to find them both breathing all right and not worn out. As she raised an eyebrow at that, Laura told her, "We'll be alright. Both Christi and I have daily exercise routines that keep us in pretty good shape. We probably can't keep up with you but we should manage to make it out of here."

Sarah nodded and stopped and listened. The late afternoon breeze had a new sound to it. "Whop-whop-whop." Sarah motioned both of the other two women under a solidly leafed tree and told them to lay down with their backpacks on their backs. This would reduce their infrared signature if the helicopter was using a system like the U.S. FLIR or forward-looking infrared.

The chopper passed behind them by over a mile and they were in no danger of being seen. They started up again and made another four miles of distance before dark. The valleys and ridges had given way to one long incline towards the twin peaks so they had been able to make better time.

Sarah carefully ranged around until she found a large burrow that some animal had made the year before. At least it didn't show signs of being occupied recently. The burrow would keep their body heat from giving them away in the cool night as well as keep them warm. It got cold in the mountains at night and they didn't have much in the way of cold-weather gear. She realized that just some sweatshirts and one jacket was very little to work with.

55

They couldn't risk a campfire even though they had matches and there was plenty of firewood available. They munched on protein bars and drank sparingly from their one canteen. After that they got comfortable and talked.

Christi looked at the size of the burrow they were in and asked Sarah, "What creature made this?"

Sarah gazed at the younger woman for a few seconds, "Probably a brown bear. You can see that it has a northern entrance. Bears only pick that arrangement when they are going to hibernate. Don't worry about it though; most bears are more afraid of us than the other way around."

Laura had been quiet for a while because she had been praying. The darkness around them in the remote mountain range was complete because the cloud cover blocked the moonlight and there were no cities nearby to give reflected light. In the starlight that filtered into the cave, Laura could barely make out the faces of her companions just three feet away.

A dim glow began in the back of the burrow. Sarah picked up the pistol and faced the growing light. It was confusing in a sense because the light grew bigger than the end of the burrow. The glow resolved itself into a bright white light with gold overtones. Laura laughed and put her hand on Sarah's arm pulling the pistol down. "It's all right, it's a friend."

Rose came into view apparently a long way off, even though the burrow ended four feet from where they were sitting. She seemed to come towards the three women or grew in size. As she drew near her voice rang out clearly in the cool night air. "Hello Laura, Sarah, Christi"

Sarah realized it was an angel of the Lord and stopped worrying about the light and sound giving them away. This message was for them alone. No one else would notice it.

Rose smiled and said, "The Lord has given me a message for you." She saw that she had their undivided attention. "Satan is going to have his demonic forces come against the three of you during this time of stress in an effort to divide and discourage you. They are going to attempt to amplify the difference between woman and man. Normally the enemy tries to make a woman afraid because she is smaller and less massive physically than a man. They use guilt, shame, embarrassment, envy, and other emotions to cause you to sin by feeling that life, or God, is unfair."

Rose seemed to become more serious. "This time they are going to try to reverse that. You are all very capable women so the envy factor is not available anyway. They will use your own pride in your capabilities, especially you Sarah, to make you think you are better than men, thereby dividing your loyalties and relationships. Regardless of the ploy they use, remember to be humble before the Lord. Pray for coverage from detection by the enemy. Also be aware of strange people who would use you for their benefit. You all will face severe trials on this journey, individually and together. Stay strong in the Lord. Pray always."

Christi sat in awe of the beautiful angel. This was the first time she had seen an angel. She asked Rose, "I'm not married, at least not yet. How do I cope with these attacks?"

Rose smiled at the young woman. She seemed to look through Christi into the distance. Then, refocusing on her, she said, "Christi, your beautiful strength is your faith in the Lord. You have always loved the Lord and He treasures your love. He believes in you too. Stand firm in what you know and rely on the Lord for your strength. You shine in the spiritual world as a bright light of the Lord's reflected glory. The enemy cannot stand the Lord's light and so they stay away from you whenever possible. Listen to the older women and remember the armor of God."

Rose looked at the group and reminded them. "Remember the word of the Lord, *"Let nothing be done through selfish ambition or conceit, but in lowliness of mind let each esteem others better than himself."* At this she faded from sight and the dark of night returned to the burrow. Laura nodded to herself and said, "That was Philippians 2, verse 3."

After a short period of quiet in the dark Sarah chuckled, "Okay then. I guess we have our challenges set out before us, right? Right now, let's pray, we "older women" need to get some sleep. Christi, you take the first watch. If anything bothers you, wake me up."

Laura added, "If anything bothers you in the spirit, like fear, wake me up.

They prayed to be hidden and then settled in for the night.

CHAPTER THIRTEEN

Laura relieved Sarah at four in the morning and kept watch until dawn filled the burrow with a filtered light. When she woke the others they set about cleaning themselves up the best they could under the circumstances. A drink of water, a short trip to the bushes outside, and another power bar and they were ready for the day.

Sarah showed them their path on the map. She had not picked the closest village or even town for them to walk to. She had picked one that would not be easy or convenient. Knowing their enemies figured they were soft American women who would head for the nearest town for help. So, that was exactly what they wouldn't do.

Sarah recalled details of the land they were in from her briefings during her Mossad days. Come to think about it, that was only a few months ago.

She decided not to think about the past right then. "Listen girls, the government, and possibly the majority of the male population of Zyngola are heavily anti-Christian, anti-Jewish, anti-American, and anti-female. Military dictatorships favoring a Zultarian-oriented government has dominated this nation's politics since their independence in 1976. Zyngola has been embroiled in a civil war since 1991. The war and war-and famine-related effects have led to more than 1 million deaths and over 2 million people have been displaced from their homes. The war pits the Arab/Zultarian majority in North which is run by Tymeria against the non-Zultarian African rebels in the south. One thing going for us is that since 1996, traditional northern Zultarian parties have made common cause with the southern rebels and entered the war as a part of an anti-government alliance. The problem here is that these people may not like the government but they are still Zultarian and they don't like us either."

Sarah noticed the stricken look on their faces and laughed. "What did you expect? Most of the third world had been warped by this form of religious zeal against the one true God and the people that follow Him." She turned the map over and pointed to the detailed map of Tymeria. "For security reasons, the United States relocated their officials at the U. S. Embassy in Tymeria to the embassy in Cairo, Egypt in 1999. These officials make regular visits to Tymeria and our best bet is to stake out the embassy and contact them when we can. See? Here on the map is the location of the embassy. Remember the address in case we get separated. It is located on Shar Elah Street."

Sarah sat back and thought for a moment. "Also remember that we are subject to Zultarian law in the northern states. Zultarian law applies to all residents of the northern states regardless of their religion and that applies to visitors too. Do not talk to men under any circumstances. Do not show any flesh or you could be stoned."

Christi asked her, "Is the American Embassy the only place we can get help?"

Sarah grinned, "Yes, my dear. It is the only place that will defend us if we can get there. You understand that no Israeli Embassy is allowed in this Zultarian nation don't you?"

Christi nodded, "Okay, what about the French or other nations?"

Sarah shook her head. "They would not be any help to Americans."

Laura picked up the map and turned it over. "Show us where we are and where we're going."

Sarah pointed to an area about eighty miles south of Tymeria. "I think that we are right about here." She then indicated the town of El Cadon about eighteen miles north of their position. "There are numerous small villages and enclaves between here and El Cadon because we are only about a mile east of the narrow-gauge railroad between the Libyan border to Tymeria and then down this way. The railroad parallels the Conmera River and is a major transportation route of the nation. We need to avoid contact as much as possible until we can find native clothing for ourselves and get transportation into Tymeria. Therefore, we will avoid the river and the railroad and cut cross country which is somewhat shorter but more difficult. Again, this is something that they will not expect us to do."

The light had gotten stronger and the heat of the day started to penetrate the burrow. Laura opened their backpacks and took out the clothing they had available. Using a pair of emergency scissors and Sarah's help, she fashioned three hoods and passable veils from their western clothing. The colors weren't right but they served to hide both her and Christi's blonde hair and their too-white faces. There were skirts for each of them so that they looked more modest even if the skirts weren't floor length. Using the one light blanket she was able to make rough shawls for each of them.

When she was done they all tried them on outside the entrance to the burrow. Sarah was impressed. "These outfits will really help us move without arousing interest. The rough cut makes us look poor. Even though they aren't black, it is more proper wear and there is some movement for color among the more adventurous women in the Zultarian world."

They donned their new clothing and took up their backpacks and headed to the northwest. Three hours later they had been making good time through the countryside when they found a road. At least it was a beaten path rather than just weeds and trees. They were walking on the dirt road for almost an hour when they ran into their first natives. Of course these had to be men, and soldiers at that. The girls kept their heads down and completely ignored the men and their comments. Since neither Laura nor Christi could speak or understand Arabic it was easy to act demure. The gestures the men made were a little harder to ignore. But the truck kept going the other way and the girls were left alone.

Grinning under their veils they kept heading toward the town. Occasionally they had glimpses of the river and the railroad but they stayed to the east, away from those areas. Eventually, around four in the evening, they came to the place where they had to cross both the river and the railroad to get to El Cadon. There were many more people walking here because the day was drawing to a close and many people were going home from work. The girls tried to blend into the background as much as possible and not draw any attention.

Sarah had been thinking about what to do when they got to the city proper. Women normally did not ride the train at night without some form of male accompaniment. If they tried that they would probably draw the wrong form of attention to themselves. She therefore suggested that they look for a Zyngolian version of a hostel because such things were available to transitory females in some places. Sarah could read the Arabic language signs and found them a reasonable place to stay that night. They were able to pay in the local currency because Laura had exchanged her dollars for the local money when she entered Zyngola and had managed to hide the folding money well enough that the Tymerian Police hadn't found it. That now seemed like a year ago.

They were able to get some food and finally get a bath. As they settled down for the evening there was a knock at the door. Sarah asked who it was in Arabic. "Fatima" the answer came back. Sarah asked her to wait for a moment while everyone put on their Arabic clothing. Then she opened the door and admitted a Zyngolian woman who was also veiled and covered in the traditional black clothing from the top of her head to the floor.

Sarah asked her what they could do for her. She lifted her veil to disclose a pretty Arabic face with full lips and deep brown eyes. "I would like to offer you women a sanctuary from the raid that is about to happen here. Are you willing?"

Sarah nodded and everyone picked up their belongings and stuffed them into the backpacks. Quickly leaving the room they sped down the hall and out the back door of the hostel. In the dimness they followed Fatima down an alley and through a deserted street. They stopped there for a few seconds as two police trucks rumbled by and came to a halt next to the hostel. They watched as police surrounded the place and then went in the front way. The women faded into the night and soon came to a large walled-in house to which they were granted admission. Fatima led them through the large room downstairs and up to a room on the second floor.

She told them that they would be safe there. Then she left to confer with the other people in the house.

After they closed the door, Laura asked Sarah, "Aren't we supposed to be wary of strangers?"

Sarah nodded her head. "But, she did save us from that raid."

Laura replied, "I'm getting some bad vibes about this whole rescue thing. I need to pray about Fatima too."

Sarah reached under her cloak and took out the pistol. De-cocking it she said, "Fatima had bettered be on the up-and-up or she won't see tomorrow."

Christi was a bit wide-eyed at that. Laura had been around Sarah enough to know she meant every word she said.

CHAPTER FOURTEEN

The three women settled down to await developments. They weren't long in coming. There was a knock on the door and Fatima asked them to join her with the rest of her council. Still wearing their veils, they followed her downstairs and through the foyer to two sliding doors which were standing open.

As they walked through, they could see a large conference room with a large, round, and very solid table in the middle of the room. There was a large segmented area in the middle of the table and everyone sat on the outside of the circle. There were eight other women sitting around the far side of the table quietly talking. The conversations ceased when Fatima and the three strangers entered the room. Fatima indicated three chairs at the near side of the table while she walked around to her seat at the other side of the massive structure.

Still speaking Arabic, Fatima asked the strangers what they wanted to do.

Since Sarah was the only one that understood the language she answered that they were trying to get to Tymeria to the home of their uncle.

Fatima listened and spoke in Farsi to several of her council. "I think they are trying to mislead us." She had no way to know that Sarah also knew Farsi.

Fatima then asked Sarah, "What are your names?"

Sarah was quickly tiring of the interrogation. "We are not worth the time you are spending on us. We thank you for helping us to avoid the raid but would like to go now."

Fatima smiled a grim smile. "I'm afraid it is not that easy. We have placed ourselves in danger by taking you in and you owe us for that.

Sarah started to understand the vibes that Laura had been picking up, distinctly unfriendly and even potentially aggressive. "We will gladly pay you what we can for your help but really need to be on our way now."

Fatima thought for a second and raised her right hand. She snapped her fingers and three more women came up behind Sarah, Laura, and Christi and put a knife to their throats. Fatima said, "I'm afraid that we want more than your money. All the women at the table removed their veils to reveal cloaks with hoods, all in black. "How trendy", Sarah thought, as she angled her pistol under her clothes to get a shot at the one holding the knife to her throat.

Laura said, "Sarah, wait one minute. I think we need to know a little more before we "negotiate" with these people."

Sarah nodded, and slipped the gun back into her waist band. The woman behind her never found out how close she came to dying right then.

Fatima was somewhat startled by the English spoken by Laura. She ordered their veils removed and was even more upset to find herself facing two, obviously non-Arabian women. Frowning, she gave a command in an obscure language. The center of the table split and slid outwards in six directions, so that the table became a ring with an empty center about eight feet in diameter. Inlaid in the tile of the floor was a pentagram. Christi thought, "I've got a bad feeling about this."

The nine women seated at the table began to chant a repetitive litany of sing-song syllables. The air took on a heavy feeling and the light dimmed throughout the room. A smoke or fog began to form in the center of the pentagram. All three of the Americans were silently praying that God would protect them from whatever evil was being brewed here.

The light in the area of the pentagram shifted to the red and a being appeared. It was deformed and really ugly. It was also grossly male. It had horns and baleful black eyes. It was staring at Fatima. She worshiped the demon and told it that she had a special treat for it that night. She pointed at the three American women. The demon spun around and stared at them. He expected that they would be like the normal sacrifices that Fatima brought him. He was used to fawning little women that were there for his pleasure. Women that were so afraid of him that they would do anything he said just so he wouldn't get mad at them. These three were different. They weren't scared of him. They were unhappy with his appearance but they definitely weren't cowering and whipped like normal. He spoke with a loud, guttural voice in Arabic, "On your knees before your master, now!"

As he spoke the three women with the knives backed up and walked around the table to their seats.

Sarah took on a bored expression and looked at Laura, "You want to handle this?"

Laura sort of smiled, "Yeah, I think so. But first, I need to get him outside the pentagram and I need him to attack us."

Sarah grinned, "I'll be glad to take care of that for you." She returned her gaze to the horrid creature. In Arabic she said, "Listen you puny little slime-ball. You should run back to your brothers in the pit and see if you can create an original thought among you. We don't kneel to you or any other, misshaped freak of Satan's spawn."

That was entirely more than sufficient to rile the demon. He strode fourth out of the pentagram to handle these rude women personally.

Fatima and the others were amazed by the stupid comments and even more inane attitudes of these strangers. They had seen what Qx'laton had done to anyone who even looked at him without reverent fear and awe. It was gory and horrid, but it effectively kept anyone else from offending him.

These people openly insulted and demeaned him. Their punishment would be horrible and very drawn out. The screaming would be the worse.

As the demon came to the ring of the table, the three women got up and backed up several steps. Qx'laton leaped onto the table surface with his cloven hooves in preparation of rending the sassy one limb from limb. A feeling of fear made him stop and look at the older blonde woman. He screamed curses and dire threats at her.

Laura began to recite the twenty-third Psalm. "The LORD is my shepherd; I shall not want." As she did, the curses and threats bounced off as they came toward her. The demon began to hurl occult sayings at her. *"He makes me to lie down in green pastures; He leads me beside the still waters."* A golden shield began to flicker in and out of sight on her upraised left arm.

The demon was furious now and hopped off the table towards Laura. *"He restores my soul; He leads me in the paths of righteousness"* The demon raised his huge left fist to smash this woman.

Laura held her ground, *"For His name's sake."* The demon was totally outraged. The coven was in fear for their lives after he destroyed the infidels because of his great anger. As the demon started to swing his fist down, Laura continued the Scripture, *"Yea, though I walk through the valley of the shadow of death, I shall fear no evil; for Thou art with me;"*

Laura's armor and the golden sword appeared. The brilliant light streaming from the sword was God's glory. The demon shrieked terribly as he realized his folly and his doom. Laura jumped forward and swung the sword from her right to her left and cut the demon in half.

As Qx'laton disappeared into greasy smoke accompanied by horrible shrieking, Laura lifted the sword into a high guard position. The light from the sword shot out and transfixed all twelve of the satanic women. They all burst into flame, and with shrieks that rivaled that of their demon master, they were consumed.

Laura's armor disappeared and she bent over in fatigue. Christi was still trying to process what had just happened and get her heart to settle down. Her opinion of Laura had just changed radically and she began to understand what she meant about "serious spiritual warfare". As the smelly, ugly demon had headed for them she had seriously questioned Laura's calmness and recitation of the 23rd Psalm. The on-rushing demon had frightened her so much that she knew she couldn't stand, let alone run. Then Laura went gold and the demon went to hell. "This was the coolest thing she'd ever seen!"

Sarah put her arms around Laura and helped her to a chair. Laura took several deep breaths and relaxed somewhat. Sarah looked into her eyes and said, "That was fantastic! I'm going to have to write a book about this one."

Laura just looked at her. Sarah smiled and nodded, "Okay, maybe not a book, just a record of memorandum so I can tell Mark and Jack every detail." Laura chuckled at that.

Sarah checked to see that Laura was feeling all right. Then she said that they should look around for more of the traditional wear so that they could look the part tomorrow morning when they boarded the train. Looking at the twelve piles of smoldering ashes she commented, "I don't think they're going to be using their other outfits anymore."

CHAPTER FIFTEEN

Later that morning, all three women, were now dressed in the traditional garb of the region. They walked the ten blocks to the railroad station and no notice was taken of them along the way. Sarah purchased their tickets for the trip to Tymeria using money they had found in the coven's house.

They acted reserved and quietly avoided the looks, stares, and tentative advances of the men that were waiting for the train. They kept to themselves and sat alone in a passenger car when the train came.

Alone being a relative term. There were sixty-four seats in the passenger car they were in. There were also eighty-five people in the car. They had secured three of the scarce seats and kept quietly to themselves while the train bounced and swayed on the four-hour trip.

Nothing of note happened and they finally were able to disembark at the main station in Tymeria around one in the afternoon of the third day after their crash landing.

They walked casually over to the location they wanted. Careful to seem uninterested in the American Embassy they saw that there were no guards and no one in residence. Laura asked Sarah, "Okay, what do we do now? Try to find another place to stay and keep checking this building until we see something?"

Christi said, "I think that would really increase our exposure and risk. Not to mention that we will probably run out of funds for food and housing."

Sarah's impression of the young woman went up a couple more notches at that. "She's right. I have to find out when the officials are going to make their next visit and if we will be able to see them when they show up."

Laura snorted under her veil, "I thought your plan was already set."

Sarah chuckled, "Yes, originally it was. But, if you will casually check out the car parked across from the gate to the Embassy you will see that the gate is being watched. I would hazard a guess that they are looking for three females. In fact we need to move on before they decide to check us out." She started moving down a side street away from the Embassy. The other two followed her. Christi looked back and said, "Too late."

Sarah casually checked over her shoulder and saw the car slowly turning the corner behind them. She thought fast and said, "Go in the next doorway."

Laura was leading and turned into the indicated doorway. The doorknob turned and admitted them into a large foyer which was more like an enclosed porch and sitting area. Sarah closed the door behind them and walked away from the door into the building and up a set of stairs. Christi and Laura followed her.

As Sarah reached the top of the stairs a man in silk pants and a tee-shirt came around a corner with a cup of tea in his hand. He stopped in his tracks. Seeing three strange women in his house didn't compute. Sarah straightened out his confusion with a well-executed, palm-heel strike to the jaw that lifted him off his feet and left him lying on the floor unconscious.

Christi rushed over to her and whispered, "Why did you do that? He didn't do anything to hurt us!"

Sarah contemplated her interference for a second. "I don't have the time to train you in Middle Eastern etiquette and propriety at the moment. Just understand that what I did was the best thing I could for him and for us. I could have killed him you know. Now let's move before the police out there start ringing the bell!"

She led them through the back of the house and a garden. That brought them to a halt at a tall wall and with an inset gate. Sarah carefully peered over the gate and checked the alley they were about to enter. Seeing nothing she was about to open the gate when she felt a touch on her arm. Laura was standing there shaking her head. She whispered, "Don't open the gate."

Sarah left the handle alone and checked the alley again. Still nothing in sight and they needed to be away from here quickly. She looked at Laura with urgency in her expression. Laura just shook her head again.

Sarah was in a quandary. She knew that Laura was hearing from God's Spirit and yet they had to move before the police entered the house and found the man. She raised her arms with her hands outspread and palm up in a gesture of "What?"

Laura leaned close again and whispered, "Look again."

Sarah looked and saw a shadow, then a second and a third one, men on foot. She would have walked right into them. They were headed for the gate to this back yard. She looked around, stooped and picked up a large nail that was lying on the ground. She quietly slid it into the handle mechanism and then flattened herself back against the wall behind some bushes a few paces away from the gate. Laura and Christi joined her behind the bushes. The handle rattled but didn't operate. It rattled harder but still wouldn't work.

There was a hushed but urgent conversation and then three rapid fire, silenced rounds blew the gate lock completely out of the gate. The gate swung open and three men ran through. Their focus was on the building beyond the garden. If any of them had looked back he would have seen the three women gliding out through the open gate. But they didn't look.

Three blocks later, Sarah was anxious to get them out of this mess. Her problem was that she didn't have any assets in place to help them and they were quickly running out of money and time. She saw another police car slowly cruising by and tried to ignore it. Since Christi and Laura were pretty much out of sight in an alley and she was by herself she didn't draw any special attention and the car went on down the block. It wouldn't be long before they started foot patrols asking for identification papers from any unaccompanied women.

She wandered over to a newsstand to look at the papers and see if there were any special announcements about them. As she checked out the papers she prayed a sincere prayer. "Dear Yahshua, I seem to have run out of options, again. I know you love me and those with me. Give me some direction on how to keep us free and get us out of here. I pray all things in your name Yahshua." She felt better after her prayer. She felt an uplifting hope and glanced around. She noticed a man leaning against the wall near the stand, reading a paper. It dawned on her that she knew him.

Sarah paid for a paper and walked over near where the man was and started reading her paper. When no one else was around she spoke in Hebrew, "Lev Greenberg, you stand out like a neon sign saying Mossad."

He didn't miss a beat or even look up. He replied in Hebrew also, "AHH! the intrepid Mrs. Connelly, good to see you too. Are you in need of assistance?"

"Is Hamas hostile?"

He chuckled softly. "How many of you are there?"

"Three"

He carefully glanced around. "Go to the end of the alley to my right. I'll meet you there with a car." He folded his paper and walked away.

Sarah kept reading for a minute and then dumped her paper in a trash can and sauntered away slowly. Reaching the alley she motioned for the other two to follow her. As they reached the end of the alley an older black Mercedes Benz pulled up with Lev at the wheel. All three of them quickly got in the back and sat on the floor where they wouldn't be seen from the outside. Lev drove away carefully. After they were out of the city he told them they could get up. He drove them to a walled property with a large house inside the wall.

After they got into the house Sarah hugged Lev and asked him to get in touch with David Zahavy in Tel Aviv immediately. He smiled and motioned for her to follow him. A hidden radio room was available in the safe house and in minutes Sarah was talking to her old boss and good friend.

He was glad to hear from her. Mark had warned him that his wife and others had been taken captive. Mark had explained that Jack, Sensei Grady and himself were being pursued but he thought they could get away. Mark had asked David to use what assets he could to watch for Sarah because he was pretty confident she would escape and be looking for a way out of Zyngola. Sarah thanked him for his efforts and passed on the thanks of the whole Crossfire Team. Finishing her conversation she went to have a bath and find some food. The bath was marvelous and she found her equally clean partners ravenously eating some chicken in the kitchen. While they were eating, Lev told her that they were going to be slipped out of the country by private plane that evening.

Later that afternoon, Sarah was still worried about Mark. She had checked their E-mail and phone logs. He hadn't checked in during the last three days. That was decidedly not like Mark.

Laura had done no better trying to locate Jack. Seeing Sarah's concern she commented, "Jack and Mark are a good team and they know the Lord. I think we should pray for their safety and inquire of God's Spirit as to their whereabouts".

They prayed for a while and then Sarah remarked that while God would take care of their husbands He wanted the women to do what they could to help. The three of them decided that they should track the men's last known location and try and find out if they had been captured or were just lying low. Sarah went back to the radio room to call David for any additional help he could provide. Laura followed her and asked if she could get a message to the President and Christi went to ask Lev about his life as a spy.

CHAPTER SIXTEEN

Sarah was concerned. "David, I know that you're limited in what you can do with your assets on non-company business. What I need is Intel. Something definitive I can use to determine where Mark and the guys are. Can you do that?"

David thought for a minute. "No, but I know who can. I will get them in the loop immediately."

Sarah thought for a second, "Who are you talking about?"

David went, "TSK-TSK Sarah, only a couple of months out of the service and you don't know about the NSA's tracking capabilities? I would think with your husband's connections you would be on top of things like that."

Sarah mentally counted to two and then said, "Since when did the Mossad have to ask the NSA for cooperation instead of having the information themselves?"

David laughed, "Since they offered to help us in our searches. I will talk to them after I hang up with you."

Sarah chuckled, "Well, if they need any permission just ask them to call the President. That's what Laura is doing right now. Bye for now."

After she hung up she went to find Laura. Laura had just talked to the President's aide. Apparently the President was locked up in a committee meeting for the next two hours. But, he would call her right back at that time. It seems that the Connelly's and the Malone's rated A-1 service since their defeat of the world threat by the Omniscience Temple.

Sarah and Laura were without purpose at the moment but, not for long. Sarah went back to the phone and called one of Mark's top investigators, next to her of course.

The phone conversation was short. "Randall, this is Sarah."

"Thank God you are safe; we were all really worried about you."

Sarah smiled inwardly about the compliment. "We are all right now. What about Mark?"

Randall didn't know any more than what David had told her. "He reported being pursued in Zyngola after your capture and then, nothing. I haven't heard a word from him since then."

Sarah considered, "Okay, what I want you to do is get a location on that last call from Mark and let me know what the GPS coordinates were."

Randall was at the Connelly Investigations Headquarters in Washington, D.C. and had access to the records she needed. He gave her the GPS coordinates and told her to stay in touch every six hours, if possible.

Sarah looked up the coordinates and determined that they placed Mark inside Tymeria. But that was three days ago, they could be anywhere by now. She went to find Laura and Christi.

After discussing the situation they decided that they had to wait for help from the NSA before deciding what to do.

An hour later the phone rang and it was the President for Laura. She gave him a quick sketch of their escape and rescue by the Mossad. Then she asked him to authorize NSA help in locating Mark, Jack and the Sensei.

The President's voice was clear on the satellite link. "Laura, I will move the NSA and the military to get Mark back. You know how much I owe him."

Laura smiled, "Yes sir, I know he would appreciate it."

The President told her to call the NSA in thirty minutes and gave her a number to give them. He then rang off and picked up a different phone.

"This is the President. Let me speak to the Director."

"Yes, Mr. President." There was a momentary silence on the line and the Director Harrison came on. "Yes sir, Mr. President, what can I do for you?"

"Tom, a Laura Malone is going to call you via sat link from Zyngola in about twenty-five minutes. I am authorizing you to give her request for a search for her husband and two other people the absolute top priority. Are we clear on this?"

"Yes sir, perfectly clear. Is there to be any limitations on our efforts?"

"No, Tom, no limitations. I want these people found and extracted immediately, regardless of the impact on other projects. Personally Tom, these three people kept the entire world from going up in nuclear smoke not too long ago."

"Yes sir. We'll find them if at all possible."

The President laughed, "Oh, it will be possible, Tom, one of them is wearing a PPM."

"Yes sir."

Sarah was describing the PPM to Laura at that moment. "It is a passive, resonant UHF locator. It doesn't do anything except reflect an extremely precise frequency 1.9GHz signal. To the searching satellite it is like seeing a teensy little bright light in a dark room. Mark has it built into his belt buckle. When the NSA sweeps the area and gets a response they tighten up the signal to the indicated area. With the additional energy in the tightened beam they get back more information including the number of the locator.

Laura placed the call and the NSA started their sweeps. It only took fourteen minutes for the locator to be found and identified as Mark's.

CHAPTER SEVENTEEN

Jack was still praying in the living room of the safe house when Mark walked into the room. Mark told him about the conversation with David and the help he was mobilizing. Mark then asked, "Do you think we need to concentrate on finding the people behind this atrocity in the making or on trying to find the girls and possibly rescuing them?"

Jack had been asking God's Spirit the same question. "Personally, I want to try to help our wives but the leading I'm getting is that we need to stay on target." Jack looked introspective for a little bit. "Between the capabilities of your wife, Laura's talents and the combination of the two I believe that they will get away from their captors and get the whole group of them released in less time than it would take us to find out where they are."

Mark had been doing some praying of his own. "Yeah, that's what I think the Lord is leading us to do also. I have great confidence in Sarah and while I'd die for her, I think they'll be all right. Since we've lost any advantage we had to start with, what do you suggest we do now?"

Jack had some leading from the Lord on that too. As Jim Grady entered the room with them he said, "I think that we need to go on the offensive rather than running and hiding. Let's see if Hiram has any Intel we can use."

They found Hiram filling out reports and he was glad to put that down for a break to talk to them. Jack and Mark filled him in on what they were tasked to do and their lack of knowledge of the situation. Hiram thought for a few minutes and then got up and went to the computer keyboard. He typed and scanned for a few minutes. Jack looked at the screen but it was in Hebrew and he couldn't read that language, yet.

Finding the article he wanted, Hiram printed it out and came back to the three men and sat down. Scanning the document he looked up at them. "This may be something that can help you. There has been an unusually large financial investment made to an individual Zulam for unknown reasons. Our investigation of this Zulam has shown that he is training a select group of his followers for some secret Jihad effort that is paying off. We don't know what it is; only that it is going to be expanded in the very near future. The reason that he hasn't moved forward with it, is you."

Mark frowned, "What do you mean *us*?"

Hiram smiled, "Please understand that our information comes from observation and from information from disenfranchised or disgruntled associates of this Zulam. We don't have any inside information at all. But it seems that this particular Zulam was the source of the information that you were coming, who you were, and when you would be here. He supplied this information to the police and said that you were spies."

Jack looked at Mark. "The only way he could know all that is from the dark side of the equation. Mark shook his head, "There are a lot of ways he could have gotten word about us. The bad guys could be using him as a front, feeding him information and letting him do the dirty work.

Hiram went on with his information. "The Zulam we're talking about is named Abdullah Hami. He was orphaned as a teen when one our missiles was deflected and struck his house, killing his parents and siblings. He was a moderate until then. Since then he has studied hard, especially with the The'an and he has gathered a following that is extremely radical. We've tried to arrest him several times for suspected terrorist activities but can never seem to get him. He always knows in advance when we are going to raid an establishment where he is. He is gone before we can even surround a place. It really wasn't important, he hasn't been very high on our list until he got seven million U.S. dollars three weeks ago. But, I would definitely think that he could be what you're looking for." He closed the paperwork and fed it to a shredder where it was hacked to pieces, reduced to ashes, and then further destroyed by water and mixing.

A small sound caused Hiram to pull out a cell phone and listen for several minutes. He then responded in Hebrew with two words and hung up. He looked at the two men. "That was one of our operatives. Fifteen of your group just showed up at the hotel. Neither of your wives nor the singer was with them."

Jack asked Hiram if there was any way they could talk to Stan Hargrove without getting caught or detected. Hiram thought about it for a few seconds and then made a call on his cell phone. After hanging up he said, "I asked my operative to see if he could get Mr. Hargrove to accompany him using your name. We can't bring him here, but we can meet them elsewhere. How much do they know about what you are doing?"

Mark shook his head, "Stan and his wife knew. None of the others except the three of us, our wives, and the singer knew about our mission. The rest of them thought that we were part of the support group for the band."

Jack suggested that they wait until they had talked to Stan before deciding on a course of action. Jim and Mark agreed and Hiram checked his watch and went to start the car.

Again they acted like there were only two people in the car. They reached a secluded park where they could meet without being seen very easily.

A few minutes later a motorbike pulled up next to their car. The passenger got off and took off his helmet. It was Stan Hargrove. Jack hugged him and Mark shook his hand. It was obvious that Stan was glad to see them still free. Mark asked what had happened.

Stan ran his hand through his hair. "We were all grabbed like chickens in a bag. They took us to this jail and locked us up. Awhile later this cleric came in with a clipboard and started staring at us. He let Debbie and I go along with the real support people and the band. But they kept Laura, Sarah, and Christi. I tried to complain but they threatened to beat me and the other band members dragged me out of the building. I'm real sorry guys, I tried."

He sighed, a big sigh, "Then we made our way back to the hotel and I met my mysterious friend here who had your name. What's going on with you and are you going to find the girls and bust them out?"

Jack told him that they didn't have enough information yet. They would contact him again as soon as they could. Stan told them to stay out of sight, "I think every cop in this town is looking for you and Mark." Then he got back on the bike and they left.

Mark stared after the disappearing motorbike and asked Jack a question. "I assume you were protecting him by not telling him what we know?"

Jack smiled a grim smile. "That's right. I don't think they need to be endangered any more at this time. I'm sure they are being watched and we'd probably better get out of here too."

Hiram took them back to the safe house and then left saying he had to check on some things.

Finding food in the kitchen the trio made a meal and then went to find some place to sleep.

CHAPTER EIGHTEEN

Apparently Hiram returned during the night. Everyone else was so exhausted they never heard him come in. Mark woke up at dawn and padded through the house. In the kitchen he found Hiram drinking some very hot and thick coffee. Hiram looked up at the commando and smiled, "Ever since I did a tour in Paris I've had a liking for this type of coffee."

Mark nodded and poured himself a regular cup and sat down at the table. "What did you find out?"

Hiram laughed softly. "How do you know I was looking for something for you?"

Mark looked at the Israeli agent, "First, I know David and I'm sure he gave you specific orders to help us as best you can. Secondly, we are a danger to you and your cover by being here. I'm pretty sure you'll do whatever is necessary to speed us on our way. This is exactly what I would do under the same circumstances. Thirdly, I feel fairly sure that whatever this Abdullah is cooking up is affecting your people as much as it is ours."

Hiram was nodding in agreement. "You are right on all three counts. But you left off one more. I want to get Abdullah off the streets and knowing your background I'm pretty sure you will do that for me. You do know I studied your techniques when I was in training don't you?"

Mark smiled, "So I've been told."

Hiram got serious. "All right, what I found out could help you. My people were able to get hold of one of Abdullah's bodyguards. He was most talkative when shown the beautiful view of Tymeria from the top of a tall building, upside down. Anyway, it seems that Abdullah has a place in the country. A really hard-to-find place and that is where he is doing his training for this special team." Hiram produced a map of the northern portion of Zyngola. He pointed to a small red circle on the map. "This is where the camp is and the bodyguard was very sure that Abdullah spends most of his time there."

Mark studied the map. "Can you get us some heavier weapons?"

Hiram nodded, "Already done. They are in the storeroom."

Mark was about to get up when Jim Grady suddenly appeared in the kitchen. Mark made a mental note to himself. "Everyone is wandering around and I don't have a clue they are there", I really have to fix that."

Mark motioned to Jim to follow him. He opened the door to the storeroom and found three of their M16Z "Snakes", three bags of both ammo and grenades to go with them. He looked at Hiram with a raised eyebrow.

Hiram shrugged, "I thought it would be faster to liberate some of the arms you brought into the country than to smuggle new ones in." He smiled at the look on Mark's face. "Don't be surprised, I'm really not that good. David told me where to find them."

Jim laughed and checked the action on his weapon. Jack leaned over Mark's shoulder and said, "I'll take one of those."

Mark added two more check marks to his mental note on detecting people sneaking up on him. Then he said, "Let's get some breakfast and do some planning. A firm target gives us some operational possibilities."

After eating and doing some travel and target planning, Mark sat back and told them. "One thing I'm worried about is their ability to see us in the spirit. I'm not sure how to factor that into the scenarios."

Jack shook his head, "Don't worry about it. Our big guy is bigger than their big guy. We'll just pray for a covering that won't disclose us to the enemy."

Hiram looked back and forth between the two of them. "Are you guys really concerned about religious interference?"

Mark looked at Hiram like a father would a small child. "Buddy, you'd bettered believe it. I was like you not so long ago. But what I have seen in the last year convinced me that the battle on the spiritual level is much more important and fierce than anything we see in this world."

This was delivered quietly and with such sincerity that Hiram believed him completely. "Wow. I always wondered about that."

Jim asked, "How soon before we leave?"

Hiram looked at his watch. "About thirty minutes is all. Let's get the weapons stored in the back of the car while it's still in the garage." He got up and picked up the bags of handguns, grenades, and other ordinance while Jim gathered up the Armalites and headed for the garage.

Jack looked at Mark and said, "Let's pray."

CHAPTER NINETEEN

Jack led the prayer for God's covering to prevent the demons from being able to warn the Zulam and his people that they were coming. "Dear Father Yahveh, In the name of Your Son, Yahshua, we pray for your protection as we do your work on Earth. Lord Yahshua, the enemy is watching us and is using this observation to hinder your work. We ask you to bind all spirits that are reporting our whereabouts and make them blind, deaf, and dumb. We pray that you will cast these spirits along with all of their backups, replacements, and future assignments into the abyss to never return. Lord Yahshua, we ask that You cover us and our activities to prevent the enemy from seeing us or knowing where we are. Thank you Father Yahveh. It is in Your name, Yahshua, that we pray everything."

Mark opened his eyes and then closed them again. "You know, I sense a lightness and freedom I haven't had for a while. That was a great prayer."

Jack smiled, "its God doing the work, all we can do is ask."

Jim called them from the garage door. "Are we hidden?" Seeing the nods he said, "Let's go!"

The old Chevy rolled out of Tymeria heading north. About five miles into the open land, Hiram turned off the beaten path onto an almost non-existent track that led over a hill and into a tree-lined opening. Sitting in the opening was a Huey helicopter gunship painted in all tan camo and carrying no markings. The three men said goodbye to Hiram and boarded the chopper which eased up into the night sky. Everything was pitch-black on the ground so the team sat quietly while the visor/helmeted pilot flew to the designated drop zone. They were flying very fast and fairly low to avoid any radar but still high enough to avoid detection from the ground. Oh, the people on the ground heard them but either couldn't see them or didn't want to know what was going on.

Forty minutes later the helicopter flared out two feet above an opening in the desert scrub and the three commandos dropped to the ground with their gear. Within seconds the chopper was gone and the team was hidden in the scrub. Waiting for an hour to see if the landing had been detected, the team assembled their weapons and packs for the five kilometer hike to the location of Abdullah Hami's training compound.

At that precise time, the object of their interest was indeed in his compound. He was having a none-too-reverent discussion with Valach, the lesser god of revenge. Abdullah was furious and it showed in his mental speech with his "god". "What do you mean? You have no idea where the infidels are? Aren't you a god? I arranged the capture of the three women and then they escape the Air Force? No one can find them and the men have completely dropped out of sight! This is not acceptable. You are my god and you are supposed to be helping me! BUT! You can't find any of them, why not?"

The voice in his head was also irritated but for more important reasons. It was probably good for Abdullah's health that Valach was so furious at his attendant demons for losing the entire Crossfire Team that he didn't take offense at the tone in Abdullah's thoughts, "Because, the infidel's God is interfering with my efforts. It is nothing but a nuisance but it can cause problems like these. I will find them. Rest assured of that."

Hami suddenly realized that he was treading on dangerous ground. You can express your irritation *to* your god but it wasn't smart to express your irritation *at* your god. One did that only if one wanted to cease living. This thought cooled his anger considerably. He redirected his anger at the Americans. "They are probably all the way back in the United States by now." he thought.

Abdullah got up and left his prayer cubicle. He padded down the wooden floored hallway to the study which was the operational center for his mountain training center. He picked up the telephone and made a call to his agents in Tymeria. When the leader of his local followers was on the phone he inquired as to their progress. "Have you located any of the three men or the three women?"

"Not yet Master." We have some interesting stories of Americans in several places in the city and we are attempting to see which ones are real." The man was loyal and very dedicated to Abdullah and there was no reason to doubt what he said. Abdullah thought for a few seconds and then said, "All right. Keep on looking for them. I would concentrate your search at the transportation centers. Remember, you are doing a great service for Zultar. Do not slacken your pace. These infidels must be found!"

Hanging up the phone, Abdullah ate some peanuts and drank some cool water. Refreshed, he contemplated his next move. He couldn't start building more assault teams until the problem of these foreigners was resolved. He thought about the women. He would gladly destroy them if they weren't such good hostages. Of course they weren't hostages any more. How they took over the aircraft they were on and still survived their crash landing was beyond his imagination. They were very lethal and needed to be subdued or destroyed. First though, they had to be found.

He sat back in his overstuffed armchair and thought about the missing men. It was reported that these men were even more dangerous than the females in their group. Perhaps he had taken on more than he really should. But, he had the same problem with the men. First they had to be located. If they had fled the country they would be trying to sneak back in sooner or later and therefore remained a problem.

Five hundred yards away from the chair Abdullah was sitting in, Mark Connelly studied the layout of the training center with some very good Israeli 40-power binoculars. He was able to determine the important staff building and the power generator building. Others included the chow hall, the motor pool garage, and the latrine. He pointed these things out to Jack. Jack looked at the center with his own binoculars. "There doesn't seem to be any fences."

Mark muttered, "Yeah, it may mean a sophisticated sensor system, or that they don't expect anyone to bother them, or that they rely on the demons to warn them of intruders."

They continued to watch the activity of the target for several hours. They had classified the guards and the workers that kept the camp working. They had also spotted five men who didn't seem to do anything but eat and relax.

About 1 o'clock in the afternoon. Jack spotted what had to be the Zulam they were looking for. He pointed him out to Mark and Jim. The teacher walked briskly to the motor pool and emerged with two armed guards in an old Jeep-like vehicle that had probably been made as a copy in China. The Zulam and his guards swept out of the training center and roared away down the side of the hill the center was located on. He was probably going to Tymeria.

Jack watched him leave and commented, "You'd think that if he had millions of U.S. dollars he could afford better transportation than that."

Mark laughed, "Did you hear the engine in that thing? It's made to look old and cheap so as not to attract unwanted attention. I'll lay you odds it isn't a year old yet. So, what do we do now that the bird has flown the coop?"

Jack refocused the binoculars on the center. "Let's get one of those other men to tell us what is going on here."

Mark shook his head, "That is risky because they will miss the man real soon and realize that there's something going on. Then they start looking for us."

Jack shrugged his shoulders. "We aren't going to do any good just sitting here hoping the head wacko will be back soon. And we aren't going to leave without some answers."

Jim snorted; "Let me "borrow" one of the non-worker types. I'll be back here with him soon." Jim left his backpack and took off at an angle to penetrate the center at the point nearest to the building the non-workers seemed to be staying at.

Jack and Mark had the highest respect for Jim Grady and his capabilities. They didn't worry about him getting observed or caught. Ten minutes later their confidence was rewarded as the big man returned lugging a slighter man over his shoulder.

Jim laid the man's body down in the sand. "He's a little unconscious right now but I think he'll be okay in about ten minutes."

Mark injected the man's arm with truth serum, "Might as well stick him while he can't feel it."

The man came to a semi-conscious state and Jim questioned him. Jim was the only one that spoke Arabic in their trio. Jack and Mark kept guard while the interrogation was under way. In about fifteen minutes, the Sensei took the man back to camp and placed him back in the chair he had been sleeping in when Jim bagged him. He had never woken up and couldn't identify them or where they were hiding. This way he'd wake up in a few minutes and only wonder why he had slept so long.

Jim got back to the other two men and sighed. "I found out what their great secret involves. It seems that there is a "lesser god" named Valach who helps a guy named Abdullah Hami, who I think is our Zulam." This demon and Hami train these people to astral project their spirits and curse and do damage to infidels. Apparently they are simply a test group that is the prototype for many more groups to come. They have killed approximately five Jews and two Europeans so far and ruined the careers of a dozen more. It seems that the expansion of their group is on hold while Hami searches for us."

CHAPTER TWENTY

Mark was all for leveling the camp and eliminating the crew of demon-worshippers. Jim was silent thinking about the problems involved.

Jack sat down on the ground. "We can't do that." In response to Mark's questioning look, he continued. "We aren't some God-appointed killing group. First of all, God hasn't told us to destroy them. Second, we don't have any legal grounds to attack that compound. They haven't done anything that could be proven in a court of law. What do we have to indict them with? An Israeli agent's comment that this Zulam told the police we were dangerous. He wouldn't testify and we couldn't prove it. To tell a jury that God has asked us to stop a terrible spiritual plot wouldn't hold any water with the court. Nobody at that training center has done anything illegal that can be shown as illegal. Since this is a spiritual matter we need to tackle it spiritually and not in the flesh."

Mark didn't like this shift in priorities but couldn't argue with Jack about the legality of the situation. "What about arresting me before and our people the other day and taking them to jail?"

Pointing at the training center, Jack said, "These guys didn't do that, the police did. All we have about the un-provable spiritual attacks is the word of an unknown man who offered the information during an illegal interrogation where drugs were used illegally."

Jim nodded. "We don't have much to back us up in this case."

Jack said, "Let's pray and see what the Lord wants us to do."

As they prayed in their prayer languages, Mark had a vision. He was standing on an open field. It was bright daylight and a few hundred feet away from him was a demon hiding behind a moon-god mask. The demon was exhorting everyday people to attack Mark. Believing that they were doing god's will, the crowd turned towards Mark and headed his way. The demon was laughing hysterically.

Mark found he had an assault rifle in his hands but couldn't shoot the people because they were being deceived by the demon and weren't really his enemies. Instead, he snapped the rifle up and fired a dozen rounds into the demon. This didn't hurt the demon but enraged the people because they thought Mark was shooting at their god.

Mark tried to run but his feet wouldn't move. He saw the crowd was almost upon him and he cried out for Yahshua to help him. Suddenly there were two glass walls between him and the crowd. The walls divided the crowd and left an open avenue between Mark and the demon. Mark realized he needed to change his attack strategy and he put the rifle on the ground and dropped to his knees. He prayed that Father Yahveh would have his mighty angels come and bind the demon and take him to the abyss to never return.

He looked up and the demon was gone. The people milled about behind the glass walls and eventually dispersed.

Mark came back to the desert scrub as early evening darkened their area. He looked at Jim and Jack and found them still praying. "Jack, Jim, I've got something to tell you." Both of them stopped praying and paid attention to him. Mark explained his vision in detail.

Jack nodded. "That's confirmation that we need to handle this on the spiritual plane until they do something that requires us to respond to in the flesh."

Jack returned to praying. As he continued to seek the Lord he felt the conviction of God's Spirit that they should not attack the training center but to wait upon the Lord's timing. After a while he told the others of this conviction. Making themselves as comfortable as possible they settled down to wait.

Around two o'clock in the morning a cold front went through the area and the desert temperature dropped quickly. This, added to the inactivity, made the waiting harder. Even Jack was feeling like they should head back to Tymeria when the rumble of engines was heard. Soon a convoy of three large, military-style trucks lumbered into view. Their lights slashed through the scattered brush and few hardy trees and made the rest of the dark even darker.

The trucks passed the commandos and turned into the compound and came to a halt. Men with guns got out and opened the backs of the trucks. Yelling and kicking, they escorted thirty five, poorly-dressed men and women out of the back of the trucks and across the parking area. They lined them up and made them walk into a single-level building with tiny, barred windows. Not long after that the guards came back out and locked the door and walked to the larger staff building. Quiet returned to the area except for the sounds of quiet crying and some moans from the jail building.

It might be kidnapping, but it still didn't give any legal authorization to the Crossfire team to intervene. The rest of the night passed slowly with no more incidents.

The affairs of a large encampment went like normal after the dawn. Some people went between buildings, and soon there was the smell of cooking and around six a.m. the troops and personnel of the camp finished their morning prayers and then wandered into what was obviously the mess tent for breakfast. Several buckets of some kind of food were taken to the jail. Prisoners were escorted to a latrine and back and the activities of the day commenced.

Around ten in the morning guards brought all the prisoners out and lined them up in front of a small stand in the open field. After making them wait an uncomfortable half-hour, one of the camp leaders came to the stand and started reading from a document to the prisoners. He was speaking Arabic and Jim translated for Mark and Jack.

"You infidels are here because you have violated Zultarian law. You have been convicted of being members of an outlawed group of extremists. The penalty for trying to spread your contemptible religion among the pure Zultarians is beheading. There is no appeal and you will be executed after prayers this afternoon." The camp leader turned to the guards and said, "Take these miserable Christians back to their cells until their execution!"

The guards prodded and forced the prisoners back into the jail. They came out, locked the door and laughed at the meekness of the prisoners as quiet came back to the field.

Jack and Mark looked at each other. Mark tipped his head to one side, "Well, we still don't have any legal grounds for interfering in local politics but I will not stand by and let them slaughter three dozen people because those people believe in Christ."

Jack had been asking the same question of God. "No, we're not going to allow this because it violates God's law which is higher than the Zultarian law." He shook his head for a second. "Okay, we get them out of that jail and back into the trucks and out of here. Don't shoot anybody that doesn't attempt to shoot you first or tries to stop you, okay?"

Mark was stretching his arms and back to shake off the rigors of lying on the ground all night. "I'd guess that there are about twenty guards and fifteen other staff personnel in the camp. It would be easier if we captured them rather than trying to make a jail break with twenty-some people and trying to fend off the attacks of the camp personnel. Don't you agree?"

Jack was about to agree when activity started up on the field again. Using the binoculars he could see them setting up a chopping block that had obviously seen service before from the bloodstained surface of the wood. He watched as the guards went to the jail and brought out one of the prisoners. In the light of day Jack could see the face of the man. It was peaceful and composed. He was ready to meet his Savior. The two guards were joined by a large Arabic man with a heavy sword and the official who had read the indictment. They tied the man's hands behind him and forced him to kneel with his head over the block.

Jack dropped his binoculars and brought his Armalite "Snake" up to his shoulder. Selecting the built-in silencer he put the crosshairs on the sword of the executioner. As the man raised the sword for the killing blow, Jack squeezed the trigger on the rifle. The bullet made no noise as it flew to its target. The 58-grain, boat tail slug impacted the sword at four thousand feet per second. The sword rang and flew out the man's hands. The other two guards and the official didn't have time to wonder what happened before they saw the three commandos coming towards them. They raised their hands in surrender. Mark and Jim used plastic riot cuffs on all four men and gagged them with strips ripped off of their own clothes. Mark said as they finished, "Well, there goes that plan."

The large, bushy-haired man on his knees looked from the trussed-up guards to the commandos with a stunned but happy expression. Mark pulled out his K-Bar combat knife and cut the ropes from the man'sds. Then Jack and Mark went down on one knee covering the building with their rifles. There had been no reaction to their interference as yet. Jim asked him in Arabic if he was all right. He nodded and then said in English, "May Jesus Bless you for your timely intervention."

Mark said, "Let's get off of this open field." The four men ran back to the side of the jail and out of sight from the other buildings. The rescued man stuck out his hand to Jim. "I'm Harry Pembroke, I'm English and I'm pasturing an underground church in Tymeria. We got rounded up yesterday and brought here without a trial or anything. Can you help me get the other church members out of here?"

Mark nodded and asked him, "If we can free the rest of them are there three of you that can drive those trucks?"

Harry nodded, "Right on, chap."

Jack raised his rifle and blew the lock off of the door to the jail. Swinging the door open he stepped in and saw the rest of the prisoners holding back in fear of death. He found that the doors were fastened by handles that could only be reached from the outside. The four men opened all the doors and got the people outside the building in less than two minutes. Mark told Harry, "Take these people and get them back into the trucks. I know this style of truck; it doesn't have an ignition key. Just turn the switch, which is on the left side of the wheel, to the right and step on the starter pedal on the floor, to the left of the clutch. Make sure the truck is in neutral before you do that. Once the engine starts, it's just like any other four-speed standard shift. Reverse is all the way to the right and toward the dash. Got it?"

Harry and several of the men all nodded at once. Mark continued, "You probably can get close to Tymeria without being stopped, but once you enter the city you will draw attention. You probably want to abandon the trucks near the suburbs and hike in. Don't go back to your meeting place and do try to get out of the country if possible. I'm sure the police will be looking for you after a day or so."

Harry said, "But if these people report the trucks as stolen, they'll be waiting for us."

Jack smiled a grim smile, "Don't worry about that. No one here is going to contact anyone for a long while. Now get going. We'll deal with the guards."

Harry nodded and pointed to the trucks. The entire group headed for them with scattered "Blessings" and "Thank you'" being given to the three men who had just saved them from sure death.

As the people reached the trucks Jim said, "As soon as the first truck starts they're going to be coming out to stop them."

Mark smiled, "Three of us and thirty of them. Doesn't seem fair for them does it?"

Jack knew that Mark wasn't being facetious.

The first truck started up, quickly followed by the other two. All three trucks started moving, turning around in a circle and heading back onto the road away from the camp.

Mark turned towards the command building. Using the built-in 40mm grenade launcher he triggered a round towards the radio antenna on the top of the building. The explosion blew off all of the antennas and supporting structures from the roof. Jack did the same thing to the telephone lines by eliminating a nearby telephone pole which snapped the two wires as it fell.

There was a yell of surprise from the staff building followed by a stream of armed guards running out onto the field. The guards started to shoot at the departing trucks. The commandos fired some rounds above the guard's heads while Jim shouted in Arabic for them to give up or die.

The guards dropped their weapons and raised their hands. The guards were disorganized and their control was erratic. In less than five minutes all the guards were tied up. When the commandos ran out of riot cuffs, they found some rope and finished the job.

Jim ran to the entrance to the staff building and entered, followed by Jack and then Mark. As they went room by room they rounded up the staff and held them in a large sitting room. Eventually Mark counted heads and they had everyone he'd been able to see in the camp over the last day.

One of the men from group that Hami had trained to do astral projection stepped forward. "You have attacked our people and you have no right!" Mark looked at Jack.

Since the man spoke English Jack replied, "By Mosaic law, you have no right to execute other people in the name of your moon-god Zultar. By rights we are supposed to stone you to death for idol worship. But since you are deceived and probably have been since birth we will withhold that sentence and give you a chance to repent and ask Yahveh for forgiveness."

That line of reasoning left the Zultarian in shock. He had many come-backs and rebuttals for everything Christian but nothing about Mosaic Law.

Most of the staff personnel sat down and tried to stay out of the argument with the armed men. But one of them stepped forward. He was a large man and obviously agile. He flexed his arms and spoke in Arabic. Jim translated, "He wants to fight us hand-to-hand in fair combat to see whose god is the better god."

Jack almost couldn't believe the situation. They had just captured nineteen people and now they were being given a challenge to determine the supremacy of God. He handed his rifle to Mark and took off his ammo belt. He didn't like having to fight in boots but wasn't given the chance to take them off. The Arab strode forth and launched a quick round-house spinning heel kick to the head. Jack blocked it with his right arm and attempted to kick the man's other leg with his right foot to the knee.

The Arab was wise to that move and jumped out of range. He threw a hard back fist at Jack's head which Jack deflected. Jack tried a side kick which the man avoided. For several minutes the two men sparred with each other, throwing punches and kicks which were blocked or avoided by the other man.

Jim Grady watched his student carefully. He felt that Jack could take the Arab but they just didn't have the time to wait. He put his rifle down and stepped into the fray. Seeing this, Jack backed up and away from the fight.

The Arab sized up the older man and launched a series of rapid front punches designed to wear his opponent down until he was able to hit him with effect. Jim blocked the first two punches and on the third one Jim used the man's momentum to effectively turn him around. The Sensei stiffened the three fingers on both hands and struck the Arab in three places on the back with his fingers. The man froze in that position. He tried mightily to move but couldn't. The nerve groups that the Sensei had struck locked the man's muscles rigidly into one position.

Jim then struck both sides of the man's neck with his fingers and the man dropped to the floor like a sack of grain. He didn't move after that.

Jim stepped back and picked up his rifle. Jack did the same.

Mark looked out the window and noticed a jeep there that he hadn't seen before. Before he could yell a warning to the others, a dozen guards came through the door behind them with their rifles up and yelled for the Americans to drop their weapons. They were outgunned and outnumbered. As the three commandos dropped their weapons, the staff and the guards rushed them and a flurry of fists and feet smashed into the three men.

CHAPTER TWENTY-ONE

Jack came to in pain. He immediately sucked in a breath and felt more pain where he was missing a tooth. As he came fully conscious he felt pain in both his body and his head. He settled himself down emotionally and tried to control his autonomic system. After he reached a place of steadiness he began to catalog his condition. His left eye was closed and he couldn't open it. His right eye was swollen and only worked half-way. He tried to see where they were and was rewarded by a blurry vision of a small window with bars. Okay, he was in the jail building.

He was chained to the wall with his arms spread apart and his feet shackled to the floor and the wall. He gently moved his head and was rewarded with a giant-sized headache and pain in his neck. Checking his extremities he found he still had all his fingers, toes, arms, and legs. He could feel bruises all over his body and he was sure his head didn't look any better. He silently prayed for strength and a reduction in the pain that was almost blinding him. After a few seconds, the pain receded and he did feel stronger.

Slowly looking to his right he saw Mark hanging in a similar pose in the next cell. Jack realized that he probably looked like Mark and Mark looked bad. He had cuts on his face and blood on his clothes. He wasn't moving and he was either still unconscious or asleep. Jack could see his chest rise and fall so he wasn't dead anyway.

Turning his head the other direction he saw Jim Grady. Jim was lying on the floor of his cell and his feet were chained to the wall. From the unnatural position of his arms Jack could tell that both of his arms were broken between the wrist and the elbow. He was also unconscious but alive.

The light was failing in the little window. Jack passed out again. Sometime later it was dark and he heard a moan. It was coming from his left. He wondered who it was for a few seconds until he remembered Jim. He tried to speak but only a croak came out. He summoned as much saliva as possible in his dry mouth and swallowed. That didn't feel good either. But he was able to rasp out a word or two. "Jim, can you hear me?"

Jim coughed twice and then responded in a weak but steady voice. "Yes, Jack, I can hear you. Are you in one piece?"

Jack had to take a big breath because of the bravery he heard in Jim's voice. "Yeah, I'm in one piece. How is the pain in your arms?"

Jim sighed, "Tolerable, but I can't feel my hands and I sorely regret that."

Mark's voice joined the conversation from the dark on Jack's right. "They apparently weren't too appreciative of your capabilities. I thought you did a great job."

Jim made a sound something like a chuckle. "They weren't too happy with any of us. I was still conscious when they were dragging us in here. They were talking about our execution tomorrow morning. Since we broke the sword of their executioner, they have decided to use our own words and stone us to death after early morning prayers."

Jack's spirit was grieved by the unstated fact that Jim must have been awake when they broke his arms. But the humble older man never mentioned that. That spoke volumes to Jack about character. He determined to somehow get loose and save both his friends.

Moving brought waves of pain from everywhere but he tried his chains and leg shackles. Nothing gave at all. Mark grunted from the next cell. "You had better summon an angel if we're going to get out of this one."

That reminded Jack of Paul and Silas's imprisonment in Neapolis as told in Acts. He remembered that God inhabits the praise of his saints. Maybe God would send an angel and an earthquake to rescue them. He began to hum the tune, My God is an Awesome God. It took a few stanzas until he got Jim and Mark to sing along with him. They had started on the tenth rendition of "I See the Lord, High and Lifted Up" when he thought he could hear a sweet voice and then the end of the jail house exploded.

CHAPTER TWENTY-TWO

Sarah was checking her weapons. She had a burning anger that needed to be released, and soon.

The NSA had followed the location of Mark's PPM with a series of photographs taken by one of the agency's low-level Keyhole satellites. The photos showed buildings in the area of El Bara, north-northwest of Tymeria. There were people shown in the photos. Close-ups revealed that there were many Zyngolian guards carrying three men towards a small building. Even though the men being carried were covered in blood and their clothes were in tatters it was obvious to Sarah who they were. She ran the picture of her husband's battered body being carried by four smaller Arab men. She couldn't tell if he was alive or dead. But God's Spirit continued to confirm her hope that he was still alive.

Christi had been smuggled out of the country by the Israelis. Her band and support staff had been told to leave the day before. They were all headed back to the United States. Christi hadn't wanted to leave but knew her people needed her.

Now Sarah and Laura were outfitted to go to war. Both of them had full combat fatigues with Kevlar vests. Besides 9mm pistols they had their Armalite "Snakes" from the band equipment. Laura, as usual, was praying for God's protection for the men and themselves. Sarah tried to put her anger on God's altar but she just couldn't leave it there. Her mood got darker as they were taken out of the city to rendezvous with an unmarked helicopter. As they boarded she was surprised to see five American SEALs in the craft. "What is this?" she asked.

The leader, Captain Willis, answered her. "Our Commander asked us to accompany you on this little outing. She has a soft spot in her heart for General Connelly and apparently some higher authority to authorize this raid."

Sarah motioned the chopper pilot to take them up.

After being dropped near the camp, they made their way to the buildings they had seen in the photos. The

SEALs eliminated four roving patrols that were between them and their objective. It was still dark but dawn wasn't far away when Sarah heard singing. She snuck close to the jail building and heard voices raised in a Christian song. She had to classify this one as "Make a joyful noise unto the Lord" because the singing was really poor. But it gave her an idea where the people were. Captain Willis showed her a thermograph view of the building through the scope of his rifle. The three images were on the far left end of the building away from the door. She took the slack out of the trigger on her 40mm grenade launcher and whispered, "Fire in the hole!" She triggered the round and as it flew to the building she said, "Knock, knock!" The 40 mm grenade exploded. The majority of the door and frame disintegrated and bricks flew.

Three of the SEALs went into the main staff building while one stayed outside as a rear guard. Sarah, Laura, and Captain Willis forced their way into the jail and lit up the place with a flare.

Seeing Mark in the nearest cell, Sarah waved and said, "Honey, I'm home!" He grinned and looked to his left where Jack was hanging from the wall. "See, God sent two angels instead of one."

Using a multi-tool, Captain Willis got Mark and then Jack free from their chains. Jack limped and moved slowly but he helped the Captain release Jim from his leg irons. The Captain spoke into his comm. link. "Jonesy, I've got two broken arms here. Can you bring me your splint?" Getting an affirmative He carefully splinted the Sensei's left arm. Jonesy showed up with the other splint and they immobilized the other arm. The Captain was about to give Jim a morphine injection when the older man said, "Save that, it isn't necessary, I can block the pain myself."

The Captain stared at him for a few seconds and then nodded and put the injection away. Jack and the Captain helped Jim to his feet and toward the door. After everyone was outside the jail building, the Captain called the other SEALs to their location and they extracted the injured back to the field. The same unmarked Huey helicopter that originally brought Jack to the camp settled to the ground and everyone loaded onboard. The chopper lifted off and headed south-southeast.

After a change of helicopters, the entire crew flew out over Sudan to the Red Sea and landed on a military hospital ship that was there for the ongoing U.S. effort in the Middle East confrontation with terrorists. Jim's arms were set and the other injuries were treated for all three of the team. Jack called David at the Mossad and arranged to get Stan and Debbie Hargrove out of Zyngola. They had stayed behind in the event they could help the team,

Two days later, Jack was sunning himself on the deck next to Laura. He still had bumps and bruises but he felt that he was back in fighting shape. Mark seemed to recover quicker and was already eager to get back to the fight. Jim had been airlifted back to the U.S. for more extensive treatment and rehabilitation. He was in good spirits when he left. He waved one of his casts and told them "I can feel my hands again, praise God."

Jack, Laura, Sarah, and Mark had dinner the evening of the second night and discussed what they should do. Again they lifted their need for direction up to the Lord in prayer. This time the answer they got surprised all of them.

CHAPTER TWENTY-THREE

Abdullah walked through the wreckage of his camp and surveyed the damage and the losses. He was outwardly calm and reserved. He offered up prayers to Zultar for the deaths of all twenty guards. He let everyone around him know that it was reprehensible the men had to die. They didn't deserve to die just because the infidels couldn't stand Abdullah and his popularity and power.

Zultar would understand their deaths. Abdullah was upset because he now had to replace them and that involved effort on his part to replace each man. He still didn't have any qualms ordering the executions of the guards the infidels hadn't killed. They had failed to stop the enemy. It had been necessary to enforce order and show that failure was not accepted. He needed bodies to show to the authorities and the press when he blamed it on the infidels. He was quite sure the next group of guards would be much more vigilant.

Actually, none of this bothered him half as much as the fact that it happened without warning, twice! Valach wasn't able to fathom where the infidels were any more now than he had been before. That shook him. That meant that Valach wasn't able to overcome the infidel's god. Of course, Valach was only a lesser god. Zultar was still supreme and it did not come as a surprise that Zultar didn't help Valach overcome the alien god. Zultar was arbitrary and fickle. That was his right. Still, Abdullah began to wonder just how much he could count on Valach in the future.

One thing was for sure. It was on Valach's orders that he had sidetracked his training and deployment of more spiritual attack teams. Well now, since Valach couldn't find the infidels then Abdullah was free to do what he wanted to do the most. Destroy infidels!

A little over three hundred miles away from the brooding Abdullah, Jack and Mark were discussing the results of their prayer time.

Jack shook his head. "If what I heard the Lord tell me is what is about to come down it will be awesome. This is something I would never have thought of." He looked at Mark, "I don't think you would have either."

Mark agreed with Jack. This concept went so far beyond his "strategies" that he was humbled in the extreme.

Mark thought back to the vision he had received in this prayer time. He had been praying that the Lord Yahshua would show him the proper approach to eliminate this threat without the Crossfire Team having to simply kill the Zulam and his followers.

Suddenly he had been transported to a beautiful island and he was standing on a field which ended in a cliff beyond which was the ocean. The sky was hazy blue and the air was warm. He looked around and was surprised to see Jack, Laura, and Sarah there with him. It seemed more real than real life. He knew he was in a vision, or was he?

The angel Caleb appeared and greeted them by name. He then seemed to darken and grow in size. His words took on a commanding tone. Mark knew he would remember every word spoken here for the rest of his life.

Caleb floated about a foot above the ground and spoke. "The Lord God Almighty has told you He will not permit this foul evil from taking place. He has given the task of stopping it to you four. Forget any feelings of failure or inability. You have been brave and kept the Lord's desires first most in your thoughts as you attempted to fulfill his will."

Caleb floated closer to the foursome. "The Lord wants all men to come to repentance and seek Him. But some, who are at first deceived, refuse to throw off their yoke of bondage because of their own carnal desires. They do not want to escape their blindness because of the power it brings them in the flesh. The Lord will give them over to their evil desires."

Caleb started to shine like the sun. His color was almost blinding. "Hear now the will of Yahveh, your God. *The enemy will rise up to destroy my believers in Africa; I will meet their challenge and show the world that I am God. You will need to stand firm in your faith and believe.*"

Caleb softened in tone and fierceness of light. "You must return to Tymeria. Do not go to do battle in the flesh, but pray constantly and be meek. Challenge the teacher of evil, the puppet of the demon Valach and his master to defeat your God in front of their loyal followers. God will be with you. Know that the battle in the heavenly will be immense as Satan contends with God's forces for domination of the deceived masses. It is imperative that you four show your belief as a rallying point for the church. Caleb reached out his hands and power flowed from him to them.

Mark felt like the power strengthened him so much that he could move mountains. But he had grown enough in his walk to realize he didn't have any real physical power on his own. This power was the power to believe and was only effective when exercised in faith in God.

Mark realized that the vision was over and opened his eyes. He looked at his wife and the Malones. They literally glowed in the perfect health of faith.

Jack opened his eyes and looked with peace at Mark. "I think our time in the furnace on Victor's island was training for this event. Don't you?"

Mark thought about that exhibition of God's power and agreed with his friend. "Yes, you're right. If the radioactive fires of an open nuclear reactor couldn't hurt us, then the followers of Zultar will not be able to shake our faith either."

Laura smiled at the discussion between the men. "I feel more at peace with myself, the world, and God than I have ever felt before."

There was a knock on the door to the small wardroom they were in. When Sarah opened the door the sailor standing there handed them a message. Sarah read it and laughed. "It's from Jim Grady. He called to tell us his arms have been healed and all his damages are gone. He ends the note with "Praise Yahveh and Yahshua!"

Jack felt his mouth with his tongue. "My missing tooth isn't missing anymore."

Mark stretched and laughed and grabbed Sarah in a bear hug. "I don't have any bruises or cuts anymore either."

They settled down and looked at each other with grins on their faces. Jack threw the discussion into the practical arena. "We prayed for guidance and we got it. Now, how do we implement the plan on the worldly level?"

Mark had been thinking about that. "We need to challenge Abdullah Hami in such a way that he can't just have us killed and bury the challenge. I think that means we need to excite public opinion and get the local Christians and Zyngolian government involved in a public way."

Sarah nodded, "Yes, this reminds me of the poisoning fast and prayer. We need to galvanize the church worldwide to pray for this demonstration of God's glory."

Laura felt the correctness of that in her spirit. "I would call the President and brief him on God's directions so that it doesn't go against administration policy in this area of the world. I'm sure if we present it properly we can get his support."

Sarah went and got a Bible, flipped it open and added, "Do you realize this could be part of Bible prophesy? I remember reading in Daniel 12:1 *"At that time Michael shall stand up. The great prince who stands watch over the sons of your people, and there shall be a time of trouble, such as never was since there was a nation. Even to that time. And at that time your people shall be delivered, everyone who is found written in the book."*

Jack said, "That is end-time prophesy. And we are in the end-times according to everything I've heard. All right, Laura and I will work to get the support and prayers of the President and the American Christians. Mark, you and Sarah do the same with Worldwide Christians other than the U.S. "

Jack organized his thoughts for a second. "Then, when the Lord releases us, we will get the word spread throughout the Zultarian world about the challenge in Zyngola. Lastly we will openly contact Abdullah himself and issue the challenge. We'll need world-wide television and computer coverage of the event. Let's get in contact with Christi again. If she has the chance I think she'll be able to work the media angle, any thoughts on this?"

Mark shrugged and said, "I'll feel undressed without any guns but I finally understand that God is more protection for me than anything on this earth."

Laura looked a bit somber. "Guys, let's remember that God didn't say that we would live through this, He only said that He would be with us. Keep that in mind as we trample out the vintage where the grapes of wrath are stored."

CHAPTER TWENTY-FOUR

Four days later, the President of the United States sat quietly behind his desk in the oval office and listened to Jack and Laura explain what they had been given as a mission by the Spirit of God and how they planned to accomplish that task.

When they had finished, he sat there in thought and prayer for a few minutes. He looked up and sighed. "We have a bunch of problems with this whole thing and some real problems with some of the specifics of it. First, I know God is behind you on this. That is confirmed in my spirit by God's Spirit. Second, just about everybody else is going to be against you in this. Do you know what it sounds like to someone who isn't spirit-filled?"

The President stood up and gestured with his hands as he walked out from behind the desk. "The United States, represented by several individuals has declared war on Zultarism. They have issued a declaration of war against the faith of the Zultarians and are going to have a showdown in Zyngola."

He shook his head, "This is not politically correct and will result in screams of horror and rage from the Congress, the Supreme Court, and the International Court, my own cabinet, not to mention every other country in the world that has a Zultarian population. How do you propose to placate them?" The President was concerned that they would be outlawed, possibly jailed, and legally barred from challenging Zultarism forever.

Laura had been praying during the President's talk and God's Spirit gave her an answer. When the President wound down she spoke. "Mr. President, we don't have to placate them because we are not going to upset them at all. The Lord is moving matters so that it will be politically correct for us to challenge them. In fact, it will be the only answer for the whole world. In the next forty-eight hours events will transpire that will demand an answer from the world. Our challenge will be that answer."

In his spirit President Bollen felt that her answer was right. He sat down behind his desk and thought for a minute. Then he asked them, "All right, let us say God moves the world to agree to censor Zyngola. What do you need me to do to help you?"

Jack sat forward, "We will need your personal prayer coverage and whatever pressure you can put on the media to cover this event. Also we may need some protection and transportation getting to Tymeria."

The President raised an eyebrow. "And protection once you're there and getting you out? That could be quite a ..."

Jack gently cut him off. "No Sir. Once we're there we are in God's hands. We aren't even taking any weapons with us. The Lord said to go there armed only with our faith."

The President could understand how that would play in Tymeria, unless there was a snag. Then it would be really messy. "All right, my prayers you will have of course. I'll move the media as much as possible to cover it although they may slant the stuffing out of the story. I'll also arrange for your transportation to wherever you want to go into Tymeria. And I'll give you one more bonus. If things play out like you say they will, the situation will be similar to the Arab Strike Force (ASF) poisoning affair. I will see what I can do to encourage the free world, especially the Americans, to pray for you also."

Jack said, "Thank you Mr. President, that is a more than generous offer." Laura nodded her agreement as they got up to take their leave.

The President came around the desk and clasped both of them around the shoulders. He bent his head and said, "Dear Heavenly Father, I ask that you go with this couple into and out of danger. Have your mighty angels fight for them every step of the way. I also pray for their success in this affair. It's in your name we pray Jesus."

After leaving the White House, Jack and Laura went to the MCI Center on F Street. A Christian Leader's meeting was taking place there over the next two days and Minister Throman was attending. He met them in the lobby and steered them into a small office near the entrance. "How are you two doing? I haven't heard from you or about you for a while. I watch all the news casts to see what part of the world has had miracles or destruction and try to figure out if you were involved." He laughed with them.

Laura hugged the elderly Minister and Jack shook his hand at the same time. They talked for a few minutes and brought him up to date with events in Africa. Then they told him of their mission and asked him to participate by alerting the Christian community when events unfolded so that he could.

He agreed to, "Of course I will. I've learned that you are as close to the Lord as anyone I've ever even heard of, let alone knew. This is an audacious plan of the Lord. You will need all the prayer coverage you can get."

Jack held up a hand, "Alan, we especially need you to pray for the angelic warriors. The battle will be the fiercest seen for a long while according to the angel that told us about it." Jack paused for a few seconds. "There is a chance that the Connelly's, Laura, and myself will not return from this trip. So, pray hard for all four of us."

The Minister was taken aback. He had never heard Jack so unsure of their future before. He couldn't talk he was greatly concerned for their lives. He would miss them terribly if they didn't come back. Of course it wouldn't do to show his emotional agreement with that possibility. He smiled and said, "Let's talk about that when you get back, okay?"

In Tel Aviv, Sarah and Mark talked to David Zahavy about prayer support of the Messianic Jews and Jewish Christians. David listened and thought for a few seconds. "I don't think there will be any reluctance on anyone's part to pray for your success and protection. I dare say that there will be many of the Jewish faith that will be offering up prayers for you also. That is because Zultarism is rapidly becoming a major threat to our way of life. You say I'll know when to make an announcement and that will be in the next two days. I'll make sure that everyone is notified."

Later that day the first warning signals flew out of Tymeria.

CHAPTER TWENTY-FIVE

Abdullah Hami was gloriously happy. Valach was gleeful. Nobody knew how Zultar felt about their victory since man could not know god or his feelings. Abdullah relished every minute of adulation he received in the ruling council after his proposal was approved unanimously by the council and approved whole-heartedly by the administration.

At the beginning of the day Abdullah put his proposal forth and waited patiently for the reactions of the council members. He was not overly concerned because Valach told him that it would be accepted. While he wasn't sure of Valach's capabilities concerning the infidels, the god had never failed when he was working with Zultarians.

Abdullah thought back over the last six days and the efforts he and Valach had to put forth to get this proposal accepted by the entire council.

Right after the infidels had been reported leaving the country, Valach proposed a radical idea to Abdullah. Abdullah had considered it and liked it. He called twenty-five other Zulams on his newly reconnected telephone system and requested a meeting in Tymeria the next day to address the problem of the infidels. Many would come because they wanted to resolve the nagging problem of the two percent of the population that weren't Zultarian and had no intention of becoming Zultarian. Most of the rest would come so that they weren't seen as dragging their feet about the issue.

Valach promised to help the reluctant ones to see the light. So Abdullah worked and reworked his original draft of the proposal on the trip to Tymeria.

The next morning, right after morning prayers, the twenty-six teachers met in a softly lit room with refreshments and attendants for any need. Abdullah noted that the most influential teachers were here. He opened the session by describing, in gory detail, the attack on his training center.

"I had come to the city to confer with the government that morning. The infidels had to know my schedule. We had been ordered to re-educate the members of a Christian church that the police had arrested. They were placed in pleasant accommodations at my school. The teachers there were going to debate the issues in the morning, starting with their leader. As the discussions were beginning, several dozen infidel warriors charged into the school and killed my leading teacher and three of his aides in a blaze of gunfire. They proceeded to kill and destroy wantonly everywhere they went.

They took the Christians with them as they left. In the last battle, several of our brave students were able to subdue three of the raiders and disarm them. We didn't cause them any injury even though they had destroyed my school's communications systems, the library, and the food court. One of these infidels had the audacity to yell obscenities about Zultar and then empty his machine gun into one of our women workers, killing her instantly.

We locked the captured raiders up in one of our buildings to await the police. But, sadly, we had no way to contact them at that time. "

Abdullah hung his head like he was ashamed. "That night an even bigger force of infidel soldiers raided the school for the second time to free the three captives. All in all we had twelve civilians and twenty-three security forces, all loyal and faithful, and mostly peaceful, beautiful Zultarians killed wantonly by the vicious horde. This is becoming a nightmare. We can no longer sit idly by as this tiny minority gives cause to these killers who destroy our people and our way of life. As long as any non-Zultarians stay in Zyngola we open ourselves up to raids or invasions on the pretext of "helping the poor Christians, Buddhists, or whatever."

There was an outpouring of anger and demands for the expulsion of the non-Zultarian people infesting their land. This was exactly the attitude that Valach wanted. An attitude he could inflame and amplify the hatred and the fear of the invaders. Abdullah let the momentum continue for as long as it was becoming more heated. When he felt the moment was right, he banged on his podium for attention. Stopping in mid-harangue or explicative the members of the meeting turned to the front to see what the fastest rising star in their community had to say.

Abdullah held both hands high in the air and shouted. "We have to send a signal to the world that Zyngola will not stand for these invasions, that we will not tolerate anyone who does not swear allegiance to Zultar!" There were many shouting agreement with him. He held up his hands again for silence. When it returned he calmly said, "I have heard from Zultar on this matter. We are to expel all non-Zultarians from our country immediately and execute any that stay. They should all be killed at one time in a great show of our faith in Zultar. This is the signal that will make the world know that the mercy of Zultar doesn't extend to these infidel dogs!" There was a more muted agreement to this suggestion. But Valac continued to inflame the attendees and to give confidence in everyone's mind that to deny a command from Zultar was to join the enemy.

Slowly, but surely the fervor returned to the entire group. In the end, they drafted a resolution and everyone signed it boldly. This was a major step of belief in the Zultar leadership and love for his people, not to mention Abdullah's. Anyone who wasn't one hundred percent behind it was brow-beaten into submission by his peers.

The meeting broke up with the agreement that Abdullah's proposal should be taken to the ruling council by Abdullah and the top five clerics attending the meeting. It would be four days until they could present it to the council and they would do their best to drum up support for it in the meantime.

After everyone left, Abdullah called the attack team back at the school. "Start putting the fear of the infidels into the minds of the council. Suggest that the only way to be safe is to destroy the infidel menace in our country."

He hung up and then called the man in charge of fifty mercenaries with which he had made a secret arrangement.

CHAPTER TWENTY-SIX

Over the next four days Hami amplified the news that there were seven raids by infidel hordes into parts of northern Zyngola. Bombs were used, and rockets and explosives blew up minarets, hospitals, schools, religious meetings. Hami would use anything that would inflame public opinion and put pressure on the council.

No one could identify what country the raiders were from, but they were Caucasians and brutal. They seemed to delight in killing women and children. Fear spread across the land. Demands for protection went unheard. The raiders always seemed to come to help some distressed infidel or group of non-Zultarians. The worst atrocity happened in Tymeria the day before the council meeting. The raiders appeared in broad daylight, seemingly unafraid of the police or the security forces and raped and pillaged a Zultarian school. Thirty-three women and children died. As the security forces rushed to the area a massive explosion went off. This killed over one hundred fifty civilians and sixty-five soldiers. The city was in shock. The streets were deserted because of the fear.

The next day, under heavy security, the council met to discuss these raids on Zultarians by these infidel terrorists. The meeting was delayed for an hour due to a bomb threat. It turned out to be a real bomb and it was defused before it could go off. It was obviously meant to kill the entire council. A note scratched in Hebrew and English on the bomb casing said, "We demand an equal voice!" It was not signed of course. Hami was glad that no one took the time to figure out that a message on a bomb was useless if the bomb went off.

Abdullah and the five clerics presented their proposal and petition to the council. The astral projection team had done their work well and Valach finished it off. The proposal was to round up all the non-Zultarian people in the country who couldn't or wouldn't leave and put them to death by firing squad in an arena to be built especially for the event. It could be built in less than a week.

Abdullah used his polished oratory skills to cement the proposal. "There is an official jihad against non-Zultarians in our country. The jihad is our way, and we will not abandon it and will keep its banner high. We will never sell out our faith and will never betray the oath to our martyrs. I know it would be impossible to round up all the non-Zultarians in the country, especially the south, but the ones in Tymeria would be a definite statement that we will no longer suffer these insults to Zultar and our people! We must show the infidels that we are strong and will not shirk from our faith! Word of this proposal has spread quickly in the infidel camp. Many of these undesirables have already fled our country. Good! I wish they all would leave. But some won't and now they are calling their killing squads down on us to force us to give them our birthright! This we will never do. Stand together as Zyngolans. Stand together under the banner of Zultar and eliminate the source of all our suffering! Kill the infidels, Jihad! Jihad! Jihad!

He had stopped at that point because he could see the agreement in many faces and he heard Valach tell him that it was done. He looked up and drove the nail into the coffin of Zultarian infidels, "Zyngolan people and their great god Zultar will wait to see if you will stand with them." He turned and left the podium to thundering applause and shouts of Jihad! Jihad! Jihad!

The word came down two hours later that the Zultarian council had agreed to the proposal and signed it. The construction on the killing field was already underway. It would be one of the most attended events in Zyngolan history.

Abdullah Hami felt sure that he was on his way to becoming the greatest leader the world would ever see.

CHAPTER TWENTY-SEVEN

The day after their first meeting, the President called the Malones back to his office. When they arrived there was a subdued atmosphere of hectic hurrying everywhere. Ushered into the Oval Office they were greeted by the President and a good part of his cabinet.

President Bollen looked at the couple and asked them, "Have you heard the news from Tymeria?" After they both nodded, he continued. "The entire government of that nation has gone stark raving mad. They are insisting that they don't care what the world says, they are sovereign and they will deal with their internal problems their own way. That way is deportation of anyone that doesn't believe their way and mass murder of innocent civilians, nearly two thousand innocent civilians who couldn't or wouldn't get away. How in the world do they justify this?"

Laura spoke up quietly but clearly. "Mr. President, they are being deceived by Satan. This is clearly a national demonic influence overriding rational thinking. The government has been seduced by a carefully orchestrated program of inflammation, murder, rape, and destruction blamed on infidels. The main player is a Zyngolan named Abdullah Hami, a cleric who is playing the entire country like a violin. We are sure that he is behind this series of attacks that has led to the jihad. This is a new twist in a perverted program he has developed that uses groups of Zultarians attacking Jews and Christians through demonic astral projection. They've killed a dozen people this way so far."

The President sat down and looked at his cabinet. The head of the Joint Chiefs of Staff stood up and addressed the room. "I can't say that I buy the satanic concept, but the details of these raids are like she says. I think that we need to get a quick consensus of world powers and go in there and remove those idiots from power." He sat down.

Jack shook his head, "If you do that you will inflame the entire Zultarian population of the world and will have a world-wide war between Zultarians and non-Zultarians. Are you prepared to handle a war with a hundred million Zultarians?"

Several other radical theories were put forward but none of them were going to save the 1,867 people that are being rounded up in Tymeria.

Finally, the President turned to Jack. "You said that you felt that you had an answer to this problem."

Puzzled, the Chairman of the Joint Chiefs of Staff, Five-star General Howard Miles, asked the President, "Mr. President, we just found out about this. When did Mr. Malone tell you that he had an answer?"

The President looked calmly at his JCS and said, "Howard, these two people came here yesterday about this time and told me that God was arranging events so that the world would have to respond to a Zultarian threat. They have an option that is out of this world but I believe is our only answer to this problem."

The JCS sat down and nodded at Jack. Jack stood up and cleared his throat. "Mr. President, cabinet members, I need to speak of a spiritual solution to a spiritual problem. This is not a battle for soldiers with weapons. That will solve nothing. Worse, it will only make the polarization between religions worse. Remember, Ephesians 3:12, *"For we do not wrestle against flesh and blood, but against principalities, against the rulers of the darkness of this age, against spiritual hosts of wickedness in the heavenly places.* This combat will be between angels and demons in the heavenlies, not men on earth. You have to understand this from a spiritual viewpoint rather than a physical one. Is there anyone here who cannot do that?"

Three people, including the Vice President, held up their hands. The President asked them to leave the room. The Vice President said, "I resent being shut out of the process because of some religious mumbo-jumbo." The President stood up and said, "Tom, you are my second in command, but I am concerned about your memory." Seeing the questioning look on his VP's face he continued, "Don't you remember the ASF poisoning of millions of our people? Don't you remember the nuclear threat to the entire world by the Omniscience Temple? Both of these matters were fought and won by faith in God and by spiritual warfare rather than weapons of war. Now, sit down and listen with an open mind or leave as directed."

The VP sighed and nodded. He sat down and paid attention to Jack. The other two people also seemed to have had second thoughts and stayed.

Jack nodded, "Okay, I want you to understand that we pray to God Almighty and try to do His will. What I am going to propose is not my idea, and not my choice. There is a high probability that neither my wife nor I will live through this, but if it is the will of our Creator, it will be done." He noticed that he now had their undivided attention.

He took a deep breath and plunged in. "The Lord Jesus has decided that the deception of Zultarism has to be challenged, openly, and for once and all. To that end He has allowed the events to transpire that are going to come to a head in Tymeria in five days. Four people, my wife, I, Mark Connelly and his wife Sarah, have been given a mission to save the Christians being rounded up in Zyngola right now, and to let Zultarians throughout the world see that Zultar is still nothing but a pagan moon-god idol and that Yahveh is the true God of the universe." Jack let them chew on that for a few seconds.

Then he elaborated, "We want to issue a challenge to the Zultarians of Tymeria and the rest of the world to a contest between Zultar and Yahveh with the lives of ourselves and the other two thousand non-Zultarians in Tymeria as the prize. If Zultar is god then we die. If Yahveh is God then we live and they release all of us."

There was a stunned silence for a good thirty seconds. Then everyone started talking at once with the exception of the President, Jack and Laura. Eventually order was restored and the primary question was put to the Malones.

The JCS asked them, "What are you going to do to prove your case? Have God pour down fire from heaven like Elijah did?" It came as a surprise to many that Howard Miles knew his Bible facts.

Jack answered him honestly, "That is a good possibility considering the precedent, but I really don't know. God hasn't revealed that to us yet. But, I will tell you what he has said. Jack prayed silently that God's Spirit would give him the exact words he had heard from Caleb.

"The Lord God Almighty has told us that He will not permit this foul evil from taking place. He has given the task of stopping it to the four of us. The Lord wants all men to come to repentance and seek Him. But some, who are at first deceived, refuse to throw off their yoke of bondage because of their own carnal desires. They do not want to escape their blindness because of the power it brings them in the flesh. The Lord will give them over to their evil desires. Hear now the will of Yahveh, your God. *"The enemy will rise up to destroy my believers in Africa; I will meet their challenge and show the world that I am God. You will need to stand firm in your faith and believe."*

You could have heard a pin drop in the Oval Office. Laura had been praying that the Lord would convict everyone there that this was His word and that it was His will they were doing.

The VP waved his hand in the air, "We're betting the lives of nearly two thousand people, plus you four on this message from God. Although I am loath to use such a slender thread in this matter, I have to admit that I can't think of anyone else's hands I would rather put their fate in than that of God's."

The President concurred. He turned back to the Malones. "What do you need from us?"

Jack said, "We need to publicize the challenge throughout the world and then present it to the Zultarian government of Zyngola. We also need as much press there that can be arranged."

The JCS asked, "What if they turn it down?"

Laura answered him, "God says they won't. Also, by then it will be on everyone's mind that if they refuse then it shows that they don't have any faith in their god and that Zultarism is a false religion. The challenge will be accepted."

The President sighed, "Father Yahveh, protect us all."

CHAPTER TWENTY-EIGHT

After Mark hung up the telephone, he went over and sat down next to Sarah. She was sitting at the dining room table in their hotel room in London. Papers and lists were everywhere, most with check marks on all the entries. She looked up at her husband and raised an eyebrow. "What is the news?"

Mark nodded his head, "Jack and Laura got the President and the cabinet to go along with the challenge. It is being distributed to the world as we speak, over the television, radio, internet, newspapers, and any other means of mass media. The duel is on for this Saturday Spy Lady, and we have front row seats." His levity was almost gallows humor considering the hostile environment they were headed into in Zyngola.

Sarah checked her lists and moved the last pile to the finished group. "We have contacted every friendly religious group outside the U.S. that we can. They are aware of the stakes involved and will pray that God will support us and the battle in the heavenlies and to provide justice for all men."

They sat there and stared at each other. This might very well be their last few days on earth and with each other. Mark realized just how much he loved his wife and what she meant to him. He knew that she would not allow him to protect her and keep her from going. Anyway, the Lord had said that the battle was for all four of them. But, Oh! How he wanted to find a way to save her from this.

Sarah had already made peace with God about their participation in this challenge and had placed both Mark's and her lives in the hands of God. She could almost read the thoughts going through his head. "Mark, I love you more than anything except for God. I see the white knight in your eyes. Don't let my safety trouble you. We are both in God's hands and only He can keep us safe. We've done all we can for now. Let's put all this on the back burner until Friday and the trip to Africa." She put her hands on either side of his head and kissed him. "Let us enjoy each other's company for the next three days. Tell Jack that we are going to take a mini-honeymoon until then and only call us if it is an emergency. Okay?"

Mark realized that she knew the odds and wanted to spend her last days in carefree enjoyment of their life together. It was not a request he wanted to deny, nor would he, even if other matters encroached. "Sure, I can't think of anything I would rather do. He winged a silent prayer to God to seek acceptance of this small time-out from the Lord's work. He felt peace and consent in his spirit. He picked up the phone and hit re-dial.

Jack took the call and listened to his best friend's plans. He hung up and prayed about it for Laura and himself. He too felt the peace and agreement of the Lord. He went to find Laura.

Mark and Sarah had toured London many times in their past lives and it didn't lend itself to their need for peace and tranquility. Nice, France was nice but crowded. So Mark made reservations and they flew to Cancun, Mexico and a private estate with a private beach. The next two days flew by in peaceful enjoyment of themselves and God's bountiful nature. They sailed on a Catamaran; scuba dived in the ocean, lazed on the beach and spent the evening enjoying each other's company. The rest and relaxation was not only a needed but essential break in their daily affairs. No phones, no guns, no intrigue, not even a bad meal. They prayed many times and grew closer to the Lord and each other. By the time Friday came, they were at peace with God and ready to stand and fight.

On Tuesday after Mark's last call, Jack told Laura what the Connelly's were going to do for the next three days. Laura smiled because she knew how much in love their friends were. She got up and kissed her husband. "I think that they have the right idea. Let's do something for ourselves." She grew somber. "I don't have any idea how this will turn out, but I want you to know that you are the essence of my heart and I will be happy to be by your side regardless of the outcome. I also know that we will win, either way."

Jack agreed with that thought. He hadn't planned on ending his life on earth this soon, but God's plans and his rarely matched anyway. He just knew that they were doing

God's will and the result couldn't be better in any other way. "So, what do you want to do for the next ninety-six hours?"

Laura knew that as a couple their affairs were in order in the event they weren't there to handle them. She had arranged a trust fund for each of her brothers so that they would be taken care of in any event. She also knew that Jack had talked to his father, mother, and even his brother, as well as his uncle in the last twenty-four hours. So they were really free to do whatever they wanted to do. She prayed. "Lord Yahshua, you know my heart better than I do. And you know Jack's heart and desires. Tell us through your Holy Spirit what we should do with the time we have left before Friday." She fell quiet and listened to her spirit. An idea formed in her mind that she knew she would never have thought of in a million years. She turned to Jack, "Why don't we go home and just relax?"

Jack realized that her idea was exactly what he wanted to do. "Okay, I'll get a plane for us."

Six hours later they arrived at Castle Malone and unpacked. Laura took the accumulated mail and put it in a drawer. It could wait. The same for the voice mail messages. She went into her bathroom and had a nice hot bath in her tub with all the bubbles she wanted.

Jack started to go to his computer and thought better of it. He made a pitcher of ice tea and took it and two glasses out onto the veranda in the small garden atrium. He went into their bedroom while the tea was cooling and had a shower. He put on a casual set of slacks and a tee shirt and his favorite sandals. He looked at the Paraordinance P10-45 lying on the counter in his bedroom. He picked it up and put it into a drawer.

Padding back out onto the cool flagstone of the atrium he sat down in the cushioned chair and reclined. He let the quiet and peace soak through him as he rested there. The late afternoon sunlight was high on the east wall and the restful shade in the rest of the garden lulled him to sleep. He woke up a while later to find his wife in her robe sitting next to him sipping tea. Smiling, he got up and got some more for himself.

As they sat there in the quietly darkening garden Jack could feel the presence of the Lord. It was so relaxing he found himself feeling like he was in the most incredible river in the universe. He realized he was experiencing the "River of Life" that flows from the throne of heaven. He let himself become one with the river and found he could sense God's Spirit in a whole new way. It truly felt like every cell in his body was adjusting to an absolute perfect alignment and he felt in tune with God. He continued to rest in this condition, communing with God on levels he didn't even know existed.

All too soon he left the embrace of the river and returned to the garden. The sunlight had returned to the garden but was now on the west wall. Jack realized that he had been near to God for the last ten hours and he was so much at peace with everything that it was wonderful. He looked over at Laura and saw her looking back at him. She smiled and stretched; a vision of loveliness.

She sighed, "That was the most refreshing night I've ever experienced. I'm sorry it had to end so soon. But, God has repaired and refreshed us so that we can go on and do it in love, not anger or spite."

Jack realized that the thought of anger was repellent to him. Obviously God had been working on him throughout the night too. "I can't think of anything that could top that. What do you want to do today?"

Laura's grin became impish, "I want to listen to Christian music, I want to dance, I want to run through the grass in my bare feet, I want to sing to God. What do you want to do?"

"Well, as unlikely as it seems, I want to jump for joy, run for miles, and breathe fresh air and see a glorious sunset."

They did all these things and more over the next two days. The love between themselves and between each of them and God was glorious and personal in the extreme. They loved each other and God's world more than they thought possible in the time they had left. By Friday morning they were ready to do His will.

CHAPTER TWENTY-NINE

The news of the challenge traveled like wild fire throughout the world. People of all faiths and all tongues debated the possibilities. There was a large cry for not allowing the challenge to occur for fear of the death toll if God wouldn't be God. But the argument lost momentum against the counter argument that God has to be God or He wouldn't be God. Therefore He will act in this case, maybe.

The government of the United States, working through the Egyptian Embassy, delivered the challenge to the government of Zyngola in Tymeria on Thursday. The President had added some incentive to ensure that the Tymeria politicians would accept the challenge. If they declined the challenge then there were eighty-six nations that were ready to intervene in the bloodbath or extract revenge on the guilty. This included eighteen nations with a Zultarian population.

Abdullah Hami was called before the council at noon on Thursday. The council had the challenge and the alternative read to him. "How do you think we should reply to this?" the council President asked Abdullah.

Abdullah thought about it and replied. "I think that they are just trying to set up an excuse to invade us. I would accept this bogus challenge and make them invade without a reason and watch the world condemn them."

The President of the council was a learned man, with several different college degrees. "What if they actually want to see something done by Zultar? Zultar doesn't care what men think and he might not respond."

Abdullah understood the situation very well and decided to prove Zultar's power over the infidel's god. "We will mass Zultarian believers at the site. When they all pray at once for Zultar's intervention, to show his might to the world, would he not respond? I think he will. Let the infidels bring their god and let the world see the might of Zultar!"

The council debated the matter for two hours and then reluctantly agreed to the challenge. Agreement required them to not hurt any of the infidels until Zultar won. Otherwise, the original alternative would be imposed. Everyone on the council knew that would mean the end of Zyngola as an independent state. If it had only been non-Zultarian countries threatening them, then they could call for a jihad against that. But, with a major part of the Zultarian world demanding the challenge, they were forced to go along.

The council responded to the U.S. proposal and asked how the challenge would be carried out. The U.S. Representative said that four people would be arriving at the designated site at dawn on Friday. They would explain the challenge. Since it was being done in Zultarian controlled territory in a Zultarian country there would be no non-Zultarian forces in attendance.

As soon as the challenge had been accepted, the Zyngola administration was beset by hundreds of request for media visas to allow the challenge to be broadcast throughout the world. Since many of the requests came from Zultarian-populated countries there was again little the government could do but agree.

The News services started arriving within two hours and continued to build throughout Thursday late into the night.

Valach's thoughts were almost livid. "How dare you agree to this challenge? You puny human! I did not agree to it and I will have no part in it."

Abdullah's opinion of the sub-god was getting worse with every word. "What is the problem? Zultar is supreme, is he not? He is the god of all gods and we will be victorious. Then we will be rid of all the infidels for good!

Valach swore in several languages that Abdullah did not know. "YOU, YOU, IDIOT! This is not what we planned. Zultar is not knowable by any man. You don't know what..."

Abdullah's oily comment stopped the flow of thoughts in mid-rant. "But, you are a god, you know what Zultar wishes, therefore you can intercede with him for us. Can't you?"

Valach fumed and fussed for several seconds. Then he said, "I will intercede with your petitions, but I won't guarantee that Zultar will see that there is any reason to be involved in any contest he didn't agree to first."

Abdullah thought for a second. "There will be hundreds of millions of believers that will see this event. If Zultar doesn't show his greatness over the god of the infidels, many, if not all, will turn away from him. They will believe that he is not god."

Valach was silent. Abdullah hoped that last argument would be the important one that would give Zultar the incentive to completely defeat the infidel's god. He got up from his prayer mat and started for the door.

Valach's thought stopped him in mid-stride. "Zultar will defeat the infidel's god, but I can promise you he might then rip out your eternal soul and slow roast it for a thousand years for agreeing to something like this before you heard from him." With that the voice faded away. Abdullah trembled at the thought. "Still", he thought, "What I did will give him great glory and he might reward me handsomely. He comforted himself with that thought.

Jack and Laura met with Mark and Sarah at Eglin Air Force Base in Florida at 2 a.m. Friday Florida time. The increase in confidence and a new serenity was obvious in all four people but it was mutually accepted without comment.

Jack said, "Are we ready to do this?" Everyone agreed they were. Mark reported to the Base Commander's office and got his permission and the orders for the crews involved in getting the four of them to the field in Tymeria.

Mark came back to the group, "Okay, we leave in thirty minutes. The flight will take twelve hours to reach a carrier in the Med off of Egypt. That will make it 2200 hours local time. We will rest there for about six hours and then leave for Tymeria. We should arrive at the designated spot just before dawn on their Friday." He looked at Jack. "Do we have any idea of what we are going to do when we get there?"

Jack calmly looked at Mark, "Follow God's lead."

Mark grinned, "I knew you were going to say that."

CHAPTER THIRTY

Harry Pembroke led his thirty-member group in a quiet hymn of thanks and then preached to them out of Psalm 91. *"He who dwells in the shelter of the Most High will rest in the shadow of the Almighty. I will say of the Lord, He is my refuge and my fortress, my God, in whom I trust."*

Their freedom had lasted almost a week before they were spied out and captured again. This time they were in the grinder. The news had come two days before their arrest that anyone that was not Zultarian had better convert or get out of the country. His flock was made up of Zyngolans that couldn't afford to leave. So he stayed too. Now he realized that he was going shepherd his whole flock into heaven personally. He looked up from the new tents they had been given last afternoon at the hundreds and hundreds of people in the wire-fenced camp. The mood of the group depended upon their religion. Buddhists were stoic, quietly waiting for their fate. Christians were sad about leaving this earth and happy to be going to God. The few people identified as Jewish were non-committal but generally seemed sad. The other people were everywhere on the spectrum of confidence from hopeless to quietly gleeful.

From the talk in the camp he heard that there was some kind of contest that would be held tomorrow and their futures hung in the balance. Now, what kind of sick joke was that? He shivered again in the evening air. The first two nights they had to sleep on the ground without even a blanket. These sudden tents and food were suspicious at first but he figured out the deal when he saw the media outside the fence. He laughed silently as he thought of the fact that the abusive government didn't want the world to think they were cruel to the people they were going to kill tomorrow. How sad. He prayed that if that was to be their end, then the Lord would make the end quick and painless for all the captives.

At the end of the service he got up and wandered over to the area near the fence and watched Zyngolian guards patrol the twenty-foot wide strip of land between the media and the fence. My Lord, there had to be a zillion media people out there with TV cameras and trucks and all jockeying for a position nearest to the fence. How horrible! Did the whole world want to see hundreds of innocent victims killed?

He watched the guards as they hurried past him on their patrol on their way back to the warmth of their heated huts. He was just turning around to go to the tent when something sailed by his head and bounced off the ground in the dark. He stopped and carefully looked around at the departing guards. None of them had noticed the object. He slowly walked forward until he could see it. It was a covering of bubble-pack around a small object. He acted like he was tying his shoe and he carefully picked it up and slowly walked away from the fence. Finding a small place where the guards couldn't see him behind two tents, he unwrapped it. It was a cell phone. Suddenly it chirped at him. He lifted the cover and put it to his ear "Ello" he said.

The man's voice on the other end was conspiratorial in tone. "Be careful not to talk too loud. I don't think the guards can pick up this frequency, but if I see them coming into the camp I'll tell you."

Harry said, "Well, thank you. I am Harry Pembroke, who are you?"

The voice on the other end declined to identify himself. "You know what they'll do if they find you with that phone? I don't want them after me too."

Harry thought, "How considerate of you." Then he said, "What do you want?"

The man wanted the local color as an exclusive for his upcoming broadcast. Harry thought, "How long do you think it will take them to figure out you're the one that lobbed the cell phone over the fence when you tell everyone what I tell you?" But instead he asked a question of his own. "Why are all the press people here? To witness another Zyngolian mass murder and televise it to the entire world as entertainment?"

The phone was quiet for a while and then the man came back on and said, "You don't know, do you? They haven't told you people! They are diabolical."

Harry sighed and said, "Diabolical you say? Let me tell you something Mr. Newsman, every day in south Zyngola roving bands of government sponsored terrorists question innocent women and ask if they are Zultarian. If they are they go free, if they aren't they are gang-raped, mutilated by having their breasts cut off and left to die as a warning to other non-Zultarians. Men are killed every day here because of their belief in the true God rather than Zultar. That is Demonic, not diabolical. The fact that the industrial west, including the U.S. and Europe, won't acknowledge these atrocities or try to put pressure on Zyngola to stop them is bad enough, but your own news services ignore the murder and rape and death as if it didn't matter."

The newsman replied, "My name is Ted. I understand what you're saying and yes, it is true, the atrocities, and yes, it is true the west doesn't seem to take a great interest in stopping it. And yes, the western press doesn't do a very good job of reporting it. There are many reasons for these attitudes and lack of action. But that is not what I was going to tell you. The reason that the press is here is because the U.S. has issued a challenge to the Zultarian government of Zyngola. They have demanded a shoot-out between the Zultarian god Zultar and the Christian God Yahveh. If Yahveh wins then everyone is to be set free."

Harry doubted that the Zyngolian government would let them go even if God himself came down and demanded it, but, anyway, he said, "How are they going to determine the winner?"

Ted didn't know the answer but said that four people are going to show up at dawn the next day to represent the captives and they would set the rules. Harry thanked the man and told him that he had to spread the news. They would talk later. He pocketed the phone and went to tell his flock first.

CHAPTER THIRTY-ONE

The radio in the Zyngolan air defense headquarters crackled to life. "This is Major Michael White of the United States Air Force. We are bringing four, unarmed civilians into your country per your agreement. We are requesting permission to cross your borders."

The permission was granted for the three helicopters to travel across Zyngolan air space and deliver their passengers, but the Zyngolan government demanded that the choppers leave immediately on the reverse of the route they entered.

On board Major White's helicopter, the four members of the Crossfire Team were quietly waiting for their entrance into the stage being set at Tymeria. Using their headsets to overcome the engine and rotor noise, Mark asked Jack, "Okay, what does God want us to do when we land?"

Jack wished he knew the answer to that question. He was really flying on faith on this one. Answering Mark he said, "No clue yet. I'm sure God will give us direction when we get there. Just believe and don't doubt. I know that I know that I know that God is in command of this situation and we are doing His bidding. He will direct our steps, all right?"

Mark nodded his head. That was what he wanted to hear. That was confirmation of the fact that no one had an idea what was to be done and therefore no one was looking to him for direction.

Laura smiled at the other three people. "This is where the rubber meets the road. Your faith is all you have now so live it and believe." They felt the chopper maneuvering to land. Everyone grabbed hold of something.

The helicopter swung in over the outskirts of Tymeria and headed for the huge crowd assembled in a field just south of the city. Even though it was still dark there was no problem finding the place. The media had enough lights and generators going to light up a small city. The helicopter flew lower and slowed. As it crossed a seven-foot high barbed wire fence held up by poles driven into the ground, its searchlight lit up dozens of large tents in the enclosed area. There was really no place to put the chopper down without hitting tents or people.

Jack told the Major that they had to land among the captives. He knew that was what the Lord wanted them to do. So they threw out two rappelling lines that reached to the ground. A bright spotlight from a guard shack suddenly lit up the helicopter and the rappelling lines. In its bright glare, Jack swung out of one side of the helicopter while Mark copied his action on the other side. They rappelled down the lines to the ground. When they were down and standing in the wind wash of the rotor down draft they secured the lines as Laura and Sarah came down. The lines were retracted and the helicopter lifted up into the night. As the rotor wash and noise abated, hundreds of the captives surrounded them. Some hugged them, others shook their hands. Mark watched the lights of the three helicopters leave with some trepidation.

Eventually Jack heard a voice he recognized. The British Pastor Harry Pembroke came up and shook his hand, and the others. "Ello again, looks like you're always showing up to save me at the last second. We have been praying for an answer from God and we are all very glad to see you. Can you tell us what is going to happen?"

Jack felt the anointing of God's Spirit come upon him. "You will see the strong right arm of the Lord break this yoke of bondage and set the captives free. When dawn comes we need everyone to start singing praise to the Lord. Use basic church songs like "My God is an Awesome God, "Nearer My God to Thee", and "I see the Lord, High and Lifted Up" for the Christians. Have everyone else do whatever they can to praise God. This will be critical because there is a huge war going on in the heavenlies which will determine the outcome here today. Can you get the group here to do that?"

Harry's heart was encouraged by the knowledge that the Lord was involved in their peril. He agreed to get others to spread the word and to organize everyone into groups so that they could sing together in the morning. Laura stepped over to him and put her hand on his arm. The anointing covering her spread to him and Harry staggered and almost fell under the power of the Spirit. He looked at her and wondered how a person could carry such a powerful anointing and not be slain in the spirit. She leaned close and the clean smell of her hair caught at his imagination after the unwashed days in the camp. She told him, "Harry, if possible, can you have some of your groups spell each other in rotation. We need the covering of constant praise, but this challenge could go on all day. Okay?"

He nodded and impulsively took her hand and kissed the back of it. Smiling he returned to organizing the captives.

Sarah saw the first light of dawn creeping over the eastern horizon. It was a ruddy red glow that seemed to be as big as the dark horizon itself. In the faint red light she turned and looked at the other three people she loved more than life itself. Getting their attention, she grinned, and said, "Show time!"

Taking off the coveralls they had worn to keep warm in the cool night air in the helicopter, they revealed clothes designed just for this event by Sarah. Each person had on a white Eton-style jacket over a simple white shirt. The legs of the white pants fell over white boots. Each woman wore a white silk scarf around her throat which floated on the warm breeze behind them. The only decoration visible on their outfits was a simple blue cross on the upper left chest of their jackets. The pure and simple outfits were not only a statement of their faith; they also showed that they weren't concealing any weapons. The bright white stood out from the solid brown of Tymeria and the various darker clothing of the captives.

As the sun continued to quickly rise above the horizon in the east, the four bowed their heads and prayed God's will be done here today. They walked towards the fence and took a position standing side-by-side in a line facing the gate.

Ted Corrant, the FOX newsman who had talked to Harry by cell phone, described the scene for his listeners who had only radios. From his vantage point to the east with the rising sun at his back he could easily make out the entire field of battle. "The view is spectacular. In the stark light of first dawn, the battle lines are being formed. Inside the fenced area, the two thousand or so captives are all facing north, towards the gate, arranged roughly in twenty rows with one hundred people in each row. They are a ragged lot having been arrested suddenly and having had to spend two or three days and nights in this field. I understand that they didn't even have any shelter or food for the first two days. My feeling is that Zyngola only gave them food or shelter because we, the press, were going to be here."

He used a set of binoculars and studied the camp. "Between the first row of the captives and the gate to the fence are four people dressed in white who arrived by helicopter several hours ago. They are standing side by side facing the gate and about half way between the captives and the fence. On the outside of the fence there doesn't seem to be much happening as yet near the small huts that have been built here for the guards. There is a small platform facing the gate and quite near the fence. Behind that are seven small shed-like huts within twenty yards of the outside of the fence and lastly, there are three gigantic tents set back a hundred feet or so."

The announcer continued describing the scene. "Several hundred yards behind that, the land rises a little and there are literally thousands and thousands of people who have come to witness this event. My contact says that these are all devout Zultarians and admittance to the crowd is controlled by the Zyngolan military."

"Okay, now there is some activity on the outside of the fence. A Zultarian Holy man is walking up towards the fence and mounting the small platform that was installed last night. I can see him with my binoculars and I believe that is one of their chief clerics. Let's see here, yes, he is a Zultarian scholar named Abdullah Hami. I believe that he is about to speak to the captives.

CHAPTER THIRTY-TWO

Abdullah stared across fence and the thirty feet of space separating him from the four Americans that arrived just before dawn. He thought to himself, "They're all dressed in white, how amusing. It will make a wonderful contrast to their bright red blood. He carefully studied the two women and realized that they were the ones he had seen before in Tymeria. No matter. They would not be leaving this place alive.

Abdullah hated this charade. He had thought of violently opposing it in the council when it had first been spoken about. It was a worthless waste of time. The hostages should be killed now! But, the council was facing the wrath of the world and knew that if they did not accept the challenge their god would be seen as cowardly. They would not have that. So Hami devised a plan to turn it to their advantage and agreed to emcee the affair himself.

He addressed himself only to the men in the crowd, which was as it should be. Speaking in English he said, "Infidels, I am Zulam Abdullah Hami. What is this challenge you bring before our great god Zultar?"

Jack felt the anointing fall on him. "We are four Christians who come in the name of Yahveh. In His name we challenge Zultar with a simple test to prove who is truly God and supreme. Since this is your land, Zultar should go first. The test is this. Have Zultar destroy us and all of these captives by his own hand without man's intervention. If he can do that, then you will have met the challenge, shown that Zultar is supreme, and solved your problem all at the same time. Can Zultar do this simple thing?"

Abdullah grinned and answered back, "We will ask him to do what you suggest."

Jack nodded and added, "If Zultar is unwilling or unable to do this. Then Yahveh will have an opportunity to respond to the challenge."

Hami nodded his agreement, grinned and raised his right arm. The flaps on the three huge tents were pulled back and large groups of people came out into the light of

133

the rising sun. There were one hundred of white clad teachers of the The'an, the Holy Book of the Zultarians. Walking behind each teacher came twenty of his most faithful worshippers.

Ted Corrant, the newsman, continued to describe the scene. "Oh this is a surprise! I see Zulams from all of the Zultarian enclaves from around the world. They must have been slipping into Tymeria over the last few days without any notice. All of the heavyweights of the The'an are here. They are marching out and forming groups twenty feet behind Abdullah Hami. I can see that they all have their prayer mats and as they get arranged they are kneeling down on the ground, facing me. Well, that makes sense. They are going to pray kneeling in the direction of Kush, the spiritual home of their god. There are probably as many Zultarian worshippers in front of me as there are captives on my left."

Hami spoke to the gathered Zultarians. In Arabic, he told them to beseech Zultar to totally destroy the infidels as it was said must be done in the The'an. All together they bowed with their heads to the ground. Thousands of the onlookers also dropped to their knees and bowed to the east. They all began to pray destruction on this insignificant group of infidels.

The scene was striking in that the white robed Zyngolans completely covered the area in front of the fence and were complimented by the thousands of worshippers on the nearby raised ground towards the city.

The prayers were being made in all the forms as every Zultarian sought his god and prayed as the prophet Blemian had instructed them in the The'an to kill all the infidels. The prayers were sincere and heartfelt. Ted Corrant estimated that there were at least three hundred thousand people praying to Zultar for the destruction of the captives.

As the sun continued to rise into the clear sky, the air became hot and the sand scorching. The captives continued to sing praises to God and the four team members stood solidly in an at-ease position with their hands behind them.

Unknown to the captives or the press, each of the seven small sheds which were spread out all along the fence line, held a tripod-mounted machine gun and soldiers to use it. At the signal from Hami, they would open fire and strafe the captives until none lived.

The volume of noise from the Zultarians praying was immense but Laura could still hear the voices of the captives singing praises to God. She subtly moved her weight from one leg to the other while praying to the Lord to give her strength to stand.

Five hours of praying had resulted in no death to the captives and Abdullah was beginning to believe that Zultar wasn't interested in accommodating the challengers. He was about to signal the machine guns when the tallest infidel called to him. He stood up and faced the foursome. The man said, "Zultar hasn't acted yet. I believe it is time for Yahveh to demonstrate his power."

Abdullah knew that with a wave of his fist he could have them all killed but was also aware that would not look good for Zyngola on world-wide television. So he decided that he would let them have their turn. It was obvious that god wasn't interested in their little games so it would do no more harm than waste a few more hours. Then he would declare a stand-off and have them killed as was originally intended. He yelled back. "Yes, We will give you time for your god's response."

Jack responded, "Thank you. I must warn you that people, who do not worship Yahveh as the only true God but instead, bow to an idol, will not inherit the kingdom of God. I urge you and all those with you to repent and seek the true creator of the universe."

Abdullah sneered and yelled back. "We will never sell out our faith and will never betray the oath to our martyrs for your infidel god. Do not demean us with your pitiful offers of salvation."

Under the anointing of God's Spirit, Jack, Laura, Mark, and Sarah held their hands up and in unison said, "Father God hear our plea. We ask you to act to set the captives free and to demonstrate your might to these people so that they may know your glory and worship you as true God."

At his microphone the newsman Ted Corrant was on the edge of his seat. Deep down he wanted to see God do something to save these people. For a long minute his hope wavered. Then, a little at first, clouds began to appear in the huge expanse of the cloudless African sky. The clouds

135

quickly began to tower upward in the sky as they multiplied. In the shade of the clouds the temperature dropped as the sun's direct light was cut off.

The BBC newscaster from London, whose booth was located next to Ted Corrant's noticed something odd and started telling everyone around him, "Look, the clouds are only covering the area outside the fence. The captives are still in the sunshine!"

It was true. As the sky darkened and the wind suddenly started to blow chill under the clouds, the sun was still shining on the area where the captives stood singing. The sounds of praise songs could be heard much more clearly now. It was as if another two thousand voices had joined in the praise to God. And the singing took on a heavenly quality of purity and sweetness.

The teachers of Zultar looked around and asked each other what was going on. Abdullah Hami stared up at the clouds and prayed to the voice in his head, "What is this? Remove the clouds immediately!" There was no answer in his mind.

An ominous dread spread through the group in front of the fence. They begin to get up from their prayer mats and some began to run.

All at once a heavy rumble was heard high in the atmosphere. It was almost like thunder, but the sound was more of a continuous rolling sound that was getting louder and closer. A technician in the press area yelled, "Look! Up over there, in the clouds! Something's happening!"

High in the atmosphere to the west of the area there was a boiling disturbance tearing through the clouds and it was moving toward the ground at supersonic speed. As the disturbance tore through the clouds the air was violently displaced which resulted in a continuous roar of thunder that shook everything. Most of the media people ducked and many tried to seek some form of shelter.

The boiling disturbance rushed at the ground outside the fence. Many of the panicked Zultarian worshippers screamed in fear and raised their arms to fend off whatever it was.

The disturbance struck the ground violently and raced east like a ninety-foot high wall between the fence and the spectators. It had come out of the west and headed directly east parallel to the fence and straight toward the media pool.

Before it reached the frightened reporters, it leaped back up into the clouds with a tremendous roar. A blast of super frigid air gusted against the trailers and vehicles of the press corp. Windshields broke, several cameras had their lens shattered. Even though most everyone had dropped to the ground, they all felt the icy chill that went all the way to their bones. This happened even though the disturbance hadn't come within five hundred feet of the press area before it raced back up into the atmosphere.

In the area where the disturbance had passed through, everything was frozen in absolute silence. The two thousand Zultarians caught by the disturbance outside the fence didn't move. A glassy expression of fear or confusion was etched into the lines of every face. The immobile postures of people showed panic and those fleeing had been frozen in flight. Everything, including the people, gleamed in the light. The liquid in every cell in the vegetation, the sheds, the tents, and the people had been instantly frozen solid as a rock. Unfortunately when the water in a cell freezes, it expands and the ice ruptures the cell walls.

A great silence filled the land with the exception of the crackling of ice as the warmer air returned to the area,.

Suddenly, everyone in the area heard these thundering words in their own language, *"I, Yahveh, am the Lord your God. You shall have no other gods before me."*

There was quiet for about twenty seconds. Then there was a tremendous shaking and shuddering. The ground split in two about thirty feet outside the prisoner's fence in a line running parallel to the fence. The end of the split stopped just feet short of the press area. As the fissure continued to widen to about thirty feet, the people in the press and the television cameras could see down into the abyss that was being created. Through the splitting ground and crumbling rock they could see hot molten lava glowing an angry red and orange in the deeps.

The shaking increased and the land on either side of the fissure tipped downward into the crevasse. Everything between the spectators and the fence line, with one exception, shook and danced toward the fissure. The tents, the sheds, and the people, all still frozen into position, fell into the glowing, steaming crack in the ground. The media people could clearly see the people melting as they fell downwards towards the fires. The spectators had been knocked to the ground by the shaking, climbed back to their feet and screamed in horror as they watched the two thousand Zultarians disappear into the ground.

The shaking and shuddering continued with everyone dancing to stay upright as the crevice slammed closed with an earth-shuddering roar. Then after the fissure came back together, the shaking stopped. The echoes lasted for several seconds.

Silence again returned to the area. The ground between the fence line and the spectators was back to normal except it was completely vacant as if none of the Zultarian forces had ever existed, with one notable exception.

All alone on his small platform, Abdullah Hami knelt and held his head in both hands. His whole body shook and he moaned. The memory haunted him. The super intense cold had passed directly behind him and as he turned to look he could see the glassy stares of men he had known for years who were only twenty feet behind him. Frozen into ice were all of the great lights of the The'an and its greatest advocates and all their people. They seemed to have been looking at him with disapproval. When the ground split and everything fell into the earth, he could see all the way to the hellishly burning lava at the bottom. When the silence returned he rose from his knees, raised his hands and looked skyward, He wailed at the top of his lungs, "Zultaaarrrrr!"

A whistling noise grew in the air and drowned out his cry which was stilled forever as the two hundred-ton statue of the moon god Zultar from the Parthenon crashed down into the ground exactly where Abdullah was standing. The statue had fallen from such a great height that it buried itself eight feet into the desert floor.

The thundering voice spoke again. *"You shall not make for yourself a carved image — any likeness of anything that is in heaven above, or that is in the earth beneath, or that is in the water under the earth; you shall not bow down to them nor serve them. For I, the Lord your God, am a jealous God"*

The stone of the idol suddenly broke into fierce flames. The rock melted and flowed like water. The entire statue melted and pooled on the ground.

In the deep silence that remained, the thick clouds covering the area quickly dissipated. The sun again shone on everything.

When the statue had struck the ground, the entire north side of the fence line had collapsed. The four members of the Crossfire Team were on their knees like most in the area, having seen the judgment of God on idol worshippers. Each person was praying thanks to God for their salvation. When they finished they stood up. Jack looked at Mark and said, "I know God did that, but what was it in the natural?"

Mark chuckled. "Man, I don't know, but I'd guess that the jet stream over Africa was diverted down to the Earth for a short period. The jet stream flows at the edge of the atmosphere and is the temperature of space. There have been occurrences of this before. The phenomenon is called a "Strider". Scientists have quick frozen Mastodons that have been caught in such a thing. That could be explained away as a freak of nature but I don't know of any technology that would allow us to lift a two hundred ton piece of rock and drop it with such accuracy." Mark looked over at the pooled rock that had frozen into position as a permanent gravestone for Abdullah Hami and his assault on God's people.

Sarah said, "Let's go home. What's our exit strategy?"

As the master strategist, Mark looked somewhat bemused. He said back, "I don't have one. I was sure we weren't going to leave here alive, so I didn't plan for it."

Sarah turned to find Harry Pembroke standing there. She smiled at him. "You can tell the people they can go home now."

Harry nodded, and said, "Thank you all for what you have done."

Laura laughed, "We didn't do anything except be obedient and pray. Your people did the praising that allowed the war in the heavenlies to be won. We all need to thank GOD. He did all the hard stuff."

Harry waved to his people and the entire nineteen hundred group of ex-captives started walking out of the previously fenced-in area, across the land where their enemies had been and headed back toward town. As they reached the line of the quiet spectators many of the people that had seen the power of God asked them, "What do we do now? Zultar wasn't real. Help us to understand." The gospel spread that day to thousands.

Mark looked to the city a mile away and said, "I guess we walk."

CHAPTER THIRTY-THREE

As the team walked along the road, surrounded by hundreds of people, they saw a man standing by an old Chevrolet at the edge of the road. They went over and shook hands with Hiram. He drove slowly along through the throng until he found a dirt road leading east. He turned onto the small rutted road and made better time. He looked at Jack in the front seat next to him. "What happened back there? The military wouldn't let me near enough to see."

Jack thought about what to say to this stalwart Jew. "The power of Yahveh God was displayed in a mighty manner such as hasn't been seen since the days of the Exodus. Zulam Abdullah Hami and a couple thousand Zultarian notables were sent to their just rewards and the people that were to be executed were set free. Zultar was shown to be what he is, simply a pagan idol that could do nothing. I think you can get to see the reruns on television tonight."

Hiram blinked several times. "I would dearly love to have been there. Do you think this will destroy Zultarism?"

Sarah answered from the back seat where she had been gazing out the window and thinking about that same thing. "No, it won't. It will be explained away as coincidental freaks of nature, an unexplained phenomenon, or anything else but God. Mankind in general can't handle a direct intervention by God in our world. Remember the Hebrews at the mountain. They said if they heard God talk to them directly they would die. Also the agendas of every nut, psycho, alternative religious group, and nation will resist the concept and deny what they saw happen. You watch, even the Zultarians will explain away their moon god's inactivity as indifference in the affairs of insignificant man."

Laura said, "It will have an effect on many that saw what God did in answer to prayer. But Satan will cast his fog over mankind and they will soon forget what happened here. The only real effect this had was to temporarily free the captives and eliminate the threat that the Lord wanted removed."

Jack smiled, "The President told me that if God moved, then so would he and the government. The Zyngolian government will repeal their anti-Christian laws or the proof that Hami hired a hit team will be broadcast world-wide and destroy the government that went along with Mohammad Hami."

Mark spoke up. "What about that team Hami had already trained?"

Sarah said, "Maybe we had better visit that training center of his again."

Jack agreed. He asked Hiram if they could revisit his safe house and get some weapons and maybe hitch a ride on the mystery helicopter again.

Hiram smiled, "Yes you can. But, this time I'm going with you. I don't want to miss any more of the action."

Four hours later, just after dusk, the four team members and Hiram leaped from the helicopter onto the open field near the destroyed jail building. There was nobody around. Weapons up and ready they made their way into the staff building. Everything was deserted and had a hasty departure look. Papers scattered everywhere, drawers dumped out and thrown on the floor. Chairs and lamps knocked over.

Mark surveyed the place and spoke into his combat microphone. "Guys, I think we're too late. We'll probably have to hunt these vipers down in the city itself."

Jack came back, "Maybe we can catch them on the road from the helicopter."

Mark was about to agree to that when Sarah spoke through using her battlecom microphone, "We don't need to chase them. They're here. Come down the stairs to the third door to the right.

The other four people joined her in the room and stared at the mess. The four men that had been using astral projection to attack others sat there with glazed eyes hauntingly vacant. Mark checked each one and announced that they were sort of alive, but barely."

Laura was praying silently to God's Spirit and asking for an understanding of what happened. She got the entire answer in one burst. She stopped and sorted out the images and impressions she had received. Then she announced. "Their spirits are gone! They were astral projecting, probably against us on the field. When Yahveh struck down the Zultarian group He also destroyed these men's spirits. They've left their temples in defiance of Holy God and they are not coming back, ever."

Mark felt uncomfortable with these harmless enemies. "If we leave them here they'll just starve to death."

Jack stopped and asked God what to do. He looked up with grave concern on his face. He told the group to get back to the helicopter now! He shoved them all out of the room and ran for the exit with the others hot on his heels. He grabbed Laura's hand and ran for the waiting helicopter. As they got close he pointed the first finger of his right hand straight up into the air and made a circling motion. The pilot had never shut down the rotors and now started spinning them up to speed. Hiram went through the opening like a bullet. Jack and Laura jumped into the open hatch. As Mark tossed Sarah onboard and jumped on himself, the chopper lifted straight up. At Jack's urgent warning the pilot tipped the chopper up on the rotors for maximum speed and hauled tail away from the center. As the last person on board, Mark hung onto the webbing. His legs hung outside the helicopter. Jack reached out and grabbed his webbing and hauled him into the helicopter.

A glow from above them lit up the interior of the helicopter. It got brighter and then a meteor slammed into the training center. It was only sixty pounds but it was traveling at meteoric speeds so it brought a great deal of energy with it. The explosion that occurred when it hit was similar to a dozen two thousand pound daisy-cutter bombs going off at once.

The training center disappeared along with the trees and landscape in a quarter mile radius of ground zero. The helicopter was slammed this way and that by the shock wave and by all rights should have crashed, but, the pilot managed to stay airborne and got it stabilized. It was an impressive job of flying in a twenty-year old Huey. The pilot kept it heading away from the blast site but for a few seconds was sliding to the left and the team got a bird's-eye view of the destruction.

After they landed, instead of taking off again, the pilot shut down the engines and got out of the chopper. Walking around the nose of the aircraft the pilot came up to Hiram. Removing the helmet, "he" turned out to be a very pretty, young Chinese Asian woman. She handed Hiram the helmet and said, "Thanks for the ride Hiram, but I quit."

Hiram looked from the helmet to her and then to the helicopter. He made a small wry face, flipped the helmet under the helicopter and opened its right hand door. He located a hidden switch and pulled it all the way out. He then walked to his car and looking back, said, "Come on, let's go!" The ex-pilot and the team climbed into the Chevy and rode in silence as they pulled away from the chopper.

Mark asked Hiram, "Aren't you forgetting something?"

Hiram shook his head, "No."

Behind them there was a blinding explosion and the helicopter, shattering into a hundred burning pieces, lit up the night sky. Mark looked back and said, "Oh, I see."

Jack looked at the Asian woman and asked her, "Why destroy the helicopter and quit?"

She had carried these warriors into several battles and felt kindred with them. She coolly assessed Jack's comment and quietly replied in excellent English. "I got rid of the helicopter because it was time. Zyngola was closing in on the bird and would have caught me sooner rather than later. This last flight was taken at an extreme risk. But I realized that you needed to go destroy something else. Boy! You do good work, but, how do you get a meteor to hit what you want it to?"

Jack smiled, "By following orders. The boss wanted that operation taken out and His Son took it out."

Laura had been appraising the young woman. "Besides a vintage Huey, what other aircraft can you handle?"

Su Li's eyes twinkled, "I can fly anything with rotors or wings, except the big commercial jets and maybe the newer fighters and stealth bombers, why?"

Mark took over. "Because we frequently have need of a top class pilot who can fly like you can. When you told Hiram that you quit did you mean you left the Mossad?" Mark heard Sarah chuckle quietly beside him.

Su Li grinned, "I'm an independent. I wasn't sure where Hiram's money or equipment came from until now."

She reached forward and gently smacked Hiram in the back of the head.

Hiram flinched and then laughed. "I think we both need a change in our lines of work. He pulled over near an intersection and parked the car. Reaching under the dash he pulled another one of those switches. Everyone piled out of the car and walked around the corner.

Unexpectedly they found themselves face-to-face with a pair of Zyngolan Policemen. Everyone was taken by surprise but the policemen were shaken the most. The two of them were on foot patrol with holstered handguns. Facing them were six people, five of which were dressed in combat black suits with grenades and knives hanging from their combat rigging. They also had Kevlar vests and each one was holding an extremely nasty-looking automatic weapon with a grenade launcher attached to it. All four weapons were pointed at the two policemen.

The strained silent standoff was shattered by a glaring flash and the roar of an explosion behind the armed group signaling the end of the Chevy.

The younger of the two policeman said in shaky Arabic, "It is required that we arrest you." But it was obvious to everyone that would be impossible. Hiram spoke to them in Arabic for a few seconds. The policemen nodded and took their guns out of their holsters and gave them to Hiram. They turned around and Hiram used one of the guns to hit them both in the head. He didn't hit them too hard but they both collapsed onto the ground and acted unconscious. Hiram threw their guns away.

Mark looked at him and asked him what he expected with them walking around dressed like this. Hiram grinned a sheepish grin. "Sorry, the other car was supposed to be here to meet us, not policemen."

No one bothered them in the next four blocks. Anyone that saw them went indoors and shut the door. Hiram opened the garage door to the safe house and let them all in. As he locked the door he said, "We have about twenty minutes to leave here before the entire Tymerian police force comes calling. He ran to the hidden radio room and made a quick call.

While he was doing that, everyone else changed clothes. Su Li didn't have any civilian clothes in the safe house, but one of the dresses that Christi had left fit her fairly well.

Fifteen minutes later they all met outside and a full-size VW van pulled up to the group. Everyone got in and rode along quietly. Sarah laughed, "Hiram, I suppose that you pulled another one of those switches in the safe house didn't you?"

Hiram was about to answer when there was a huge fireball several blocks behind them. He looked back, smiled, and said, "Of course."

Reaching a field thirty miles from the capital, the driver let them out and reversed back onto the road. He headed back to the city.

Several minutes later engines were heard overhead and a Bell/Augusta BA609 tilt-rotor aircraft settled to the ground. The BA609 was a commercial, 9-passenger version of the V22 Osprey military VTOL. The BA609 was fairly new and its appearance here with Arabic markings was a surprise. The six passengers boarded the aircraft which quickly took off vertically and did a twenty-second transition to horizontal flight. It accelerated to a cruising speed of 250 knots. Mark had noted the auxiliary fuel tanks which gave it a 1,000 mile range.

It was a luxurious ride compared to the Huey that Su Li had flown them in and much quieter. Jack and Mark talked for a while and then Jack got up and came back to where Su Li was sitting next to Hiram. Jack squatted in the aisle. "How would you like to work for us?"

Su Li stared at him for a few seconds. "Well, I am without work at the moment but I have a few questions first." At Jack's nod she continued. "Who are you? What do you do? Is any of it legal? What would I have to do? How much does it pay? And, of course what benefits do you offer?"

Jack was used to this type of honesty and he responded in kind. "We are called the Crossfire Team. We are a select group of people who respond to threats and challenges around the world. I'd say we are quasi-legal. We have good connections in Washington D.C., Tel Aviv, and other countries. You would be tasked to provide air transportation at any time, to any place, many of these missions will be like the ones you recently flew. The job will pay more than you will have time to spend, and the benefits are out of this world. You will of course need to pass some security checks and other tests and take some military weapons training from a guy named White, if you want to join."

Su Li told him, "Let me think about it for a while." Jack nodded and got up and went back to his seat. Laura looked at him with a raised eyebrow. "Well, what did she say?"

Jack told her, "She wants to think on it."

Laura nodded, "Smart girl. Jack, I'm telling you that God's Spirit almost yelled at me to have her help us. It was one of His strongest directions I've ever gotten on the spot like that."

Jack looked at his wife. He hadn't seen her in make-up and a nice set of clothes in a while but she still looked lovely to him. "Is that your discernment operating or did you get a heads-up from God?"

She smiled which lit up the cabin, "It was definitely from God."

CHAPTER THIRTY-FOUR

As the tilt-rotor headed southwest towards the Gulf of Guinea, Jack placed a satellite phone call to Denver, where it was around noon. The phone was answered cautiously on the second ring. "Hello" A very neutral voice without any accent or inflection.

Jack looked at the tell-tale indicator on the sat-phone receiver. He had the right party. "Charlie, this is Jack Malone. How are you and Linda doing?"

Charlie Wu was one of the Crossfire Team's partner operations. Charlie and his wife Linda Wu were American citizens with a shaded background. They both used to be Chinese Internal Security Agents, or more commonly, spies. They had found Jesus and fled from mainland China to the U.S. where they had met with Sensei Grady who they knew by reputation. They had been instrumental in helping the Crossfire team before it was a team. Jack and Laura were indebted to them for the inside work they had done to undermine the criminal operation of Don Miland, who was trying to kill them.

"We're fine Jack. I got to see the show you four put on this morning. God really showed some stuff didn't He?" The ex-Chinese agent had never been concerned that his God would let them down. He and Linda had been delighted at the results.

Jack laughed, "Yes he certainly did. Listen I have a little project for you if you are free at the moment." After ascertaining that was the case, Jack continued. "We're looking to incorporate another person into the team and we don't know much about her. She is definitely Chinese lineage but we need all the data from her great-great grandfather down. Especially any associations we would want to worry about. God seems to want this to happen so I doubt that you'll find any armed skeletons in her closet but she is one fine pilot and I'd like to know where she got her training."

Jack plugged a microchip board into the side of the phone. "Here comes what we have. He pushed a button and the data up-linked and down-loaded to Charlie's black box which was connected to his computer. Charlie checked the data and mused, "Su Li. Okay, we'll get back to you but this may take some time." Linda Wu came on the line. "Wow, Jack, she's some looker. Does Laura know about her?"

Jack laughed and repeated Linda's comment to Laura and then handed her the phone. Laura chuckled, "Linda, how are you?" After some pleasantries she said, "Yes, I know about her. I'm the one that suggested we hire her. She can really handle a helicopter under the worst conditions. And I'm not worried about Jack getting lured away. He knows I'm the best thing for him in this world." They both laughed at that. Then they broke off.

Jack looked at Laura, "Want to bet how long it will take them to have her whole history?"

Laura smiled, "Sure, I bet they'll have it in twenty-four hours."

Jack chuckled, "Less than eighteen is my guess."

Jack was interrupted by Su Li coming up and sitting across from them. She smiled, "I was talking to Hiram about working for you to see what he thought. He and I have worked together for three years now. He gives you guys his highest rating and knowing him that has to be something. I'm okay on the flying and the dangerous stuff, but I don't know about all this religious involvement. How would you feel about hiring me with me being an atheist?"

Jack looked at Laura and then answered Su Li. "Your beliefs are your own concern and we will not try to change them. But how will you feel working with a bunch of Bible-believing, tongue-talking, Jesus freaks?"

Su Li smiled, "You mean a bunch of well-paying Jesus freaks, right?"

Laura reached up and did a high-five with the smaller Asian woman. "You'll fit right in, don't worry."

Su Li sobered up a bit and asked Jack again. "Really, how will you handle my atheism?"

Jack said, "Su Li, it takes more faith to not believe in God than it does to believe in Him. You may not believe in God, but He believes in you and He wants us to work together. You're welcome to your beliefs like I said, but you are going to see things that will make you really wonder."

Su Li pursed her lips and then smiled, "I'll wait until then to wonder, okay?"

Jack nodded. "In case you're wondering, we are running a security check on you at the moment. Is there any skeletons in the closet we should be aware of?"

Su Li shook her head, "Not really. I'm just a normal girl who likes to fly." She hopped up and stuck out her hand. As Jack shook it, she said, "I'm intrigued by this "training" you were talking about and I am looking forward to meeting this mysterious Mr. White." She walked back to her seat and sat down.

Laura smiled at Jack. "She's got a lot of eagerness for someone who doesn't think there is anything after this life."

Jack smiled back. "It should be interesting to see how she reacts to this morning's events when we get to see them. Listen, I'm going to put her under Mark and Sarah's care for the time being. You are there to catch her if she bumps up against them too much, okay?"

Laura nodded. She realized that Jack had come to grips with the necessity of giving other people room to make their own choices and he wanted to make sure this woman didn't get hurt by the strong personalities represented on the team.

CHAPTER THIRTY-FIVE

Charlie printed out the information that Jack had sent him on his color printer. He looked at the picture of the young woman in a seat in an airplane. She was a classic Asian beauty. Almond eyes, full lustrous black hair, beautiful lips and a gentle curve to her nose and cheek bones. She had ample charms that were somewhat unusual for the Chinese. Yes, she was pretty. Now to find out whom she really was and what she represented for the Crossfire Team.

He brought up a clandestine program on his computer and displayed her picture. He cropped it to show just the head and shoulders and then activated the IDENT program. The program mapped two thousand points on the face and then went on-line and slipped into one after another security data base to compare her identity. He started with the U.S. FBI and CIA files. He drew a blank there. He then checked the records with the Mossad and Interpol. Again, he didn't find anything. He checked the British and French secret services with no better fortune. He ran through the data bases on the Pacific Rim including Japan and Korea. Still didn't find anything, now for the interesting one. He used some new passwords he'd just received from contacts in his native country. Two bombed but the third one worked.

He was into the Chinese Internal Security data base. The western world thought of China as woefully behind them in computer capabilities. He knew better. Many of the top programmers in the world were working for the government in China. Heck, the U.S. had trained most of them.

He ran the indent program and got a hit. He requested the file as a bulk download. He had just finished receiving it when his computer disconnected from the link. He hit two keys and watched as the program reconstructed, showing the reason why it disconnected. His request for this particular record had raised a computer flag and that initiated an immediate trace.

His computer had gone through twenty-seven links to reach the mainland computers. They had come back through eighteen of them before his computer broke all the links. He was still unknown and secure but they were getting closer every time he used his Ident program and it raised a flag. He would have to find a better way to insinuate his program into theirs, later though.

He decrypted the download and brought the files up on his screen. The information was in Mandarin, the high language of the Chinese. He was quite familiar with it and didn't even notice the switch from standard.

He started with the state summary. Su Li had quite a history on the mainland. She had almost been aborted but her older brother had been killed in an accident so her parents were still allowed to have a child. Why they wanted to keep a female wasn't recorded but a black mark existed against her parents because of the irrational decision.

Su Li had a fairly normal childhood with the exception that her father, Cho Li, had trained her extensively in the martial arts. Charlie thought that the man had been smart. Su Li would need to defend herself if she wanted to survive in China. He started checking again. He noticed that she had several awards for merit and skill in her matches. Charlie raised an eyebrow. She had taken first place in two major competitions, way ahead of her competitors, which he noted were men.

Charlie made some notes and returned to the records. She had been approached to join his old service but her father forbade it. She may have been involved in a major intelligence operation in a negative manner. There wasn't sufficient proof that she was involved so they had simply noted her file in the event something else should appear. He noted the dates of the report and the district. He could see if he could find out what had happened.

The next report was a surprise. Her father and her mother had been arrested but it was for nothing that involved her. It seemed that her father was suspected of having contacts with western security services and could even be a spy for them. Su Li had protested but had been instructed to stay out of the investigation.

Charlie saw the two marks in the margin which told him a lot. Even though the record stopped talking about her parents, the marks meant that they had died under interrogation. It seems that Su Li knew though. She was nineteen then and had ownership of her family home and her father's dojo. Right after they died, she suddenly sold both the house and dojo and dropped out of sight.

The next record entry showed that she had fled the mainland and had become romantically involved with a smuggler named "Thor" who was very successful and into advanced technology. He taught her English and paid for her to take flying lessons which showed that she had an incredible talent for the art.

Charlie looked back at her medical information. Ah, yes. Su Li had the human equivalent of a hawk's vision. She could see farther and in dimmer light than ninety-nine point nine-nine percent of the population. She also had a gift for spatial relationships, two necessary talents for a pilot.

She had progressed from single-engine light planes to multi-engine, night flying. It was then that she started flying jet aircraft. The only ones that her boyfriend could get were surplus military jets. So her talents were even further honed in the use of flight characteristics. These aircraft had their attack radar and airborne weapons removed before Thor got possession of them. So she developed her flying to give her an edge against an armed enemy. Then she had changed courses and started flying helicopters. She apparently had even more talent for this form of air flight.

He noticed that the service had taken a new interest in recruiting her and had sent a pair of agents to bring her back to China to explain the advantages of working for them. The agents were never heard of again but a message was appended to this file that had been received from an anonymous E-mail address. It read, "If you continue to plague me I will turn my attention to eliminating you like you eliminated my mother and father. Don't bother me again."

There was an insert from the high command to kill her if possible.

There were no further entries and that was where her record stopped as far as the Chinese service was concerned.

Charlie sat back and considered what he had found. It was possible this was all fabrication. Then again the records were normally not used to mislead anyone because no one was supposed to have access to them except officials. But, they may have determined he could penetrate their files. But if that was the case, why would they alter this particular file. They would not have had any reason to connect Su Li and his efforts.

Well, he had two pieces of information he could use to check against her story. He would go back to the western services and see if he could find any reference to Cho Li. Also, he could see what he could find out about the smuggler Thor.

He started researching those records with his usual determination and perseverance.

CHAPTER THIRTY-SIX

The Crossfire Team finally got to go home. They said goodbye to Hiram on the U.S. aircraft carrier the VTOL had left them on the day before. Hiram was getting a ride back to Israel in an American F-18B. He shook each of their hands and wished them well.

The V-22 Osprey that the team rode was a military version of the earlier VTOL and while it lacked the amenities of the Bell BA609 it was an acceptable ride. Su Li was a probationary member of the team and as such was riding with them. She had been quietly awed at the U.S.S. Abraham Lincoln and its fleet of F-18s, F-14s and other aircraft. It was definitely a mobile air base that would rival any land-locked air base. She had almost asked to fly one of the fighters but knew it wasn't going to happen. She kept her mouth shut and her eyes open. This Crossfire team had some real pull. She had watched the Captain of the carrier give them whatever they needed. Now she was intrigued. What is so important about this group of soldiers? She intended to find out.

After two mid-air refueling connections the V-22 settled down at Eglin Air Force Base in Florida. She was granted a work visa to enter the United States and her sponsors were responsible for her conduct and whereabouts. She had no delusions that they would be remiss in their duties. She recognized a dedication in the women that rivaled the men when it came to duty. She liked that.

Transferring to a staff car the team traveled across the base to a large hanger. The car drove inside. Su Li got out with the others and went up the stairs to enter a four-engine Jet Commander business jet. She heard a "ten-hut" from behind her on the hanger floor. She stopped at the top of the stairs and turned in time to see the assembled Air Force personnel all come to attention. A sergeant said, "Hand salute" and the thirty or so uniformed men and women all brought their right hands up in a military salute. What surprised her was that they were all looking at the boarding ramp she was on. The next surprise was when all four of her companions came to attention and returned the salute. She had more things to mull over in her mind. The civilians and the military treated these people with honor. The salute meant that they were, or had been, in the military. It was all very confusing.

Everyone took a seat and the stair ramp whined-up and sealed shut. The engines were started and the plane began to taxi out of the hanger. She could hear the tower chatter coming from the cockpit. Deciding that she ought to start earning her keep, she unbuckled her belt and headed for the front of the plane. No one stopped her or said anything. They all acted like it was perfectly normal for her to head for the controls.

Actually, Jack would have been disappointed if she hadn't taken the initiative in this case. He understood her reluctance in the VTOLs and on the carrier. But this was non-military and really fell into her expertise.

Su Li stepped into the cockpit and saw that the right seat was empty. There was only a pilot in the left hand command seat. Knowing the courtesies, she knocked on the bulkhead. The pilot looked at her in his mirror and she pointed to the co-pilot's position. He grinned and nodded. She put her purse on a hook and slid into the seat. It took her little time to strap in and put on the headset. Immediately she was listening to the tower's instructions for their plane, "Alpha Bravo Three Niner Five" taxi to R1, you are third in line behind two fast movers.

Su Li watched the two F-22s roll out and jump into the air. Then she watched as the pilot taxied to the main runway and turned the jet into takeoff position. He had a light but sure touch on the controls, very comfortable at the stick. The tower gave them clearance to take off, climb to angels three and come to a heading of 295.

The pilot ran the engines up to full and released the brakes. The lightly-loaded bizjet accelerated quickly and rotated well within the parameters. The actual leaving of the ground was soft and fast. The plane's four engines had enough power to allow an almost vertical climb. She watched as they flew out of the pattern. Her eyes were drawn to the radar display. This was no ordinary bizjet radar. There were military icons and displays that she didn't recognize. She could however, understand the basic information being displayed and she saw two blips coming up quickly from behind. Seconds later, the two U.S.A.F. F-22 Raptors that had taken off before them came along either side of the civilian jet. Again she was surprised when the pilots turned their visor/helmets towards the bright white aircraft and saluted. The pilot returned the salute and the two fighters pulled away from them at a fast pace. In seconds they were just specks in the distance. What she didn't know was that the two F-22s were their escort. They would stay out of sight but within forty seconds by afterburner.

Su Li decided that she liked the F-22 and hoped she'd get a chance to fly one someday. She picked up the flight chart and read it all the way to a place called Denver, Colorado. This was her first time in the United States and she had never heard of the place. "Oh well" she thought, "A flight path is a flight path."

The pilot spoke to her directly without using the head set. "Have you had time in this type of aircraft?"

She nodded, he told her to take the controls. She had adjusted her seat automatically when she got into it so that the controls and foot pedals were in the correct position for her hands and feet. She took the control yoke and said, "I've got it."

The pilot watched her fly for a while and saw that she corrected the flight path after they passed a navigation beacon. He took off his headset and unbuckled his safety harness. Slipping out of the command seat he went back into the main cabin. Su Li shook her head. These important people don't have the slightest idea who I am or what I represent. Yet they are willing to let me handle their lives with no regrets. This makes this opportunity even more interesting.

She handled the call sign hand off from Cincinnati to Denver. That was another city name she didn't know. She had been flying the plane alone for almost two hours when the pilot came back and strapped into the command seat. He looked at her and said, "I've got the controls." Su Li immediately took her hands off of the control yoke and her feet off of the pedals. She relaxed and looked out the window at the terrain five miles below. It was all so green and lush, but it wasn't jungle or forest. Mostly fields and a good portion of those were crops, another amazing thing.

The pilot smiled at her. "Su Li, I like the way you handle the controls. You know what you're doing and have a good touch. I'm Major Michael White of the U.S. Air Force. I understand I'll get to help you get used to some of the aircraft and weapons systems you may need to handle. Can you tell me what your experience has been so far?"

Su Li thought, "AHH, the mysterious Mr. White. He is an officer in their military no less. This is also impressive." She grinned back and listed all the aircraft and helicopters she had trained on and flown. It was an impressive list that made most other pilots envious.

Mike nodded as he contemplated the holes in her education and all the things she hadn't done yet. "Okay, I take it you don't have any air combat experience?"

That set her back a bit. "Air Combat, no, not really, I've dropped a bomb but the aircraft I have flown generally didn't have any weapons or systems I could use."

Mike looked at her with a grin reminiscent of the one the canary sees on the cat. "If you hire on here that will certainly change. You'll need to train in long-range missile defense and attack, close-up cannon combat, ordinance selection and use, well as air-to-ground missiles. Fire and forget ordinance as well as a couple of other techniques such as radar evasion and jamming, IR and radar air-to-air missiles." He looked at her stunned expression. "You game?" She nodded.

He spent a few minutes talking to the ATC and adjusting their altitude as they begin to drop down for landing. He looked at her again. "You want to land it?" Again she nodded.

He handled the communication and flaps. She handled the engines, wheels, and brakes. She hadn't landed one of these except twice in training and that was four years ago. But she wasn't going to ask for help nor mess up.

The plane came in at the right speed, on the glide path and she cut the power as they came over the end of the runway. Pulling up just as they reached touchdown made the landing a soft one. She eased the power back on slightly and brought the nose down gently. Then she applied the retro engine braking and used the brakes softly because they had so much runway in front of them. The plane was a honey. She turned off at the designated taxiway and gave it back to Mike. She got up to go back into the main cabin and was startled by applause. All four of the people were clapping and smiling at her. So, what the heck, she raised her hands and clasped them together over her head in a symbol of "victory!"

CHAPTER THIRTY-SEVEN

Su Li had never seen a city like Denver. Everything about it amazed her both in her senses and in the casual way the others acted. How could they not be awed by the wealth and the nice houses they traveled by as they headed for something called "Castle Malone"?

She saw manicured lawns, huge shopping malls, thousands of new automobiles like the one she was riding in. She ran her hand across the leather of the seat and felt its luxurious surface. They entered another area of exclusive homes that were like castles to her. She hoped she was acting blasé' and unaffected as the others on the outside because she was thrilled on the inside.

They pulled around back of a two-story building that didn't have any windows. They ended up in a garage that held three more vehicles. They exited the garage and entered the house.

The inside was amazing to her. The decoration, the automation, the softness of everything was wonderful. She met David Zahavy and realized that he was probably Hiram's boss in the Mossad. She was taken by his graceful manners and dry humor.

Sarah took her to a bedroom on the second story and took her measurements. She went to a computer link in the room and went on-line to an exclusive women's store. She had Su Li use the fashion designer software to select a variety of dresses and clothes that she liked.

Sarah then ordered shirts, underwear, and other clothing from the measurements and Sarah's evaluation of Su Li's tastes from the purchases she had selected earlier. The store said that they would be ready by the next morning.

The two women went back downstairs and rejoined the group for dinner. It was delivered to their door and everyone dug into the Chinese food. Su Li thought that it was a lot different than the food she had when she lived in China.

The conversation was interrupted by a phone call.

Jack answered his cell phone on the second ring. "Hello?"

The construction manager's terse comments reflected his military bearing. "Mr. Malone?"

"Yes"

"Sir, we have completed the objective. I am requesting a review."

Jack thought for a few seconds. "Good work, it's too late today but we'll be there at about two p.m. tomorrow."

"Yes sir. Thank you, sir."

Jack went to find the others. "Hey guys, remember that I told you that Laura and I wanted to make Castle Malone more secure after that RPG raid?"

Having gotten all the people's attention, Jack went on, "Well, tomorrow morning you are going to be the first to have an opportunity to see the new Fortress Malone."

David smiled, delighted at the opportunity to see how Jack was going to top this amazing house that they had developed. Mark simply nodded since he and Sarah had been in on some of the designing of the new "fortress".

Sarah got up and came over to Laura and hugged her. "What did you decide about the little white picket fence?" she asked in jest.

Jack shook his head, "No picket fences, way too provocative."

Su Li was continually amazed by the house and the things she was able to manage in her room. She loved the view from her window and had forgotten completely that the building didn't have any windows.

She snuggled into a bed that was softer than anything she could remember and drifted off to sleep with happy thoughts.

The next morning the purchases arrived and she was stunned by the quality and amount of the clothing. She wondered if they were going to take it out of her pay.

After lunch, all six of them piled into Jack's new Cadillac Escalade SUV. This one was a replacement of their first CIA Escalade after a running gun battle left it a wreck. The fact that both Jack and Laura came through the fire fight alive and intact was a testimony to the battle worthiness of the class.

Jack took Interstate 70 West out of Denver and into the mountains. Just before Silver Plume he left the highway at exit 228. Driving down a newly paved, concrete road he came to a circle in the road with an island planted with trees and plants. Halfway around the circle was another road with a sign on either side. The signs were in green and white like the state signs in Colorado. Both signs said, "Private Property - Do not enter". The signs and the convenient circle back to the road out were obvious indications that illegal trespass was discouraged.

Beyond the signs the road climbed a slight grade and disappeared over the top of the hill. There were rising rock walls on each side of the road that also discouraged trespassing.

If one was daring and ignored the signs they were in for a less subtle reminder over the rise. There was a new sign in stark black and white that spoke volumes about disobedience. "UNAUTHORIZED VEHICLES AND PERSONNEL WILL BE DEALT WITH SEVERELY" In smaller print there was a warning about tire damage and vehicle impoundment.

Towering vertical walls rose on either side of the road and there was nowhere to go except back or forward. This was a single lane road with ditches on each side and carbon-arc lighting for the nighttime.

After crossing the three sets of tire-shredding grills, the road turned to the right and then arched back around a curve to the left. At this point, signs were no longer needed as the road ended in a twenty foot gap that had to be thirty feet deep. Across the gap was a granite cliff with a massive gate set flush into the cliff. Several TV cameras were visible as well as a variety of ominous closed ports that concealed weapons.

Jack operated a remote control. They waited several seconds until the gate had swung outward and up from the bottom and the top went inward and down. The entire assembly moved outward and descended into the gap to form a bridge across the open span. The bars of the gate were twenty-four inch square beams with six-inch thick walls. This would allow the heaviest truck or tank to cross it but would also resist all but major military ordinance attempting to breach it.

As Jack drove across the bridge/gate, a series of lights came on in the tunnel behind the gate. The marble walls rose twenty-five feet to the arched ceiling in the thirty-foot wide tunnel. The tunnel made a gradual turn to the left and then another turn to the right before resuming a straight path for two hundred yards. At the other end of the tunnel was another bridge/gate combination that was already in the lowered position.

Jack drove past the second gate and turned left into a large enclosed parking area. It was obvious that the tunnel and parking area were built deep inside a granite mountain. But upon exiting the SUV Su Li found the air was fresh, flowing, and smelling of mountain greenery such as spruce and pine trees.

A well-lit entrance stood at the end of the parking area. As they approached it a NovaStar sign lit up requesting identification. Jack identified himself and one-by-one had everyone step up and say their name. After this, the sign went out and a satin-chrome finished set of elevator doors opened. The six people got on the elevator.

David smiled and said to the Malones, "I see you've learned from the best."

Laura grinned, "Oh, you recognized the elevator arrangement?"

David nodded, "And the vehicle, bio-mass, ID inspection outside the first gate too."

Jack looked at his good Israeli friend and added, "I liked your concepts but we've taken them considerably farther in this installation. We'll go over it later."

The elevator had been moving like the one they had ridden at Mossad headquarters in Tel Aviv. First it went downward, then forward, then down, then forward again. When it stopped and the doors opened there were several gasps. Even though they had planned it, the Malones and Connelly's hadn't seen the actual development and it was way beyond merely visually impressive.

The elevator opened directly onto the living room. The living room was a circular-shaped open area of over two thousand square feet of floor space. The entire far side of the circle from the elevator was floor-to-ceiling windows. The ceiling was twenty feet above the carpeted floor. The ceiling was almost polished stone in a light brownish-white color which added to the spectacular view of the valley below the dwelling and the mountains on the other side of the valley. Again the air smelled fresh and mountain clean.

Comfortable furniture and dramatic art was placed strategically around the room. The lighting was subtle with recessed lamps providing back lighting and tasteful use of light panels throughout the room. A large rock fireplace and chimney graced the right wall and a large display television screen was prominent on the left. The colors and scents and accents were done with class and it was obvious that the same interior designer that had finished the first two NovaStar-equipped homes had also done this one.

Jack led the crew through an automatic doorway into the room next to the living room. Equally tasteful, this large room had a massive conference room table dominating the space. Jack looked at David, "I think you'll recognize the War Room decor."

David nodded. This was a plusher version of the table and systems he had at the Mossad. He went to the table and touched the lit button by the seat. A panel in the table slid noiselessly out of sight revealing a computer monitor and keyboard and communications gear. After examining the station he turned to Jack, "Where are the headsets?"

Mark answered him, "We don't use them with this system. The microphones and speakers are designed to be completely secure and isolated to each station. What you say will only go where you indicate you want it to go. To another member or group here at the table, to anyone with a phone or a wireless connection anywhere in the world. The keyboard will connect you to almost as many places as yours at home."

David nodded his approval. Su Li was overwhelmed with the grace and beauty that was designed into the efficient electronics and the decor.

The crew inspected the bedrooms and facilities a level above the living quarters. The upper floor was reached by multiple stairwells, two escalators, and two elevators. It was an interesting arrangement because there was a large gathering room at the top of the stairs with more comfortable furniture and a TV/DVD/Stereo and a small kitchen. Radiating off of this room were twelve short hallways that each led to a master bedroom, bath, and study. It was obvious that each of the bedroom suites were hallowed out of their own part of the granite which gave privacy to the occupants of each room.

The level below the living room housed the exercise gym, laundry, storage areas, a firing range, and additional rooms for food and supplies.

In a separate area on the living room level were the arsenal and the control room that defended the fortress.

Then Laura took them through another tunnel and they found themselves in a huge, sunlit green house, arboretum, and garden. There were several birds flying around in the area. Laura then walked them over to another hall that led to an Olympic-sized swimming pool with changing rooms and a sunning area. They toured the mechanical equipment area that controlled all of the systems and then wound back up at the living room.

Jack showed them the two studies, library, and a room for private worship that were off of the living room. All of the rooms they had seen were well lit with large windows and gorgeous views of the surrounding mountains.

They finally gathered back in the living room and were introduced to Major Gary Danning, the officer involved in the construction of the fortress. Laura went into the kitchen and with Sarah and Su Li's help brought out drinks and snacks for everyone.

Settled comfortably in one of the conversation areas, the group listened to the military man who had constructed the defensive features of the fortress.

CHAPTER THIRTY-EIGHT

Gary Danning was given the floor to describe the details. Gary was a handsome young officer in his late twenties. A military cut styled his brown hair and his face showed eager honesty. Even in civilian clothes his military bearing was obvious in his straight back and economical motions. That he was proud of what he and his men had created was evident but he didn't act possessive or defensive. He spoke from the heart with an experience of professional excellence and with the joy of a true craftsman.

Standing up with his hands clasped behind his back he addressed the group. "To begin with, let me explain my presence on this project. Under direct Presidential Order my construction crews were assigned to build this facility. As the commanding officer I was instructed by the people who sign my checks to make this my finest effort."

He loosened up some and started to walk back and forth and gesture with his hands as he endeavored to get the complex concepts communicated.

"After being assigned, I met with both Generals, excuse me, Mr. Malone and Mr. Connelly and went over their concepts. I have to admit that I was given a major head start on my finest hour. Also, I am well aware that there is no man-made nut some other man can't crack. But in this case we may have achieved a revolutionary new level of crack-proof nut."

Gary stopped pacing and smiled at the group. "First off, this dwelling sits directly in the middle of a five-mile square military reservation. That means that the government can restrict it in many ways from intrusion. The Civil Air Rules have been amended to prevent any over-flights of this reservation under 10,000 feet altitude. Mounted in the top of this granite cliff are three batteries of surface-to-air missiles which are maintained by the Marines. They are federally approved for use against any hostile aircraft violating the zone."

He stopped and took a sip of his cola. "The room we are sitting in has a minimum barrier of six thousand feet of solid granite between it and the outside world at any point, and nothing less than a full nuclear strike will breach this defense. As I understand it, that is unlikely since whatever the enemy would want would be destroyed and that is not the scenario they want."

"I want to congratulate Mr. Malone on his "Viewport" vision systems. I understand that his company, Technology Alternatives, is now working with all branches of the service to supply this technology to other projects as needed. Personally I have never seen such clarity and detail in a non-electronic, direct vision system. The new innovations for the sun rooms and the tropical garden are going to change horticulture in the future."

Gary sat down again and picked up some diagrams that he referred to and pointed out details. "The entry gates have been tested to 360 percent of load and still did not fail to prevent access. This was still true even when one gate was partially destroyed by tank fire. The Planax Weapons systems will destroy all but the most armored vehicles and have shown the capability to knock down all shoulder or vehicle-mounted missiles prior to impact and then redirect automatically on the launch position. If an enemy does breach the outer gate then the monitoring systems will allow the force to fully enter the tunnel and flood them with an inundation of over six hundred tons of water. We call this the "royal flush".

Pointing to the ceiling Gary continued, "Other than a single, well defended elevator shaft, there is no route between the top of this mountain and this dwelling. Parachutists and Para wing invaders will find themselves in a devastating cross fire from automatic weapons. If they survive that they can only rappel down to below the dwelling and face another nine hundred foot drop to the valley floor or they could possibly end up at the front gate again."

Waving his arm in a circle he smiled, "The upgraded NovaStar System2 used in this fortress is extremely deadly, and I do mean that as in lethal. Never forget that, and always keep this id tag on you as a backup if there is a penetration. If you have your id tag then you can fight from room to room in full cooperation and safety from the NovaStar system." He picked up a package and took out six medallions on titanium chains. He looked at each one and handed it to one of the team. They all examined them and then put them on. Jack had called him to have an extra one made for Su Li. David looked at the tag and smiled his thanks to Jack for the trust it represented.

He looked at each of the six people in turn, "That covers the general description. What questions can I answer for you?"

Mark suggested, "Gary, why don't you explain your terms "extremely lethal" for the new people."

Gary nodded, "The NovaStar System2 has the capability to respond with six different forms of projectile weapons. Those are fleshettes, 12-gauge shotgun rounds, .223-caliber auto fire, Claymores, 2KW red lasers, and, in some cases, 40mm grenades. Selected consoles can also deploy 8GW blue laser bursts and lethal-level MASER emissions. Hallways are also protected by cross-electrode electrical discharge devices in the 20 kilowatt, 50-amp range.

Everyone looked at each other as they considered the amount of damage the system could do. This system was developed by Jack and Mark, so the hope was that they would make it as mistake-proof as possible.

David asked, "What about helicopter or VTOL access?"

Gary grinned slightly at the Israeli. "This one is my own design. I hope you'll like it. When we were installing the air defense system at the top of the mountain we made a remarkable discovery. So, rather than use a remote, open-air landing base with armored hangers as Jack and Mark suggested, I was able to eliminate the vulnerability in traveling between the helipad and the fortress."

Gary produced another diagram with photos attached. "Buried 200 feet below the top of this mountain we found a large cavern which we enlarged to accommodate a five-pad heliport with full service and fueling capabilities. The fuel will be monitored by the Marine force as far as delivery via Chinook helicopters and delivery to the fuel cells inside the hangers.

The cavern is protected by two fortified entrances. One or both of these entrances can be opened to allow an air operation. One or two landing pads can be extended up and out of the roof simultaneously depending on the number of choppers granted permission to enter the area and to land."

Gary pointed to the photographs. "Once the helicopter or helicopters have landed on the pads, they are retracted into the helio entrance center and the entrances are closed. The chopper is then moved laterally two hundred feet into the cavern itself. In the event someone tries to forcibly enter the way the helicopters did, the entrance covers are a larger version of cold-war Titan missile silo covers. These are hardened sufficiently to survive all but a direct nuclear strike."

"The excellent Israeli Bio-mass ID system has also been installed with some modifications to scan the choppers and determine passenger identifications, potential explosives, and other parameters. The heliport is protected from above by the SAM emplacement and has two, additional remote control, auto fire Stinger sites for low-level protection. All of the weaponry and facilities are concealed and not discernible by the public or by satellite for that matter. I need to stress again that all these systems are controlled from the fortress control center.

Once the helicopter is safely in the heliport, an elevator similar to the one you rode in on will take the people to an access room. After they are scanned and approved, another elevator will bring them here."

Mark asked, "Did the design we supplied for the first elevator work out as last ditch elevator warfare in this case also?"

Gary nodded. "Yes, your design concept was excellent. I did add two small modifications which alter the final destination."

Mark's brow crunched up a bit. "What do these modifications do?"

Gary sat forward, eager to explain his unauthorized part of the design. "In the event that the sophisticated detectors in the elevator discern explosives or weapons that had not been detected before, we gas the elevator car and monitor heart activity. If everyone is rendered unconscious then we stay to your design and deliver them to the holding cell. If they are prepared to avoid the gas then your design left them stuck in the elevator until they would surrender. I see this as a way to cripple your system and take away one of your assets. So, I modified the operation so that the passengers are placed on a shelf on the face of the cliff with nowhere to go until they give up. The elevator stays in service that way."

David's face looked doubtful. "Do you ask them to politely step out of the elevator onto the shelf?"

Gary smiled, "Who's asking? The doors open and the back wall of the elevator rams to the front, shoving anything or anyone inside, out."

David grinned and nodded.

Mark also nodded and asked, "What was the other mod?"

Gary smiled again, "You know the part where you have a recording giving intruders a last chance to surrender?"

Mark nodded.

Gary shook his head. "Not necessary. This is government property and is so marked at all points. No second warnings needed."

Mark pursed his lips and decided that Gary had a point there. He also liked the additions and told Gary that.

David raised two last points. "Gary how is all this powered and how did it become designated as a military reserve?"

Gary thought for a moment. "The primary power for daily living is from four horizontal wind turbines supplemented by a three acre solar cell farm near the top of the mountain on the southeast side of the crest. Backing those sources up or in the event normal sources are compromised, there is a five-hundred megawatt nuclear reactor buried twelve hundred feet below and six hundred feet north of the bottom level. It is serviced by Navy technicians on a bi-monthly rotation. There are some weapons systems that we are planning to install that will require that level of energy."

David nodded knowingly, "Pulsed Megawatt Lasers?"

Gary made a maybe-so, maybe-not gesture. "There are several suggestions in the mill right now and I don't really know what we will end up with at this point. Understand that this is an ongoing program which we will continue to upgrade as new systems become available."

Gary thought for a few seconds. "As to the military designation, it was assigned by the President through Executive Order. But for public consumption, this is an advanced mountain training base for SEAL, RECON, Green Beret, and Navy nuclear units that your team paid for. They will be training all year around here but will primarily utilize the mountain face and hills exclusively. They won't interact with the fortress, unless they are needed."

This last was quite an admission that the present administration considered the Crossfire Team and the crucifixion nail a top priority and worthy of true national defense. Su Li had overloaded on wonder and sat quietly in awe.

Mark asked one more thing. "Gary, did you use our plan for the secure vault?"

Gary nodded. "Yeah, I liked that. It gave me a strange peace in my heart to do that exactly as designed. If you don't mind, I would like to use that type of design in other work I have planned.

Mark thought about it for a few seconds. "I'll agree for the majority of the design but not for the core portion. That will remain an "eyes only" secret for the foreseeable future."

Gary shrugged, "That's fine. I don't think that part would work anywhere else anyway because it is so specific. I'll get a set of the basic design plans and delete the core information. I'll run them by you before taking them out of here."

Gary stood and shook hands with each of them. "I've been privileged to work on this operation and in the future if you need my talents they will be available whenever you call." He saluted and all four of the team returned his salute. They congratulated him on a job well done. Mark told him that he would make sure that his superiors knew that he had achieved his finest hour with this facility. Gary then left on the elevator.

Jack took over at that point. "Even though Victor covered most of the costs, this base is far too expensive and elaborate for Laura and I to use as our personal home. We will live here and we want you all to live here as you need to. There is sufficient room and board for everyone in the Crossfire Team. You and the other members of the team can consider this your home as of now. I also suggest that we change the name from Fortress Malone to just the Fortress"

Mark looked at Sarah. "What do you think spy-lady?"

Sarah went over and took Jack and Laura's hands. "Of course we accept your offer and I like the new name. While it is true that Mark and I have become targets in regard to God's Holy treasure, I like the idea of sharing a safe house with you two. But, how do we handle all of Mark's company operations?"

Jack grinned because he had planned on that exact question. "There is one room I didn't show you yet, come here." He got up and walked down a side hall off of the living room. Reaching a double set of doors with a covered name plate on the right-hand door, he removed the tape over the name plate. It read, "Connelly Enterprises Incorporated". Jack then pressed a remote control which opened the doors by sliding them into the walls. He stepped aside and let Mark and Sarah walk in first. It was an expansive five-room suite of offices that had every communications device imaginable easily available built into glass-topped desks and a wall-sized display that could track all of Mark's worldwide company activities at once. It even included a small eating and sleeping area for long periods of duty.

Mark had never known that Jack had included this and was obviously not expecting it. He walked around and touched this and that and looked at the furniture and the equipment. There was room for a 4X expansion of operations as needed. He walked back and gave Jack a bear hug. Holding Jack out at arm's length he grinned and said, "Thank you. I really can't express how much this means to us." Sarah came over and gave Jack a kiss on the cheek. Then they repeated their thanks with Laura. "It's beautiful, thank you."

Jack held out a set of golden keys. Mark took the keys and asked, "What are these for?"

Jack said, "Your office door and your filing cabinets."

Mark flipped the keys over his shoulder. "Forget it, I trust you guys and I doubt that there will ever be anybody in this fortress that I can't trust."

CHAPTER THIRTY-NINE

Jack, Laura, Sarah, and Mark were seated at the war room conference table looking at an image of Charlie Wu. He was giving his report on his investigation of Su Li to the team.

Charlie smiled into the camera. His computer showed four small screens with each one of the team represented in them. "I must admit that you guys find the most unique individuals to incorporate into your team. I spent a bunch of your money researching your pilot and I think it will be worth it to you."

Laura grinned at Jack. "The Spirit of God doesn't make mistakes." Jack nodded in agreement with her.

Charlie sent a file that appeared on a second screen at each of their positions. He began to report his findings. He told them everything he had discovered and backed that up with files from the NSA and CIA on both her father Cho Li, and her sponsor-lover, Thor.

Cho Li had been a mole for the CIA as had Su Li's mother. They had been burned by a counter-mole in the CIA. Charlie said that he had the impression that her father was training Su Li to become an operative but had been arrested before he had a chance to tell her.

When Su Li escaped from China she had spent two years roaming the Pacific Rim nations but couldn't seem to find a place she was comfortable in for long. Charlie had a whole report on Thor whose real name was Zhou Liang.

Charlie gave Su Li a clean bill of health as far as being a counter agent and thought that they should hire her with the understanding that she was very good at martial arts and probably good at smuggling too.

The team talked it over and decided that both of those capabilities fit into their operations. They all agreed to give her a place on the team. They would watch her for as long as their Father in Heaven said it was necessary.

While this was going on, Su Li was in the garden waiting. She really wished there was a God because she wanted to stay with this group so much she would have asked Him.

She thought about Thor. She missed him a lot even though the memories were fading after the last four years. She thought back to when they met.

-----------------------✱✱✱✱✱-----------------------

One night she had been walking in Hong Kong. She had been trying to understand what it was that she wanted to do with her life. At that time Hong Kong was still in British hands. She happened upon what she thought was a hold-up. Four men had a large Chinese man backed up against an alley wall. He was unarmed but each of the others had a handgun.

Su Li was taken by the handsome features of the victim and angry with the violent cursing of the attackers. She waded into them with all the martial arts ability she had. She disarmed and crippled two of them. The man being attacked reversed the tables on the other two men when they turned to shoot her. He stepped forward and slammed their heads together so hard they dropped to the pavement like stones. Su Li and the man ran away from the scene together before the police got there. The handsome young man told her his name was Thor and that he was an independent businessman. He had been very grateful for her rescue. All the time he talked he guided her through streets and alleys away from the scene of the attack.

She knew she didn't want to be arrested and taken in for interrogation. That hadn't worked at all for her parents. Thor didn't want to be arrested because he knew he was wanted up and down the Chinese coast for smuggling arms and almost anything else his ships could carry. His smuggling did not include slaves or drugs. He personally hated those things as he had seen first-hand the damage they did to people.

Thor's childhood had been very rough and he had watched Opium and some of the newer drugs ruin his family. He had grown larger than most Chinese and excelled at sports when he finally got a chance to go to college. In the business world he saw the corruption and politics that destroyed an honest man's labor of a lifetime. After school, he got an offer to make a great deal of money by running some guns to a rebel group. He found that he had a knack for smuggling. He also liked the thrill and the danger. He took the name Thor from Norse Mythology to hide his real identity and set about building a small empire of his own.

After their shared adventure on the streets of Hong Kong, Thor realized that the young woman was enamored of him and he wined and dined her. She decided to follow this adventurer and fell in love with him. He took her into his organization and his bed. He was a gentle and considerate lover and loyal friend. In Su Li, Thor found a companion soul that hated the Chinese government and wanted to live daringly.

It was two months after they met before he told her that their initial meeting hadn't been a mugging. The four men had been Chinese agents tasked with bringing him in for crimes against the state. Su Li was even happier that she had helped to foil their schemes.

One time he took her with him as he was flying his twin-engine Beach aircraft between Hong Kong and an arms drop on the mainland. Su Li wanted to know what it was like to pilot an airplane. He got her behind the co-pilot's controls and was amazed at her innate ability to fly. He talked to her about it and then paid a pilot to train her in single-engine aircraft. She soloed in less than four weeks. She rapidly moved through multi-engine props and took on jets. She was a speed junkie and always pushed the aircraft to their limits.

But she knew her limits and that of the plane she was in at the time. After two years of flying Thor and his cargos all over the Chinese coastal areas she got a ride in her first helicopter. Routine flying had become somewhat boring so she nagged Thor to buy a helicopter and teach her to fly it.

Thor didn't know how to fly one himself, but he knew who did. He made a bargain with Su Li. If she would learn English, then he would buy her a helicopter and get her trained to fly it. Su Li agreed and was a quick study. In less than a year she was speaking and writing English as if she had always done so.

Thor held true to his word because he had developed some serious affection for the young woman. Not enough to suggest marriage though. Even though his business was in decline, he found a helicopter and bought it. He figured that it could only improve his business.

The Chinese had apparently decided that he had become a large enough nuisance and set aside some serious resources to deal with him. He was losing shipments and ships and worse yet, his men. These were people he knew and they were being hunted down and killed. He knew his time was short. But, he had promised Su Li and on one gray Monday morning he took her to a field and introduced her to a vintage Huey helicopter from the days of the Viet Nam war. It was still in good shape and even had been modified to carry a bomb inside the body above the landing skids with a quick release trap door below it.

Her instructor was Phil Orman, an American. Kicked out of the U.S. Army for racketeering, he had good reason he didn't want to go back to the states. He was a good pilot and a reasonable instructor even though he was a little friendly with his hands. One time she had had enough and did a finger jab to a nerve that left him incapable of moving for a long ten minutes. During that time, Su Li explained in gory detail what she would do to him if he ever touched her again. After that he was all business. After six weeks training, which included some bomb runs, she headed back to Thor's boat.

After that she continued to improve her flying in the helicopter. She had noticed Thor's preoccupation with his business and it didn't take her long to realize that the Chinese government was closing in on them. She determined that she would talk him into retirement and they would leave that part of the world.

One Thursday around noon, the two of them were on the aft deck of his boat which was moored near the shore awaiting a shipment of guns. Su Li heard an angry aircraft engine and looked up to the sky behind the boat. What she saw scared her into immobility. An older, propeller-engine warplane was diving on the boat. She screamed and Thor spun around. Taking in the situation in a glance he took two steps, grabbed Su Li and threw her off the boat into the water on the shore side. She didn't go deep because she was all akimbo when she hit. As she broke the surface of the water on the way back up she saw Thor with a shoulder-mounted surface-to-air missile launcher. Thor was running towards the front of the boat when the machine guns on the plane strafed the water behind the boat and marched across the deck. Thor was hit multiple times and staggered to his knees. The sight of the bullets punching through him turned her heart ice cold. He managed to stay upright on his knees long enough to fire the missile before he died. The missile was a heat-seeker that was designed to take out jets, not propeller aircraft. But its little seeker head detected the hot exhaust from the aircraft engine and blew the plane to bits in mid-air. Thor had managed to kill the man that had killed him.

Su Li watched as Thor collapsed to the deck and the boat began to settle into the ocean as water ran into the holes the bullets had made through the hull. She wanted to cry but was too angry. She swam to the shore. By the time she pulled herself out of the water the only part of the boat still visible was the top of the mast. She turned away from her pain and headed inland for the landing field where the Huey sat.

It was fully fueled and had a five-hundred pound bomb in its special compartment. She warmed the chopper up and took off. She decided to make a pass over the boat to say goodbye to Thor. As she approached the coast she saw a Chinese patrol boat approaching the sunken boat. She didn't even think about consequences. She curved around behind the patrol boat and approached it at a thousand feet. She could see the winking of rifles on the patrol boat as they shot at her. She ignored anything but her objective. As the boat was centered in the rough crosshairs on the bottom windscreen she pulled the manual release lever. The bomb fell true and the patrol boat was reduced to fragments. What was left sank a hundred feet behind Thor's boat.

Su Li flew over the spot where the boat had gone down and blew a kiss to Thor. Then she flew away and headed for friendlier skies before the Chinese sent some fast movers after her.

Thor had set up stashes all over the Pacific Rim in the event he had to run. She knew where they were and accessed several of them. This would give her funds for the next few years. Then she started looking for people who wanted to hire out her flying services.

------------------------******------------------------

The memories ended as Jack came into the garden looking for her. Actually he knew exactly where she was because the ID tags were tracked by the central computer and included GPS chips.

Jack came over and stood next to her. His smile was enigmatic and made her unsure of the result. He resolved that by offering her his hand. "Well, we've decided that we want you to join our team if you are willing."

She jumped up and hugged him. "You got yourself a pilot!" She was happier now than she had ever been.

Jack nodded and grinned. "Okay then. I am going to let Sarah handle your training and scheduling. Major White gave us a good report on you and said that he would get you approved for simulator training and then actual weapons training. I will work with you on self-defense and small arms. I know that you have some excellent training and experience in martial arts but having done the same thing, I can assure you that the transition from dojo player to street combat is a big one and we'll try to make it as easy as possible for you."

Jack smiled at her because of her obvious enthusiasm concerning her position with the Crossfire Team. He asked her if she had faced serious situations such as combat before. She told him truthfully that she wasn't trained as a warrior and her experience was limited.

Jack told her that they would train her as a warrior depending on her capabilities. Then he got more serious. "Su Li, I know that you claim that you're an atheist and don't believe in the existence of a higher being. How did you get to that spiritual position?"

His question was open and honest and she thought about it for a few seconds. "I followed the faith of my parents which was Buddhism. When they were captured I prayed to all my ancestors and to the gods for my parent's deliverance. They were killed anyway and no amount of prayer meant anything.

After I was with Thor I asked him about his philosophy about God. He told me that tomorrow isn't sure and yesterday is forgotten. That leaves only the present that we live in. One day he knew his life would be scattered like dust in the wind and he would be no more. So, he lived for the moment and I have learned to do that too."

Jack shook his head. "I'm sorry about your parents and for Thor too. But, I want you to understand that this team is the caretaker of an important Christian object. We have been, and most likely will again be attacked on the spiritual plane and in this world by demons and those they control. This is not theory or somebody's concept, it is reality. Between flights with you in Zyngola we were present when God moved and destroyed over two thousand Zultarians right before our eyes. I told you that we would not try to convert you to our faith and we will not. But you need to be aware that part of our battle is in that realm. Can you accept the idea of evil spirits trying to hurt you?"

Su Li sat there for a few minutes. Then she said, "I'm confused by this concept, but I will follow your lead in these matters. I seek truth and will not shut my mind to your concepts. Please don't worry about me. I can carry my part of the load."

Jack grinned, "I'll bet you can. But if possible, follow Laura's lead. She is the anointed one when it comes to combat with demonic forces."

Su Li returned to her gleeful state and asked, "You said we would talk about my salary. What will it be and how do we handle payment?"

Jack realized that she wasn't used to western ways. "We will help you open a bank account in the bank of your choice. Your basic pay will be $100,000 dollars U.S. per year. But, since you will get all your housing, food, clothing and equipment from us at no cost to you it is actually a lot more."

She did a quick calculation to the present Chinese Yuan. She realized that her salary was almost a million Yuan a year. That was five times what she made when she worked for Thor and she was his number two.

When she calculated the benefits of all her daily cost taken care of it came out way beyond a million Yuan a year.

Jack also pointed out that she would share in all bonuses that the Team received. Last year they distributed over nineteen million dollars to the nine members of the team. This distribution was an equal share for everyone involved in the team's activities. Each person had received a little over two million dollars.

Jack went on, "There is also the life insurance, medical insurance, dental and vision insurance where we cover everything and it costs you nothing." Seeing the look of unbelief on her face he told her, "Don't worry, you'll earn it. The things we get involved with affect the entire world and each one we solve successfully leads to new challenges."

Su Li shook her head. "I find it hard to believe my fortune. I'm a twenty-six year old, ex-patriot Chinese woman with no formal military training and to tell the truth I don't even have a license to fly. To get a chance to work with this team is most improbable. I realize that you got a chance to see me work in Zyngola, but to make a decision based on that seems strange.

Jack laughed, "If that was all it was, it would have been strange. Actually, the God you don't believe in told us, specifically my wife, that you would be good for us on our team. We've learned to follow His leading, He doesn't make mistakes. He wants you on the team and so do we. Believe me that it will work out for the best for all of us."

CHAPTER FORTY

The next morning, Su Li was up early and still trying to believe her great fortune to be where she was and with the group she was now employed by.

She turned on the giant television that had been hiding behind one of the closet doors in her room. She knew that she could crank it up as loud as she wanted and no one else would hear it because of the solid granite surrounding her room. She watched as scenes of life in America were shown in documentaries, advertisements, and other programs.

She found a world news channel and watched the events of the world unfold as told by the cable channel reporters. There were new developments in the relations between China and Taiwan which could still go either way. Peace or war, like normal.

All at once she saw the four people that she knew as the Crossfire Team. They were all dressed in white and standing side by side with their hands behind them. She recognized the area as Tymeria in Zyngola. She listened with great interest to the commentary by the newscaster.

She watched as the two thousand Zultarians were frozen into ice cubes, swallowed by the ground and the statue fell on one man and then burned to a crispy puddle. The commentator was trying to explain it in human terms. "As you saw the events it certainly looks like an act of God. But was it really an otherworldly happening? My research team has uncovered the truth of the matter. Through a set of coincidences, a "strider" occurred. A strider is an abnormal shift in the jet stream. This jet stream flows over this part of Africa and is responsible for the weather patterns and storms across that continent."

A graphic of the jet stream over Africa was shown on the screen. "In an occasional freak accident of nature, the super cold air in the jet stream touches the Earth's surface for a short time. This is called a strider. Well, all that happened here was that an untimely strider fell to earth and caused a lot of Zultarian people to freeze to death.

That super cold caused a reaction in the surface of the planet and caused it to expand at the point of impact. This in turn caused a mini-earthquake and resulted in the frozen people and things falling into the open earth. The "voice" supposedly heard at the site was only thunder that people, who were traumatized by the event, thought was the voice of God. It was only thunder."

A portion of the idol burning was shown. "My researchers are still puzzled by the appearance of this statue which weighed in the two-hundred ton range and crashed to earth killing one person. They also don't know why solid stone would burn. But they were sure there was a natural explanation for these things and they are working on them now."

Su Li turned off the television. She was really quite intelligent and the explaining away of the events in Zyngola as simple acts of nature didn't ring completely true to her. She was sure there might be a reasonable explanation that didn't require a supernatural being but she didn't think that this was it, too many coincidental happenings in too small an area.

Sarah knocked at her door and Su Li let her in. They talked about the schedule for her training and then decided to go shopping. Laura was tied up right then so the two women went to the garage, got a car, and drove to the Cherry Creek Shopping Center Mall.

Cherry Creek Mall is one of Denver's most exciting shopping environments. Su Li walked through the mall with Sarah and gazed in awe at the mall which had over one hundred and sixty of the most exclusive and distinctive stores and restaurants in the world. Compared to her survival existence in China it was bewildering.

Su Li caught at Sarah's arm and said, "There's so much here. How can you choose?"

Sarah was amused by the naive attitude of the Chinese woman. "It takes a little getting used to. But, you'll soon see that each store caters to different tastes or provides different services. You'll find yours and those are the ones you'll shop at most of the time."

Su Li eyed the glitz and the glamor and the color and crowds. "I don't know if I'll ever get used to this."

Sarah laughed, "You'll soon find it is commonplace and everyone here is only after your money. Come on, I want to show you some clothes in the nicer stores."

The day flew by as they shopped and had lunch. They took their packages back to their car and were going back to see what else they could find in the way of personalized things for Su Li.

As they headed back into the mall, three young men whistled at them. Su Li's lips compressed and she was about to show them some manners when Sarah reminded her that there are different standards in different countries. In America their attention was usually a compliment, not an insult. She led Su Li back to the doors and into the mall.

The encounter with the young men had knocked Su Li's focus from shopping to defensive curiosity. She walked along with the tall Israeli woman but she used the windows in the shops to keep track of the people behind them. She quickly spotted the three young men from outside and they were definitely following them. She hesitated to tell Sarah because it might be all right here but, she didn't like it.

They went into and out of several stores and were walking down an aisle that was being renovated and most of the shops weren't open yet. Su Li checked and saw that the three men now had two more friends and they were closing in on the two women quickly.

They entered a section that was under construction and completely deserted by other shoppers. That was when the men decided to do, whatever they had in mind. Su Li stopped and swung around to face the five toughs. The men had been hurrying up to catch the women and the sudden stop brought them together suddenly.

Showing traditional Oriental calmness, Su Li asked the lead guy. "Why are you following us?"

That was all she said. It was sufficient to determine their interest.

The lead guy leered and spoke to one of the other young men. "The Asian bird wants to know why we're following them." All five men laughed. The lead guy stepped forward and put his hand on Su Li's shoulder. "We just want to have a good time with you two birds."

Su Li didn't flinch and didn't attempt to knock his hand off of her shoulder. Instead she asked quietly, "And what will you do if we don't want to have a good time with you?"

The guy got real serious and growled at her, "Then we'll just have a good time with you anyway!" He started to reach for her with his other hand when she struck him with her right fist with the first two knuckles extended. She hit him just below the diaphragm with such force it paralyzed his ability to breathe. She then used her right hand and reached over his right hand on her left shoulder and used a Jui-Jitsu technique to pull his hand down and rotate it over. The pain in his wrist, elbow, and shoulder were so intense he fell to his knees and would have moaned if he had any air to do it with. He started turning bright red as his struggle for air reached a panic point.

Using his arm as a lever, Su Li flipped him over onto his back and stomped her heel into his chest to start him breathing again. She let go of his hand and stepped back. She had kept an eye on the other men, but they hadn't tried to help their friend.

As she stepped back by Sarah she saw why. Sarah was holding an automatic pistol pointed at them. Sarah smiled and said, "You guys wanted to have a good time, okay, let's play. Take off all of your clothes, now!" It was obvious that she wasn't kidding. The four guys standing complied quickly and in seconds were standing there in their birthday suits.

Sarah pointed back at the busy mall. "Now, get lost before I have to exterminate the lot of you." The guys all took off at top speed. Sarah made the gun disappear under her skirt and went to pick up the clothes the men had dropped. The man on the floor had recovered enough to try to grab Sarah's foot as she walked by him.

Without breaking stride, Sarah side kicked him in the head hard enough to turn out his lights and left him there. She picked up the clothes and motioned Su Li to follow her. They walked back into the active part of the mall where she dumped the clothes in a trash container.

As they walked along the mall they could tell where the naked men had gone by the noise of the crowd and the yells of the security personnel. She steered Su Li into a fashionable pub and diner on the lower level of the mall.

She carefully selected a booth for them and ordered a couple of teas.

Su Li had been watching Sarah and saw her grin as the waiter walked away. Thinking back she realized that Sarah had known the men were there all the time. She had deliberately led them into that deserted part of the mall to see how she, Su Li, would handle the situation. Su Li was at first upset and then she realized that her training had already begun.

Su Li looked up at Sarah and grinned back. "Okay, I misunderstood the situation. I thought that you weren't aware of those guys and I was going to have to save us."

Sarah nodded. "Su Li, I spent eight years as an Israeli Mossad field assassin. I have had training and experiences that you aren't aware of in the slightest. It's all right, no one told you about me and I am not being superior. I just want you to know that each of us is an expert in some or many of the capabilities needed to do what we do. You have a lot of raw talent but it hasn't been molded into a complete package as yet. We intend to help you mature into the role if you will let us."

Sarah watched Su Li's face and body language to see if she would be defensive or accepting of this change in status. Su Li swallowed her pride and understood that she was the least experienced in the team. She would learn and be able to rise to the heights of her capabilities by watching these people and accepting their training.

Sarah thought, "Good, she understands."

The tea came and after the waitress left, Sarah told Su Li that she had almost deliberately set that up with the unwilling involvement of the thugs. "I remember when I was just a new agent and only about twenty-three years old. I was in Egypt on an assignment and had gone to the store for some supplies. I was cornered by four men. Now, understand that the men today were only looking for some sexual diversions. In Egypt these men wanted to kill me because I was an Israeli. How they knew that I am not sure. I just know that I was unarmed and alone against four large, very tough men who wanted me dead."

Su Li asked, "How did you get out of it?"

Sarah frowned, "Three dead, one seriously damaged." I walked away and didn't look back. I got the supplies and went back to work and didn't mention it to my supervisor. They did find out somehow and I got chewed out for leaving the last one alive. Since then I don't tend to leave any enemies behind me that are breathing."

Su Li re-evaluated her concept of Sarah. "Are the other members of the team as deadly at unarmed combat as you?"

Sarah smiled, "Jack and Mark can beat me, hands down. Laura doesn't have any exceptional combat skills. Her talents lie along other lines."

About that time, a two-man team of Denver police officers came into the pub and looked around at the patrons. Sarah had selected a place that was not viewable from the entry area so she kept an eye on the policemen until they had satisfied themselves and left. "Did you see the police?" She asked Su Li.

Su Li nodded.

Sarah said, "Okay, lesson number two. If you get involved in a fight, then either leave the immediate area if you can do so without attracting attention, or go to ground nearby but keep out of sight. In the United States they have an extensive and very competent police force. If you do get arrested, don't try to explain anything, it won't help much. You are legally entitled to a phone call after you are arrested. Call the fortress. We'll get you released and go from there. Understand?"

Su Li nodded. Sarah took out a blouse and skirt that she had purchased before their melee and changed clothes while she sat there. She was able to do it without disrobing or causing a disturbance. She looked at Su Li, "I made sure you got some different clothes also. Why don't you try changing and I'll talk you through it." It wasn't as difficult as one would have thought.

In a few minutes they had entirely different outfits on. Sarah reached into her purse and pulled out a small package. She shook out a blonde wig and pulled her hair back tightly and pinned it in place. She then put on the wig and a pair of dark sunglasses. Su Li was impressed; Sarah looked like a radically different woman.

Sarah told her how to change her hair from the loose free-fall it was in. She tied it up in a bun on the back of her head and put on a scarf that Sarah had purchased. A pair of sunglasses and she looked different too.

They paid their bill and quietly walked out of the pub and through the mall to a different set of doors than they had used on the way in. Sarah kept up a running commentary on the things to watch for and things not to do. The whole thing was an education for Su Li who had thought of herself as pretty sneaky when she wanted to be. Sarah was sneaky super-sized!

CHAPTER FORTY-ONE

Su Li continued her training with each of the team members. She went to the gym to work on her martial arts with Jack. She quickly realized that he could easily defeat her but instead he continued to train her in advanced techniques that she had not been exposed to in her training at home with her father. She was quick, trained hard and consistently won some points.

Jack was pleased with her capability and passed her on to his teacher, Sensei Jim Grady. Jim took the easy route to determine what she needed by testing her to see what she already was capable of doing. She extended herself to the limits of what she thought was possible but never penetrated his defenses nor caused him to work up a sweat.

Then Jim went back to the basics and showed her things as simple as different stances during a particular series of defenses and attacks. He added many new kata to her collection and she began to see how combat martial arts didn't even resemble dojo work. There was an inherent violence involved that was required in a life and death situation. For example, she was used to using control to hit an opponent with sufficient force to indicate she could have broken a bone. Jim trained her to follow through the actual bone breaking and how to move into the next move or how to re-center her body after the strike.

This was an exhilarating experience and she was finally able to see the poetry in motion that martial arts was meant to be. Dojo practice and sparing were simply training and never followed a movement through to its logical conclusion. This was the true art and it was designed to defend oneself by being able to maim, disable, and destroy another human being.

Su Li's basic ethical goodness was starting to war with her capabilities to inflict this type of damage to others. She was afraid to tell the Sensei or Jack about her misgivings for fear of losing her job.

On the third day of her martial arts training, she had a chance to have lunch alone with Laura. Su Li broached the subject of hurting or killing other people and whether or not it was right to Laura. Laura listened to Su Li and silently prayed that the Father's Spirit would give her the right words.

Laura looked at the young Chinese woman and told her, "In our line of work it is frequently necessary to defend ourselves against deadly attacks. In this case, and only this type of a case, it is moral and right to strike with full power with the intent to do damage or deal out death. We don't want to hurt anyone but at the same time we have to respond in kind to defend ourselves. Usually we use our fighting ability to help defend others. Like Jack says, we are all sheep and the Lord is our shepherd. But as long as there are wolves around, the Lord needs some sheep dogs. That's us."

This made Su Li much more comfortable. She liked the idea of only using her skills to defend. To herself, she vowed to be the best and deadliest defender that she could be.

She learned a lot of field craft from Sarah. Laura and Jack took the same lessons because they hadn't come from a spy school either. There were some interesting field trips for the three of them. It all worked surprisingly well, even their mistakes. Their abilities to blend in, disappear, trail unseen, and leave no sign regardless of the terrain were greatly improved.

Mark took Su Li, Jack, Laura, and this time Jim Grady, and trained them on basic combat handgun, rifle, and scuba techniques. They made four solo runs under the ocean off of the California coast. Two of them were at night. Mark made sure they learned their lessons and was always there to see that they stayed safe in the process.

Su Li had the unique experience of seeing a large Mako shark up close and got over the fear of being under the water, something that she had built up a fear of for years. Mark knew that experience and training normally would reduce or eliminate the fear. But for Su Li, at first it got worse. She was thinking of bowing out of either the water training or if necessary, the team because of the debilitating fears. She recalled what happened then.

-------------------------******-------------------------

Laura came to her room at the hotel the evening that she had quit trying and gave into her fear of the water. She talked to Su Li for a few minutes and then she asked, "Su Li, I understand your position on the existence of God but I would like to pray with you anyway. Look at it this way, if there is no God then it won't cause you any problems, right?"

Su Li didn't really care one way or the other because she felt Laura was right, it wouldn't change anything. So she agreed to allow Laura to pray for her.

Laura started out asking Yahshua to cleanse them both and then for the Lord to bind up and cast out any demons of fear that were pestering Su Li. Laura listened to the Father's Spirit and asked Su Li to repeat after her. "Dear Lord, I break any and all agreements made knowingly or unknowingly with fear. I ask you to burn up in the fire of your Holy Spirit any demons of fear immediately and forever. I ask you to replace those fears with Your peace, joy, and love. I ask you to assign angels to keep the enemy away from now on. Thank you Yahshua, it is in your name we pray all things."

Su Li was uncomfortable doing this but she did it because she didn't want to rebuff Laura or to have to quit. Then Laura smiled at her and said good night. She excused herself and Su Li went to bed.

As she waited for sleep to come she thought about what Laura had prayed for her. To test the efficacy of Laura's plea she closed her eyes and imagined herself deep under water in the dark. She waited for the absolute terror to come. And she waited. Nothing was happening. She fell asleep trying to determine if she was not sensing any fear because of auto suggestion or because she really wasn't under water and she knew it.

Laura spoke to Mark the next morning before Su Li joined them. "I prayed for and with her last night about this fear of the water. I believe that the Father's Spirit told me that she has been cleansed of the demons of fear that were terrorizing her. Why don't we just proceed like we would as if nothing happened out of the ordinary yesterday?"

Mark agreed. After breakfast the five of them suited up with their wet suits again and got on the boat. Mark checked everyone's scuba gear and when he got done with Su Li's he looked her in the eye and asked her, "Are you okay? If you want to put this off we can."

Su Li was in a strange place. She was waiting for the fear to return but it hadn't. She wanted to continue with the training but was worried about having to give up again. The grit that allowed her to fly away from Thor's boat rose up in her. "Let's do it!"

Everyone went over the side of the boat backwards and joined up for the day's lessons.

That evening Su Li found Laura studying the tidal charts that Mark had assigned for all of them to learn. "Laura. I want to thank you for praying for me last night. I'm more confused than ever. I'd like to believe that there is a God that could get rid of my fear. But I was really sure that it would come back and it didn't. I wasn't one bit afraid of the water or the dark. It was the best time I've ever had underwater." Su Li was fairly conservative when it came to personal interactions but she wanted to hug Laura and she did.

Laura smiled, "I'm glad that you are free of that spirit. We will continue to pray for you and ask Yahshua to extend his protection over you. Thank you for telling me that you had relief from that plague."

Su Li wondered just how she was going to integrate this event into her ability to avoid God.

CHAPTER FORTY-TWO

At the time of their last night dive off the California coast it was two p.m. at a jail outside of Beijing, China. Chief Investigator Chun Xiaoping was overseeing a pleasurable task. He was ridding China of subversives.

The man had been tortured until he had nothing left to tell. Unfortunately, he turned out to be innocent. His broken and burned body would not be a good advertisement for Chun's squad if they released him.

The man was completely deranged by the delicate techniques that had been applied to get him to reveal his role in the ongoing espionage against China. Chun frowned; the delicacy of the water torture may be slightly excessive. He pondered this while he stared at the miserable sack of bones that used to be a vital twenty-three year old student. He noticed that the man was focused on him. Chun smiled and nodded. His main interrogator, Zhiping stepped forward and ended the man's life. The mutilated man seemed to look with pity on Chun and then he jerked once and collapsed.

Chun walked back to his office concerned that this failure took far too long to reach its climax. They should have known that he hadn't been guilty much sooner. It would not look good on his excellent record.

One fact that few knew about the Chief Investigator was that he was a direct descendent from the last Emperor of China. His pride and obsession was to restore the dynasties to the rule of China. He had decided also that he would be the first new Emperor. Thinking back on his career he realized that he was truly gifted in the arts necessary to rule. Absolute indifference to any other person's needs or wants with an active brain and imagination to chart the course for a nation of two billion people. Many people called him pure evil but only behind his back, never to his face.

Satan's minions had taken note of this potential and had nurtured his fleshly desires and ego to the point that he was very useful to them. They now turned his attention to a matter of great importance to them.

Chun couldn't remember when he had put the pieces together of the plot against his future as the next Emperor. But it no longer mattered because it was now obvious. This "Crossfire Team" was working with traitors from China. But more important, they had possession of the one thing that could make his elevation a sure thing. He would move heaven and earth to acquire this symbol. He was brilliant and worked out a fool-proof plan to resolve all the loose ends in one operation.

He knew that he needed to have a lever to accomplish his goals. The only problem with his lever was that the United States had really heightened their capabilities against smuggling people in and out of their country.

But, that was all right, he had come up with an excellent method that would not compromise his agents and still give him the necessary leverage.

He placed a call to one of his associates in the U.S. and set things into motion. He had been setting up his operation in America for several months now and he now knew the target's schedules and routines. There should be no problems.

CHAPTER FORTY-THREE

Events had remained quiet for the three months following their return from Zyngola. This allowed the team to rest, recover, and to get their new pilot trained by Mike White in air combat. After she had completed the training, she finally got her chance to fly an F-22. Although it was a two-seat trainer and Mike was in the back seat, she still got to fly it. The way she put it afterward was "It was pure excitement, the best ride I've ever had. Mike is right; she is the sweetest piece of work that's ever been made."

That week she received her American citizenship, her pilot's license, and her first charge card. She quipped to Sarah, "I can fly combat jets but still don't have a driver's license!"

One day she was working out at the fortress gym when Jack interrupted her. "Come with me Su Li, I want to show you something."

She followed him to a room in the fortress that she hadn't even known was there. It was obviously a vault and it had another vault inside of it. Inside the second vault was a curious arrangement. She studied it but couldn't make heads or tails out of it. She looked at Jack with a raised eyebrow.

Jack walked over to the device and placed his head against a rest and put both hands into two other niches. He said something she couldn't really understand and there was a series of clicks and a motorized vault top opened up and locked. The lights came on inside the small vault and she stared at an old box. Jack reached in and picked up the box and undid the crude latch holding it closed. He showed it to her. It was a crude spike made of old metal that was discolored on the sharper end. Again she looked at Jack with a question on her face.

Jack gently closed the box and replaced it into the small vault. He pressed a small red button and the vault door closed and latched. Stepping outside, she watched the other two vaults close and lock. They walked back to the gym.

Su Li could tell from the security precautions that whatever that was it was extremely important. She waited quietly for Jack to explain. She had found that silence brought forth answers that words couldn't.

Jack told her about the history of the nail and its importance to both sides of the spiritual battle. He watched her struggle with the concept. "Su Li, I realize that some things don't seem to add up right now but I wanted you to know that crucifixion nail is why we are under attack much of the time. The enemy of mankind wants it very badly and will do anything to get it. I want you to always be on your guard against the temptations and false promises that will be used on you since you aren't saved. Can you do that?"

She thought for a few minutes. "I believe that I can. I have sworn to protect the team and its goals with my life and my word is more important to me than anything I can think of in this world. Is that sufficient?"

Jack nodded. "I know you will."

Three days later Jack got a disturbing phone call.

It was from Martha Knowles, Minister Alan Throman's secretary. "Mr. Malone? I hate to bother you but I don't know who else to turn to. Alan was just escorted from his office by two men. They weren't police or anything official but I was scared by them. Alan told me not to bother about them but he did ask me to tell you that he couldn't make his appointment with you and that you would have to talk to God's Spirit yourself."

Jack told her, "Thank you Martha, I'll look into it right now."

Jack hung up and called Mark and Sarah who were on an investigation somewhere in Canada. They said that they would be back as soon as possible.

Jack prayed and asked God's Spirit to help find the Minister. He had a sudden thought about the church abduction and decided to follow it up.

First though, he called each and every one of the part-time team members. He couldn't get an answer from his Uncle Larry or from Carol Nolan. That could mean they were in trouble also or that they were just out of touch. Dang, he missed Mark and Sarah right now!

He and Laura drove out to the church. As they walked in he saw what he expected. Getting Martha to help him, he got the tape from the security camera in the lobby. They found the places where the tape had recorded the two men as they had come in and where they escorted the Minister out. The second clip wasn't too helpful because all three men were facing away from the camera. Jack took the tape back to the fortress and digitized it. He then enhanced the frame that held the best picture of the two men as they entered. He called Jim Grady and gave him the pictures when he arrived.

Two hours later they had a match on one of the men. Jack looked at his mentor and asked, "Jim, are you sure?"

The Sensei nodded, "Yes, this man is definitely a Chinese agent stationed in the states. He is supposedly a "diplomat" assigned to their Denver Embassy. But he is the Chinese equivalent of an old school Russian KGB operative."

Jack shook his head, "What are the Chinese doing grabbing a member of the Crossfire Team?"

No one had an answer to that. Jack put a call into Charlie Wu and asked him to come to the fortress.

An hour later an attack helicopter got permission to land at the fortress. In less than ten minutes Mark and Sarah walked into the war room. Mark looked at Jack, "What's the latest?"

Jack smiled that his friend was back and already into business mode. "We've identified one of Minister Throman's abductors; he's a local spook for the Chinese Police. Secondly, follow-up calls have revealed that my Uncle Larry is missing as is Carol Nolan. We don't have any information concerning how or if it is the same group."

Sarah shook her head. "If the Chinese internal security group is behind the Minister's kidnapping you can be sure they will be behind the others as well. They don't plan these things casually. I'll bet they're looking for a handle on the team."

Mark picked up his cell phone and made three short calls. When he was done he told them that he was having the NSA do a search for their ID tags which would passively respond to the satellite transmissions.

There was a knock on the war room door and Charlie Wu was admitted. Su Li came in at the same time. She kept a wary eye on Charlie.

Jack filled them both in on the abduction and possible abductions. Charlie asked to see the photo of the Chinese agent. When the picture was thrown up on the big screen Charlie almost spat on the floor. "That is Wufan, one of Chun's thugs."

Su Li's eyes brightened up in anger. "Chun Xiaoping?"

Charlie nodded. "He is one of the fastest climbing vultures in China. He is totally sadistic and relentless. If he is on your case then you have a real problem. It will be like taking on the entire nation of China."

Su Li swore under her breath. "That's the devil
1 that killed my parents!" Charlie looked at her with compassion. "Yes, he is."

Su Li glared at Charlie with a look that could wilt a steel pole at twenty paces. "And just how do you know that?" Obviously the answer had better be a good one or there would be some aggression right in the war room.

Charlie looked at Jack and answered her, "Because I used to be in the Security Service and when I reviewed your file I saw his mark authorizing their deaths. I saw it many times before I fled from China. In fact his mark is feared by many as being deadly all by itself."

Su Li looked like she was relieved and furious at the same time. She whirled on Jack. "How can you allow my life to be pawed over by HIM?"

Jack prayed fast for an answer. "Because he has found a way to hack into their files and I needed to know about you from all sources. Charlie has proven himself many times over as an ally and friend to the team."

Somewhat mollified, Su Li slumped down into a seat at the table. It was quite apparent that there was still a lot of emotional baggage she was carrying concerning the death of her parents.

Jack was about to start making assignments when Laura opened the door and came in. She walked up to him and gave him two pages of internet E-mail printout. She shook her head and sat down next to Su Li.

Jack read the text twice and sighed. Looking at the team he motioned them all to sit down. Then he read the text to them. "Crossfire team:. I have Mr. Throman, Mr. Lawrence Malone, and Miss Nolan in my possession. I will contact you soon concerning a trade I desire for their lives.

It is signed, Chun." The exterior military force phone rang and Jack answered it. After listening he said, "Okay, patch it through." He handed the phone to Su Li.

She listened to the clicks and silences of the transfer and then she heard a voice she thought she'd never hear again. Phil Orman said, "How you doing Su Li? Listen, I've got a couple of real surprises for you, are you sitting down?" After she told him she was sitting down he continued.

"I've got three people here you might want to talk to." There was a rustle as the phone was passed between people. Then Su Li almost fainted. She heard her mother's voice in Chinese saying, "Su Li, I've missed you Wren."

Wren was her mother's private name for her. Nobody else knew about it. She stammered, "M-m-mother?"

Her mother's quiet voice came back over the phone, "Yes dear, I'm sorry that the Chinese' government made you think that we were dead. They locked us away for a long time because of our mistaken loyalties. But I think they are going to release us soon. I hope so. Here, your father wants to speak to you."

Hope upon hope almost crushed her heart. She heard her father's voice speaking to her and asking her if she was all right. She asked him one question, "Father, do you still recommend hand techniques over foot techniques?"

He laughed, "No my sweet little girl. You know that foot techniques have much more power than hand techniques. Don't confuse an old man."

Su Li was so filled with happiness that she couldn't bear it. She started crying and handed the phone to Laura who was next to her. Laura couldn't understand the conversation and handed it to Jack who spoke Chinese.

Jack talked for a few seconds and listened and then tapped Su Li on the shoulder. When the young woman looked at him he said, "I've got somebody named Thor on the phone for you."

Su Li looked at the phone as if it were a snake. She knew what she had seen. Thor had died on the boat. He had taken at least three or four machine gun bullets through his chest. There was no way a person could live through that. She took the phone and said, "Hello?"

Thor's throaty voice came back to her. Su Li, I am glad you are all right. I thought that I was dead but I came to in the sea and found all kinds of wreckage. I hung on and the cops found me. Nothing critical had been shot through and they patched me up. I've wondered where you've been ever since then. Unfortunately they've kept me locked up since then. I've really missed you."

Su Li said, "I thought you were dead for sure. I've missed you every day since then."

Another voice came on the phone, very oily and repellent. "Let me talk to Mr. Malone. The voice was also very commanding. Su Li handed the phone to Jack. Jack said, "Yes?"

"You don't know me Mr. Malone but my name is Chun Xiaoping. I am the one that has your uncle and the others as well as Su Li's parents and her lover. Now, I am going to give you one chance to save all of these people. I want you to give the spike to Zhijian Cho, who you know as Charlie Wu. He and Su Li are to bring it to me at my suite in the Hong Kong Hilton by this time Saturday. If they don't, then I will personally slit the throats of everyone and they will all die this time. If the traitors are too cowardly or you deny them the nail, then I will dispose of these people, then up the ante, and we can have this conversation again. Good day."

CHAPTER FORTY-FOUR

The recording of the conversation was played back several times and everyone discussed the calls. There was dissension between the people on the team.

Mark, Charlie, and Sarah calmly stayed with their original thoughts on the matter. It didn't matter how much they complied with Chun's requests, he would kill them all and steal the nail. His history was clear. He would not keep his word.

Su Li was just as absolutely sure that if they didn't do as he said then her parents would really die and she just got them back.

Laura and Jack silently listened to all the arguments and prayed as they listened. They prayed for wisdom and peace.

Su Li finally stood up and said, "The lives of my mother and father are more important, at least to me, than your silly nail." She stormed out of the room.

Laura was praying that God's Spirit would enlighten her as to what should be done. She sat back in her seat with her eyes shut and attempted to still her mind and emotions so that she could receive whatever the Spirit of God wanted her to have.

The noises and voices in the room faded away and she felt the organized, calm, and wonderful peace that was there when the presence of God came near. She prayed in the spirit as she let the peace strain out all the nervous tension in her body and the confusion in her mind. As she floated in that calm place she sensed God's Spirit giving her direction. When the quietness returned she opened her eyes and found everyone looking at her. "What?" She said.

Jack smiled, "Your armor and sword appeared for a little while."

She smiled, "Oh."

Charlie stared at her with open admiration. "That was the most beautiful sight I've ever seen. I wish Linda had been here."

Laura looked at Charlie. "Don't worry; I think we'll see it again soon."

She looked at Jack. "I think I have an answer to our question."

Everyone watched her. She continued, "The Lord is again going to use us and the nail for his glory. As far as the Hong Kong meeting is concerned, we need to insist on a different location for the meeting. One that we can "feel safe" in, rather than the one he wants. Don't worry, he will complain but he will comply also because the enemy wants the nail so badly that they will make him comply. We need a place that allows us some combat stretch."

She sat up fully and looked at Mark. "Alan, Larry, and Carol are still here in the U.S. They haven't had the time to move them to China and would have a seriously hard time getting them out of this country. Let's find them and be ready to rescue them as soon as the Hong Kong meeting takes place."

Laura looked at Jack. "We need to give the spike to Charlie and Su Li so that they can present it to Chun in Hong Kong. But that doesn't mean that we can't be there too, but maybe not as obvious as the pigeons."

Charlie shook his head and said, "I've got a small variation on that plan, if you don't mind." When nobody said no, he went on. "Instead of Su Li going with me, let my wife act like her. I'm offering to put my wife in harm's way because I think we're going to need Su Li's talents in the air as a hawk rather than on the ground as a pigeon."

Jack and Mark agreed with that. Jack called Su Li back and they explained the plan to her. She looked at Charlie and asked him in Mandarin, "Why are you agreeing to jeopardize your wife? Neither of you know me, my parents, or Thor. How will you recognize them, or they recognize you?"

Charlie shrugged. "Linda can be made up to look very much like you and we have pictures of all three of them. I really feel that we will need your capabilities in the air if Linda and I are to survive this."

Su Li said that she wanted to think about it but it could work.

After that, Sarah asked Mark to help her do some research and analysis and they left.

Laura had a light lunch prepared and told everybody that it was available if they felt like eating. Most did.

Mark and Sarah came to Jack with their findings and then he called Su Li.

Jack looked at her a little sadly. "Su Li, I'm sorry to tell you this but, it doesn't look like Chun is playing fair with you. After some research, we don't think your parents or Thor are really alive. Mark and Sarah did an analysis of the voices and we are all quite positive that the voices you were listening to were computer-generated and not spoken by real people. As far as the personal information they shared with you, the consensus is that it was probably extracted during your parent's interrogation."

Su Li wanted to get mad and to hang onto the hope but she had started having her own doubts after she left the meeting in the war room. Neither her mother's nor father's voice had been any different than she remembered the night they were taken. The "interrogation" and the years would have changed them. She had an excellent ear for music and could pick out unique individual sounds without a problem. There had been an artificial sound to the voices. She nodded and looked up at Jack. "How did they get Thor's voice though? He told me that he had never been arrested."

Mark pointed out, "You said that the first time you met him he was being attacked by four of the security police, right?" She nodded and Mark continued, "It's pretty routine to make recordings of people's phone calls when they are under surveillance like he apparently had been. They could have used those tapes to compose a computer equivalent."

She nodded at that too. Then Jack added one more item. "Didn't you also say that you dropped a five-hundred pound bomb on a patrol boat that was directly behind Thor's sunken boat?" Again she nodded. Jack held up his hands, "Thor, wounded by gunfire, and that from an aircraft which use much larger and higher-speed rounds, couldn't have stayed underwater very long. If he had surfaced, then he would have been on top when your bomb went off. The concussion would have killed him like it killed everyone else on the patrol boat. I think what you saw was true. He died like a hero."

She felt the hot tears running down her cheeks. She had found and lost her parents and her friend again. She sobbed uncontrollably for a few minutes. Sarah came over and put her arms around her and held her. Sarah just let her cry. After a while the tears dried up and she felt like she had finally let her parents and Thor go. Su Li felt an anger building up as a heat inside of her. She scrubbed the tears away with the back of her hands and patted Sarah's hands to let her know it was all right. Looking up at Jack she said, "What's the plan?"

CHAPTER FORTY-FIVE

Chun contacted Jack six hours later for their answer. Jack told him that they would agree to his terms but they wanted the meet in a more public place because they didn't trust him

At first Chun said no, but when Jack wouldn't compromise he finally agreed. He asked where they wanted to meet. Jack told him that he should contact them on a cell phone two hours before the meeting and they would tell him where. That was not negotiable and Chun agreed, but assured them that they had better deliver the spike as directed or everyone being held would die. Then Chun hung up and Jack looked at the others and smiled.

Mark, Charlie, and Jack brainstormed the best location with Charlie giving the local color about each location. They then set their plans down in writing. Everyone collected in the war room and went over the plan. Linda was there in her disguise and even Su Li admitted that she couldn't tell the difference between Linda and herself. They were both similar body types being young Chinese and it only took a little bit of work to convert Linda's face to look identical to Su Li's. This primarily was in the color of the eyes, the lines of the mouth, and the overall age difference of about ten years. Colored contacts and makeup were sufficient without the need for any sculpting.

Jack stressed the need for absolute precision in timing to make the plan work: especially the timing between Charlie, Linda, and Su Li. This would require a special communication capability which Mark had acquired from David Zahavy and the Mossad. All three of the principals would wear a belt-mounted unit that interconnected to a bone-conduction speaker and microphone. The unit would amplify sub-audible words and impress them on the listener without external sounds or visible microphones or ear pieces.

The role Jack and Laura would play would be determined by the variations to the plan by enemy action or unforeseen actions.

Mark, Sarah, and Jim Grady were to locate and free the domestic hostages if possible.

After several dry runs and rehearsals the Hong Kong team left for the Orient by chartered jet taking the crucifixion spike with them.

Mark was running down all the leads he had but not finding much in the way of real data. Jim Grady's contacts had supplied them with a list of known locations that the identified Chinese agent had been seen. Again, nothing came of any of them. No one had seen him for a week prior to the abductions.

Sarah was considering abducting some Chinese agents herself and applying a little persuasion to get information when Stan Hargrove shoved open the door to Mark's office and whistled to get her attention through her headphones. Sarah pulled the headphones off and went to see what he had.

Stan had a map and a set of coordinates. The NSA had finally gotten a reading on Alan Throman's ID tag. They had been getting intermittent readings but had finally been able to pinpoint a location. Sarah called Mark and took Stan and Debbie with her to meet him. They had called on the Air Force and had been given the services of Mike White for the duration of the next several days. He brought his favorite toy with him. The hyper-advanced combat helicopter now nicknamed "Overlord".

The black helicopter was almost indiscernible flying in silent mode in the dark. As it approached the designated location in the mountains eighteen miles west of Colorado Springs the team eliminated the sporadic indications of people they saw in various locations. Mike held it at an altitude of two thousand feet above ground level while the advanced electronics inspected the suspect premises from a distance. He was able to count eight people in, or around, a cabin. Most were apparently asleep and there were three outside in the freezing sub-zero cold of the mountains. Mike pointed at the three white shapes in the FLIR/Thermal Imaging display. "Those are guards walking their beats."

Mark agreed and gave Mike a special code to enter into the FLIR system. Mike entered it on the keypad and a red dot began flashing on one of the white shapes lying down in the cabin. Mark pointed at it and said, "That's the

Minister's ID tag. Now if they haven't switched it to another person we have the right place and the right people."

Mike toggled a switch and the area ahead of them on the forward glass of the helicopter lit up with a contour mapping of the terrain of the general area around the cabin. This was an extremely clear "heads-up" display that would allow a pilot to fly "nap-of-the-earth" at very high speeds in complete darkness. It was created by a processor that took the twenty gigabytes of data input from the FLIR/Thermal Imaging sensors, radar, side-looking radar, and a variation of sonar and gave a three-dimensional picture of the land ahead of the helicopter. It was in real time and moved as the chopper moved. Mike pointed to a position several thousand yards from the cabin. "I can put it down there and you can do that commando soft-probe thing you do."

Sarah was impressed with the electronics but asked, "Will they be able to hear us that close?"

Mike pushed another button. Echoes of the sound being produced by the rotors were being monitored by the electronics and a blue ring showed up on the front windscreen. The blue ring was several hundred yards short of the cabin. Sarah said, "Okay then."

Mark nodded and Mike carefully flew away from the cabin and came in from the other direction. As they neared the ground, the display started showing details that weren't detectable from a greater distance. Mark pointed at one thing that didn't look right. Mike stopped their progress and used a free-hand mouse to highlight the object. The helicopter was linked by satellite to an Air Force base that had an NSA installation on it. There were nine CRAY super computers networked together which had access to one of the largest data bases in the world. All-in-all it took seven seconds for the system to identify the device and present the information on their windscreen.

Mike's eyebrows went up a notch. The computers had identified the strange thing as a Chinese variation on the American Claymore mine. The major variation was that it was twenty-five times the size of the normal anti-personnel mine. Mike said to Mark, "Thanks for spotting that. I didn't have the system on auto or it would have spotted it and warned us. They obviously expect us to put down there and have the means to destroy any vertical descent aircraft. What do you want to do?"

Mark asked, "Can you determine what the triggering mechanism is?"

The Major typed the question into his keypad and the computer system chewed on the request for about two seconds. Suddenly a cross-grid of infrared laser beams showed on the windscreen. Mike looked at Mark with a question as to procedure.

Mark studied the arrangement for a few seconds and then told the pilot. "Put us right behind the mine and we will rappel down. Find another location that is clear and we will meet you there when we are done."

That was accomplished and the black helicopter disappeared into the night sky. Mark pulled his IR goggles down and led the three person team through the pulsing beams. Once free of the field they used their night-vision goggles and avoided several other pitfalls and traps as they approached the cabin. They rendered the traps inoperative.

Spotting one of the roving guards they hid behind rocks and studied him. He too had on a set of NVGs. They waited until he had passed and then slid in behind him and closed on the cabin.

Once there, Mark carefully climbed the side of the structure and looked through a window and found it clear of alarm systems or visual optics. They had scanned the area for cameras and hadn't located any watching this side of the structure. Mark used his NVG and studied the people sleeping in the cabin. He then motioned the others back and climbed back down. They avoided the next guard and got away without detection. After they were safely out of sight of the guards and the cabin Mark explained.

"There are two guards asleep in the cabin with Larry, Carol and Alan. This is definitely the right group. Now what we have to do is make sure that they don't switch locations or harm them before the Hong Kong meeting, which is..." He checked his watch and calculated the difference in time. "...in less than six hours. That will be noon in Hong Kong and nine a.m. the day before at this location."

Stan studied the closer side of the cabin which was raised on stilts and said, "Then we had better find a high point and keep an eye on these guys."

Mark agreed and called Mike White. "Mike, we've got the right people. We are going to stay local. Go back to the fortress and get Debbie. We'll identify a drop point by the time you get back. Make sure she brings the XPR."

Mike gave him an affirmative.

The three of them returned to the area of the cabin, careful to avoid detection of their body heat. Stan scaled a large tree and found a good position on a major limb that had two other limbs for concealment. He carefully concealed his heat with an IR cloak. Mark and Sarah moved as close to the cabin as reasonable and concealed themselves with IR cloaks. The three of them settled down to wait. Mark scanned a relief map of the area and found a good place to have Mike set down.

Time dragged on while they waited. When Mike called back it was close to early dawn. Stan took the coordinates and checked out the landing site. It was further away but it was clear of any scanning equipment or weapons. Mike set the chopper down and shut it down. Then he and Debbie came back near the cabin. Debbie scaled the same tree as her husband and found a suitable location for the XPR.

The XPR was a new development of the Army research division. It was a sniper rifle that extended the ability of the shooter way beyond whatever had existed until then. It was a fifty-caliber with a free-floating silenced barrel and a gyro-stabilized aiming and firing capability. Debbie had worked for twelve years as a sniper/ assassin and could drive nails at eight hundred yards with this rifle. She could even knock a target down at three thousand yards. She checked the laser range finder and found that she was only four hundred yards from the door of the cabin.

As the sun climbed the eastern sky the activity at the cabin picked up. Nine a.m. was only two hours away.

CHAPTER FORTY-SIX

The chartered jet landed in Hong Kong at three a.m. local time. Jack and Laura waited as Charlie and Linda Wu exited the plane and took a car to a hotel. Then Jack and Laura donned mechanic's outfits like Su Li wore. They exited the plane on the far side and begin servicing the plane. After a while, Su Li left the area of the plane and walked into a hanger. Jack and Laura headed in a different direction. Entering a pedestrian walkway they parted company and went into the rest rooms. Five minutes later, a tall business man with a brief case and overcoat came out of the men's room and strode off into the general aviation building. Holding a flight ticket and heading for the check-in counters he joined many other people doing the same thing. He stopped and checked his pockets as if he couldn't find something. He reversed his path and exited the building at the front and caught a cab to a five-star hotel.

At the same time, an elderly Chinese woman had come out of the women's rest room and walked slowly to the front of the terminal. She was met there by a driver who opened a door to a Lincoln and helped her get inside. He then went around to the driver's door and pulled away from the curb. He took an entirely different route and eventually ended up at the same five-star hotel. A young American woman exited the vehicle which left immediately. She walked into the hotel and went to the elevators. On the fifteenth floor she got out of the elevator and went to room 1540. Tapping at the door got it opened by the tall business man. He took a device out of his briefcase and set it up.

Jack hugged her and without a word they prepared for bed. Turning off the lights they were quiet for thirty minutes. Then Jack went to work ensuring that they weren't being spied upon. He found three miniature video cameras and two audio microphones. Connecting leads from his device to the cameras and the microphones he pushed a switch. He then turned on a small light. Laura came over and he said, "I think we're clear now. They will only see us sleeping. That thirty minute loop should keep them unworried until tomorrow morning. Taking a cell phone out of his briefcase he punched in a number. He let it ring twice and hung up.

Five minutes later there was a soft knock on the door and Laura let Jim Grady and three other men with bags into the room. They distributed the equipment they had brought with them and then synchronized their watches. At exactly six a.m. five business men with large brief cases and their secretary left the suite and took the elevator to the garage level. Two minutes after they left the suite, the electronics and digital memory unit they had left were melted into ash by a thermite charge that also destroyed itself. The room was clear of any tampering and clues.

The men and woman were met by the same driver and Lincoln that had met Laura at the airport. The windows were darkened and they drove through thick traffic until they exited the main part of the city and came to a large arena area southeast of the city towards Stanley.

The Lincoln parked near the concession area. There were only a few people around at this time. There shouldn't be too many more by noon since there was no event scheduled today. The occupants either settled down or exited the vehicle and found locations nearby that were not conspicuous. Then the waiting began.

At ten in the morning at the Metropole Hotel, Charlie Wu heard the cell phone ring. He picked it up and said, "Zhijian Chochim".

Chun's voice was clear on the other end. "Ho ho, you don't want to use Charlie Wu here? Well, no matter. Do you have what I want?"

Charlie said he did. Then he said, "Do you know the sports arena southeast of the city towards Stanley?"

Chun agreed that he did indeed know of the place. Charlie said, "Please bring your hostages to the concession area at noon. Su Li and I will be there with the nail." Then he hung up and turned the phone off. That should prevent any sudden changes by Chun.

Charlie and his wife had spent the evening together quietly. They had prayed and knew that God was with them and regardless of the outcome they knew He would never forsake them. There was no more to say between them. They had made their peace with God and each other and now it was simply time to do what they had come here to do. After they were dressed, with Linda in her Su Li disguise, Charlie picked up the old box and they checked out of the suite. They knew that they had been under observation from the minute they had left the plane. They also knew that Chun would probably try to take them and the nail before they got to the arena. So they had planned on that. Precisely at eleven a.m. they got into the farthest left elevator for the eighteen floor drop to the lobby.

When the elevator arrived at the lobby the middle-aged Chinese man and the young Chinese woman walked across the lobby and had the Concierge get them a taxi. They told him to take them to the sports arena. The man set the old box on his lap as the cab pulled away from the hotel. At eleven-thirty the cab was boxed in on all sides by police cars. The man and the woman were taken out of the cab and driven to a local police station. Inside the station one of Chun's men took the box from the protesting man and opened it. Inside was a roll of paper. He took the paper out and read a report on Chinese food. He cursed and stormed outside. Pulling out his cell phone he called Chun. The context of his comments was that these people were not the ones they were after and they would have to find the nail where they said, when they said.

Chun wasn't surprised. Zhijian had been one of their top agents before he became a traitor. In fact, it would have been a real surprise if they had achieved their goals this easily. It really didn't matter. The evil force he acknowledged as his god and the number of his own people would make sure that the trade at the arena would go his way.

In a private car on the way to the arena, Charlie had seen the secret signal the decoy Charlie had sent when he had been stopped. He mentioned it to Linda. They would be there in ten minutes. Under his breath he said, "Su Li, are you ready?" They were using English on the odd chance that less people would know this language than any of the Chinese dialects.

The bone-conduction speaker vibrated and Charlie heard the typical CB radio response, "Ten-four good buddy." This answer would drive most Chinese crazy anyway.

Charlie chuckled and saw from the sparkle in Linda's eyes that she had heard the same message.

As the car pulled up to the arena Charlie saw the rest of the team that was on the ground in Hong Kong scattered around the concession area of the arena. He gripped the box on his lap more tightly as everything came to a head.

The car stopped and they got out. The car left the area as Charlie and Linda walked into the concession area. They looked around and saw that they were alone. Behind them four cars pulled into the parking lot and slid to a halt at the concession entrance.

The men getting out of the cars weren't a concern to Charlie; it was the demonic oppression that came with them that worried him.

CHAPTER FORTY-SEVEN

"Qualpian" was the equivalent to an Archangel in God's hierarchy. He had control of the entire operation. He had the full services of over three thousand demons at his fingertips for this event. He had them doing all the things needed to ensure the capture of the nail. Qualpian himself possessed Chun Xiaoping and was able to coordinate the worldly actions with the demonic plan. He watched the events unfold through Chun's eyes.

The major sub-demon to Qualpian was "Red-one control". ROC as he was known, rode Zhiping, Chun's number one enforcer. But he wasn't alone. He had sixteen other demons with him and the demonic force of many more backing them up. The supporting demons were battling with the angels and archangels of God and had been able to possess the area of the exchange and impose darkness over the place to give them control of events.

ROC himself had seen to the ousting of most of the angels that were trying to support the Christians who had walked into their trap. He had assigned two of his best demons to oppress the two Christians who had the nail. These two demons were named "Failure" and "Depression" and they were hard at work as Chun's humans walked in to meet the nail possessors.

ROC remembered what Qualpian told him about this meeting. Qualpian had been thundering, "ROC, the master himself is watching this action. He greatly desires the crucifixion nail for his use. I am giving you the opportunity to secure it from the Christians! Don't fail us. Don't give them a chance. Drive your slaves to destroy the humans and secure the nail for us."

ROC remembered that Qualpian had also told him personally to secure the nail if the humans failed. For him to fail would be unpleasant.

ROC watched and waited as the humans came together.

Rose and Caleb watched ROC as he prepared to physically enter the human world to do his master's bidding. Rose said to Caleb, "We must be ready to force our way to the scene and prevent ROC from acquiring the nail. I and my group will drive the wedge into the demons. You come behind us and battle ROC himself."

Caleb sought the will of the Creator for the proper battle plan. He realized that a direct conflict with a demon of ROC's capabilities might be beyond his range. This concerned Caleb more for the loss of the crucifixion nail than for his future. God smiled on him and told him that the battle would be the Lord's and that if God's Son was involved then victory was theirs. Grateful for the knowledge, Caleb prepared to enter the battle as it developed.

Rose had been probing the demonic defenses for the most vulnerable spot to drive the wedge through and found one. Rose rallied her angels and they charged the demons holding the outer wall of darkness over the arena concession area in Hong Kong. The sky was full of battle as the enemy poured more and more demons into the fight to maintain control over the conflict below.

All the angels suddenly got the word "Victory" and redoubled their efforts. The demonic wall buckled and collapsed inward as the angelic host fought through. Caleb was not far behind Rose and reached the human meeting just as things got out of hand spiritually.

CHAPTER FORTY EIGHT

As Zhiping led three hostages and sixteen of his men into the concession area, a local policeman walked over and spoke to him. He showed the man a badge and the policeman saluted and left talking on his radio to move all police forces at least ten blocks away from the sports arena.

Zhiping walked slowly over to the couple standing there. He gestured and the three hostages were brought forward. The older man and woman closely resembled Su Li's parents and the man could have been the Thor of her past. The broach that Linda was wearing hid a very powerful miniature color video camera. The live picture it took of the hostages was relayed to the display in front of Su Li. She didn't have to look too closely to know that these people weren't her parents or her old friend Thor. The faces didn't have the stamp of dignity and pride in them, and the posture of the man playing her father was so wrong in basic composure that there was no doubt on her part. She spoke into her microphone, "They are imposters, definitely."

Linda heard that comment and locked eyes with Zhiping. "Where are my parents and Thor? These fakes are really unworthy."

Zhiping didn't seem concerned that the sham was discovered. "We only had to fool you until we got close enough. Give me the spike, now!"

Charlie saw the six-man Crossfire team close in from both sides behind Zhiping and the larger bunch of his men. Charlie spoke Mandarin quietly. "The agreement with Chun was that we would provide the nail in trade for her parents, Thor, and the others. You have failed to provide them."

Zhiping rolled his eyes and was irritated by having to deal with stupid people that couldn't figure out a simple ruse. "Her parents and friend are dead and have been for years. I am rewriting the deal." He pulled a pistol out of a holster on his belt and fired three rounds in rapid fire. All three of the imitators of Su Li's parents and Thor died with a bullet to the head. Zhiping said "Give me the nail or die where you are and I will take it any way!" Zhiping's men drew their handguns in a show of force.

Charlie said sub-vocally in English, "Now would be good."

There was a roar-whoosh and all four cars that Zhiping and his people had come in exploded in huge fireballs. Guns were pointed outside the entrance to the huge tent, while Charlie and Linda quickly dropped to the floor.

An ear-splitting scream of explosions was accompanied by the whiz of bullets and screams as Zhiping's men were knocked off their feet and blown away. Zhiping dropped to the floor and crawled towards Charlie and Linda as the bullets ceased to fly. He had a pistol and he was bringing it up to aim at Charlie when it was kicked out of his hand. He rolled over on his back and stared up at Jack Malone standing above him.

All of Zhiping's men were either dead or dying. Zhiping looked out the entrance of the concession area and stared at the Chinese military helicopter hovering a foot above the concrete. Steam rolled off of the barrel of the minigun mounted under the front windscreen as the rotors whipped through the air above. Capable of firing two thousand rounds a minute, it had only taken six seconds to fire two hundred rounds and destroy the troops he had brought with him. His eyes locked on the face of the pilot which he could clearly see through the Plexiglas. It was the face of the woman that had been standing in front of him seconds before.

Knowing that he had been fooled and that his reward from Chun Xiaoping would be a slow, torturous death, he drew a hideout gun from an ankle holster, kicked Jack to one side, and rose to his feet. As he aimed the gun at the helicopter the minigun spoke again and Zhiping's worries about his future stopped bothering him.

In his luxury suite Chun Xiaoping had been watching the event on his own hidden camera in Zhiping's belt buckle. The last blast of the minigun shut off the camera but not before Chun had seen Su Li's calm face. Chun slammed his hand down onto his chair arm. He was not to be made a fool of by anyone! He ordered the police to arrest the people with Charlie Wu. He contacted the military and demanded that they find the helicopter that had attacked his men and destroy it. Then he told his communications person to tell the crew holding the American hostages to kill them immediately!

As he sat there, Qualpian taunted him for his failure and incompetence and lack of vision. Chun just got madder by the minute. Heads would roll and blood would be spilled because of this.

The helicopter sat down on the ground and Su Li jumped out and ran into the concession area. The carnage wrought by her minigun sickened her but she focused on helping Jack and Laura get Charlie and Linda out of the place.

There was a sub-dimensional shaking and like an image stepping out of a mirror, Red One Control transitioned into the human world. ROC was a particularly large and ugly demon. He had horns and scales and was a twisted image of a human being that stood seven feet tall and about four feet wide at the shoulders. His fingers ended in very functional claws and he had one goal. He was going to get the crucifixion spike. His odor could knock people over and his long red tongue flicked in and out of a mouth full of functional yellowed fangs.

Trapped between ROC and Charlie, Su Li was terrified and frozen in place. Her brain refused to accept this sight as real. But ROC didn't care what she thought as he brushed past her and knocked her to the ground. She didn't interest him. Charlie Wu did interest him because he was holding the box with the spike in it.

ROC could feel the power nexus that surrounded the nail and he lusted to get his hands on it.

Su Li stared at the back of the demon as he stomped towards Charlie. She had a gun and fired it into the back of the demon. It didn't seem to affect him at all. He ignored the shots and reached out to grab the box.

There was a glitter of silver and pure white light swung in an arc. ROC's left arm was struck from his body above the elbow. He screamed in frustration and pain as red greasy smoke poured out of the wound. Caleb became visible next to Charlie.

If ROC was ugly, then Caleb was beautifully handsome. The sword he held at high guard position was streaming with the glory of God. ROC pulled a large ebony blade with his right hand and blocked the next swing of Caleb's. ROC then quickly parried and swung a mighty one-handed blow at Caleb's middle section. Caleb blocked that blow but was staggered by the power in the stroke.

Su Li screamed when two smaller but even nastier looking demons materialized behind ROC. Then she stopped screaming when she saw Laura praying and her armor, shield, and sword appear. Laura went at the two new demons while ROC and Caleb battled. ROC was beating Caleb down by sheer power while calling on more reinforcements when Rose appeared next to his right side. ROC turned to parry her blow and was cleaved almost in half by Caleb's sword. Laura cut the head off of one of the smaller demons and started for the other one when it disappeared.

As ROC and the first smaller demon vaporized into oily red smoke, Caleb and Rose vanished in pursuit of the other demons.

Suddenly the battle was over. Laura's armor faded from sight and they helped Su Li, Charlie, and Linda out of the concession area and to the waiting car. The car rushed away from the area just as some police were beginning to arrive.

Crushed between three other people in the back of the limousine, Su Li reached into her shirt pocket and brought out a small electronic transmitter. Pushing up a lock she pressed the exposed red button and five blocks behind them the helicopter exploded. Jack looked at her and said, "Learned something from Hiram?"

She nodded. "But, I think I have a lot more to learn." She had just had an abrupt introduction into spiritual warfare as it is waged in the heavenlies. This was a major paradigm shift in her belief structure. She looked at the seat ahead of her and put her hand gently on Laura's shoulder.

Laura looked back at Su Li and smiled. She reached up and patted Su Li's hand. Laura knew the shock that Su Li was going through at the moment. She had done the same thing not too long ago.

CHAPTER FORTY-NINE

When Jack saw Zhiping and Charlie arguing before the battle, he keyed his cell phone and sent the prearranged execute signal to Mark via satellite.

Mark spoke the battle order into his combat microphone. It was received by the other members of Mark's team; including Debbie Hargrove perched in a tree, thirty feet above the ground.

Debbie's career had covered more than a decade of protecting people from other people with guns. She had been scanning the scene inside the cabin through a side window since she had arrived at her sniper's position.

The two Chinese assassins she saw in the cabin had been well known in the circles that Debbie moved in during her foreign assignments. Both Hung Yansi and Wan Kei were stone cold killers with a large number of victims on their souls. She had run afoul of Kei on an assignment in Spain. He failed that day and she was going to see that he failed today also.

Debbie squeezed the delicate trigger mechanism on her .50 caliber rifle. The rifle was a marvel of accuracy for a semi-automatic sniper rifle. Debbie was quite familiar with this rifle and could put five bullets into the same hole at three hundred yards with it. The distance here was just a little over that range.

She fired two shots in rapid fire. The first round punched through the window glass and hit Wan Kei in the forehead, ending his career in a split second. The second round was just as effective, catching Hung Yansi in the right temple as he turned to see what happened to his partner.

The three guards heard the breaking glass but didn't get a chance to do anything as Mark, Sarah, and Stan each took one out with a single shot.

Mark ran up to the cabin and pushed the door open. He burst into the main room and stopped. Larry, Alan, and Carol were tied to their bunks. All of them were alive and obviously happy to see him. The two Chinese executioners were lying on the floor, quite beyond caring.

Sarah came into the room and helped Mark loosen the hostages. Getting everyone out of the cabin and into the woods took only a few minutes. Mark and Stan then pulled the outside guards and their weapons into the cabin. Stan rigged a demolition charge. All of them headed back to the helicopter as the cabin exploded and caught on fire. The entire operation was completed in eight minutes with no loss to the Crossfire team including the hostages.

Mark called Jack and told him that the packages were safely in the air and on the way to the fortress. Jack said thanks for the good effort. They were in the extraction phase and everything went according to plan except the spiritual warfare fireworks which, thankfully, had also ended successfully. The Hong Kong team expected to be back at the fortress by tomorrow afternoon.

As Mark broke the connection he looked at his lovely wife and grinned. His thumbs-up sign was cheered by everyone in the helicopter.

Suddenly their ride felt like the bottom dropped out of it. The advanced helicopter fell towards the earth like a rock. Mark was essentially in free fall and felt like he was in space, but he grabbed hand holds and pulled himself into the co-pilot's seat and locked in the straps. He was staring at the Major as he did it.

Mike White was doing everything he could to keep them all alive. He had gotten a heads-up from the electronic counter warfare panel just in time to dodge two air-to-air missiles that were now banking around to come back at the chopper. Mike tipped the chopper onto its nose and flew it towards the mountain below as fast as its turbines would push it.

He pulled it out in time to fly between two stands of pine trees, one of which exploded in a fireball as the pursuing missile slammed into the trees. Mike instinctively tipped the helicopter onto it's right side and rotated right between more trees. While that sounded simple, Mark was stunned by the maneuver. There didn't seem to be enough distance between the trees for the helicopter But, since they were moving over eighty knots when the Air Force Major slung them to the right there was no time to worry about it. Mark punched up the counter weapons display and found the second missile looping back up into the air for a third pass at them. Mark selected the jamming and chaff dispensers and pushed the button for execution.

The helicopter jammed the radar frequency that the missile was operating on and it lost lock on the whirlybird. The chaff flew up above the trees behind them and the missile slammed into it and the trees around it.

Their problem was quickly obvious. The vertical drop and quick dodge into the trees had allowed them to escape the two missiles. But left them without much speed and vulnerable to an air attack. Mike was trying to find an exit from under the trees and still keep them airborne. They were skimming the rocks below as it was.

Mark saw one of the fast movers vectoring towards them. He primed a hellfire missile and targeted the blip. Punching the button when he saw a clear space in the trees launched the fire-and-forget missile out of the vegetation and into the air on a collision course with the attacking jet plane.

Mike had also been talking non-stop on his combat frequency while driving the bus through the bushes. He found a clearing and popped up into free air again. From the sound of sighs in the back he figured that everyone had been holding their breath while they were among the trees.

The Hellfire missile was chasing the enemy jet but probably wouldn't catch it as it gyrated over the sky. But it did keep the jet from trying to kill them for the moment.

Mark saw another attack run from a different aircraft suddenly broken off as the aircraft wheeled to the right and went full afterburners. He knew why when he picked up another flight of four aircraft rushing into the area. The Identification-Friend-or-Foe (IFF) electronics tagged these as U.S.A.F. planes.

The first plane was also attempting to leave the area with all speed but hadn't shaken the Hellfire. That plane became flaming fragments when the pilot turned the wrong direction to escape the oncoming aircraft. Two of the new aircraft went after the fleeing jet. The other two flew cover for the helicopter in the event there were more enemy aircraft around.

Major White brought the helicopter up to five thousand feet and pushed it to over three hundred knots as they headed toward Denver.

Mark keyed his radio and talked to the flight leader of the F-22s that were flying cover for them. "Thanks for coming to the rescue."

The Air Force pilot shot back "You are more than welcome! I've been itching to blow something up for quite a while."

Mark asked, "Who were they and what were they flying?"

The answer surprised him. "Apparently they were enemy pilots that stole two F16Cs from the 120th Air National Guard squadron at Buckley AFB outside Denver. We were on the lookout for them when we got your call. Man, I'll tell you that it is unpleasant hunting our own aircraft. The Falcon is a formidable piece of machinery. But I don't think they wanted to dance with our Raptors."

Mark agreed with that assessment. He was again thanking the pilot when the F22 commander overrode his communication. "Blue flight caught up with the remaining F16C. It won't be coming back."

As they reached the area of the fortress and were cleared into the hanger, everyone felt safe for the first time in quite a while. A Marine medic was called in to check over the hostages while Mark gave Mike White a tour of the facility. Mike was more than impressed.

CHAPTER FIFTY

The Chinese underground and the British Secret Service worked together and got the Hong Kong team back to their aircraft and out of Chinese-controlled air space through a series of ruses that would probably rate a place in an intelligence manual someday.

After hearing about the attack on the Colorado team, Jack had Su Li fly to Australia instead of heading back to the states. This was to throw off anyone who might be waiting on their assumed path.

Jack and Su Li were able to secure a ride home for everyone on a MATS flight that had stopped over in the down under nation. It added time to the trip but it was completely unexpected and therefore, uneventful as well.

It was almost midnight of the second day when the Hong Kong team finally got to the fortress and had a brief reunion with the rest of the crew. The talk went into the morning and finally everyone crashed in bed for the duration.

After reading the results of the various efforts his people hadn't accomplished, Chun Xiaoping had sixteen people killed slowly to show his displeasure with failure of his subordinates. He then sat down in his office and contemplated his revenge. Unknowingly aided by demonic advice he started putting together an effort that would give him the crucifixion nail and result in the gruesome death of everyone involved in the cursed American Crossfire Team. He chuckled when he thought of the way that he would personally dispose of the various females of the group. "Oh yes" he would use all of his might and resources of the Chinese government to destroy this group. In the darkness of Hong Kong he began refining his plans.

Thirteen hours away in the fortress in Denver the Crossfire Team cleaned up after breakfast and sat down in the war room to determine what had occurred over the last few weeks and what it meant for all of them.

Jack summarized the events of God's mission against the Zultarian group that was using astral projection to attack non-Zultarians and the trials they all went through. Then he covered the challenge between God and Zultar and the freeing of the captives. Lastly he welcomed Su Li as a full-time member of the team and recounted the abductions and the battles in Hong Kong and in the Colorado mountains. Then he asked everyone to contribute their thoughts about the ramifications of these events.

Mark started it with his usual alacrity. "I think Chun is going to try to get even with us with both barrels, and soon.

Sarah added her professional opinion. "I've known about Chun for the last eight years. He only has one trait bigger than his ego and that is his pride. We openly faced him down on his own turf, freed his foreign captives, then we rubbed his nose in it, and lastly, we slipped out of his grasp and suffered no damage. There is no doubt in my mind, none whatsoever, that he will attempt to destroy each and every one of us."

Major White commented, "Chun is playing big time and you can get a hint of how big by the fact that he was able to steal two, fully armed and operational, F16s from the Air National Guard and fly them to attack you as you were coming back from the cabin in the mountains. Very few people have the moxie, the contacts, the money, and the vision to do that."

Larry added his comments to the previous ones. "His people were able to kidnap the three of us without any fuss. They transported us to that cabin in the woods and were going to slaughter us without a qualm. Chun's organization is very capable and professional. As a pastor I can't stay here in this wonderfully safe place, I have to tend to my flock. I can't see how you will be able to protect me from whatever Chun wants to do to me."

Alan agreed with Larry.

Carol Nolan shook her head. "His agents got into a restricted building, into an armed camp of law enforcement, identified me and abducted me without raising a sweat or an alarm. I don't see how we can protect any of us for long."

Debbie Hargrove looked at her husband and he nodded. She stood up and said, "I would like to propose that we preempt the situation. You are all correct in saying that we could not protect ourselves against constant attempts to kill us. I suggest that we eliminate the problem before it eliminates us. I will volunteer to handle this if we agree that this is the proper course of action." She smiled and sat down.

Su Li said, "I'll fly you there and back. I'm ready to rid the world of this evil.

Laura's appreciation of Debbie's skills and Su Li's will just went up several notches. "You're proposing that, as a team, we put Chun away before he can find a way to do it to us?"

Debbie nodded.

Jim Grady spoke up. "You do realize that Chun is a fairly highly connected part of the Chinese government and that he is actually in line of secession to the last Emperor of China. Killing him could have serious complications for the United States. I doubt that you could get permission from the government of Israel let alone our own administration. And I'm pretty sure that they wouldn't help even if they would let us do it."

Mark added, "Not to mention that he might not be that easy to ID and take out as you'd think. He is reported to have several duplicates and you saw how he didn't even take part in the operation to get the nail."

Su Li looked at her new friends and laughed. "I can promise you that I would be able to find the man that ordered the deaths of my mother, father, and Thor." She sat back in her seat and dared anyone to argue with her.

Debbie said, "I've removed more important and secure people than this pretender to the throne of China. Do you remember two years ago, the dictator of a Latin American country that will go unnamed here?"

Mark stared intently at Debbie. "He died by accident in a high-speed car crash. They still aren't sure he's dead because he had a dozen look-alikes and it could have been any one of them."

Debbie's cute little housewife demeanor seemed out of odds with the words coming out of her mouth. "He died with my bullet in his brain just before he "died" in a car crash because I also shot out his front tire just as he was going into a deadly curve. It was him because all fourteen of his look-alikes were already dead. I know because I took them out one after the other until he was the only one left. He was fleeing me when he died. Please remember also that he had personally killed six American nuns with a hammer the week before he died."

Su Li got a grin on her face. She got out of her seat and came over and high-fived with Debbie and then went back and sat down.

When she saw everyone looking at her she said, "Hey! I saw that on television." The laughter eased the tension of the meeting.

Jack looked at Laura and said, "We need to pray about this."

The Crossfire Team will be back in
"*Chinese Crossfire*".

If this story has awakened your spirit or moved you to seek the love of Christ and His power for your life, whether you've never accepted Jesus as your savior or you've fallen away, repeat the following prayer and begin a most wonderful journey into eternal life with Him today.

Father God in heaven, As You said in Your Holy Word, (Romans 10:9) that if we confess the Lord our God and believe in our hearts that God raised Jesus from the dead, we shall be saved.

(The prayer on the next page is a sample prayer when asking Jesus into your heart as your Savior. You can also pray this in your own words.)

Salvation Prayer

Dear God in heaven, I come to you in the name of Jesus. I confess to You that I am a sinner, and I am sorry for my sins and the life that I have lived; I need your forgiveness. I believe that your only begotten Son Jesus Christ shed His precious blood on the cross at Calvary and died for my sins, and I am now willing to turn from my sin.

Right now I confess Jesus as the Lord of my life and my soul. With all my heart, I truly believe that your Holy Spirit raised Jesus from the dead. Today I accept Jesus Christ as my personal Savior and according to Your Word, right now I am saved.

I thank you Jesus, for your unlimited grace which has saved me from my sins. I thank you Jesus that your grace that never leads to license, but rather it always leads to repentance. Therefore Lord Jesus, transform my life so that I may bring glory and honor to you alone and not to myself.

I Thank you Lord Jesus, for dying for me at Calvary and giving me eternal life.

Amen.

If you just said this prayer and you meant it with all your heart, believe that you are now saved and have been born again.

You may ask, "Now that I am saved, what do I do next?" First of all you need to get into a spirit-filled, bible-based church that teaches the Scriptures, and you need to study God's Word.

Once you have found a church home, you will want to become water-baptized. By accepting Christ you are baptized in the spirit, but it is through water-baptism that you publically announce your obedience to the Lord Jesus. Water baptism is a symbol of your salvation from the dead. You were dead but now you live, for Jesus Christ has redeemed you for a price! The price was His atoning death on the cross. May God Bless You!

www.ingramcontent.com/pod-product-compliance
Lightning Source LLC
Chambersburg PA
CBHW071312250626
47159CB00004B/1398